fanatics

Also by

WILLIAM BELL

Crabbe

Absolutely Invincible

Death Wind

Five Days of the Ghost

Forbidden City

No Signature

Speak to the Earth

Zack

Stones

Alma

Just Some Stuff I Wrote

The Blue Helmet

Only in the Movies

WITH TING-XING YE

Throwaway Daughter

fanatics

A novel

WILLIAM BELL

Doubleday Canada

Library and Archives Canada Cataloguing in Publication

Bell, William, 1945-
Fanatics / William Bell.

ISBN 978-0-385-67027-2

I. Title.

PS8553.E4568F36 2011 jC813'.54 C2010-905728-7

This book is a work of fiction. Names, characters, places and incidents are products of the author's imagination or are used fictitiously. Any resemblance to actual events or locales or persons, living or dead, is entirely coincidental.

Printed and bound in the USA

Published in Canada by Doubleday Canada,
a division of Random House of Canada Limited

Visit Random House of Canada Limited's website: www.randomhouse.ca

10 9 8 7 6 5 4 3 2 1

For Ting-xing

PROLOGUE

A LONG TIME AGO, when my grade eight teacher got so fed up with my behaviour that she kicked me out of class, she had no idea—she was so knotted with anger she wouldn't have cared—that her outburst of frustration would lead to a crime.

Mrs. Sykes was cursed with wide, wet rubbery lips. When she talked, water gathered in the corners of her mouth and her lips shone with moisture. If she was irritated, as she was that day, the spit machine went into high gear and produced a tiny rainstorm that made you feel as if you'd stuck your head out a car window on a drizzly day.

"Go away!" she shouted.

The classroom door slammed in my face. I shrugged my shoulders, wiped my cheeks and forehead on my sleeve, and ambled down the hall to the library. Mrs. Tanner greeted me with a sour, unsympathetic look and heaved her bulky body from her chair behind the checkout desk. Muttering that this was the third time in a month, she thrust an old book with a blue cloth cover into my hands and ordered me to sit in the corner farthest from her desk but still in her line of vision.

"Read," she commanded. "Quietly."

The collection of ancient Greek myths hooked me right away. I read until the end of the day, then checked out the book and took it home. I renewed it so many times that Mrs. Tanner eventually gave up trying to get it back. When I graduated and went on to high school, the blue volume remained on the shelf in my room.

I guess you could say that I stole the book, but since Sykes and Tanner were accomplices the theft wasn't my fault. If Sykes hadn't kicked me out of class, I wouldn't have gone to the library. If Tanner had pressed a different, less interesting choice into my hands, I would have left it on the library chair when the end-of-day bell rang. You could say I was fated to read the book and like it enough to re-read it many times. Maybe Sykes, Tanner, and I were committing acts according to a plan we had no control over. We were like train cars pulled helplessly along tracks laid down by the gods long before we were born.

I found this notion in the blue book of myths. There were three old misshapen hags with ragged clothes and hearts as cold and spiky as icicles. They were called the Moirae, or Fates, and they controlled the destiny of every being on earth. The ancient Greeks seemed to swallow this idea calmly.

Not me. Even in grade eight I saw through the shabby excuse that the events in our lives are decided by semi-divine beings. I knew I had ended up in the library that day because I had pushed the grumpy Mrs. Sykes too far. I was bored by her tedious vocabulary exercises, and bugging her was a way to pass the time. I, not a warty trio of half-demented old crones, was responsible.

It's true—life has its surprises. Sometimes the first link in a chain of events you'd never have imagined is forged by an ordinary routine action—like walking down Mississauga Street one morning, stepping into a cafe, and ordering a cup of coffee.

PART ONE

Flee, flee from those who speak in the name of God.

—Eduardo Corbizzi

One

I

IT STARTED ON A MONDAY MORNING in early summer. As usual, I pushed through the alley door into the cramped room at the back of Olde Gold Antiques and Collectibles—the Mississauga Street store owned by my parents—where I was the official restorer, refinisher, and repairer of furniture. The store was closed the first day of the week, so I could toil away without being distracted by the tinkle of the doorbell.

I slid an *autorickshaw* CD into the player and began to repair an antique bird's-eye maple chest. Somehow the upper-right drawer had been smashed—it takes a mighty blow to break a dovetailed pine drawer—and Dad had asked me to make a new one. He had sold the chest and promised delivery in a couple of days.

Soon I was lost in the fragrance of pine shavings and sawdust, the rasp of steel teeth on wood, the familiar vibration in the saw's handle as the blade cut kerfs along the lines

I had scribed to mark the dovetails. An up-to-date cabinetmaker would have used an electric router to make the dovetails, but I preferred hand tools.

When the dovetails were done, I chiselled out the slots that the drawer bottom would rest in, cleaned up the edges with a bit of sandpaper, then painted the corner joints with glue and fitted the drawer sides to the front. After I slid the bottom into its grooves—without glue—I eased the back into place and clamped the completed drawer, setting it aside to let the adhesive dry. Good for another hundred years or so.

I hung my apron on a hook beside the curtain that separated the shop from the showroom, brushed sawdust off my sleeves, and left by the front door, crossing the street to the sunny side to get a good view of Olde Gold's display window and the small walnut cabinet I had designed and made myself. On the store's sign, OLDE GOLD ANTIQUES AND COLLECTIBLES, there was room for another line of print: Fine Custom Furniture.

With the ink on my high school diploma barely dry I had spent most of the past year as unofficial apprentice to Norbert Armstrong, a well-known local cabinetmaker. I wanted to design and make furniture, not spend my life working only for my parents, and although it had taken Mom a while to come around, they supported my ambition. When I "graduated"—the ceremony was a picnic of ham sandwiches, potato salad, and Norbert's foul-tasting homemade beer on the patio behind his shop in Hillsdale—Norbert had grumbled good-naturedly that for the first time in many years he might have some competition. I took his remark as a compliment.

I headed down Mississauga Street, bought a copy of the local paper from a box outside the Shepherd's Crook pub, and re-crossed the road where it began its descent to the park on the shore of Lake Couchiching. The *Mariposa Princess*, a double-decker sightseeing boat, was backing away from the pier to begin its morning tour of the lake.

I stepped into the Half Moon Cafe, with its fragrance of ground coffee and fresh baking. It was a popular place, with maybe a dozen wrought-iron tables, the original plank floor, and a stamped-tin ceiling painted light grey and criss-crossed with pipes and ducts.

I took a table near the coffee bar and opened the paper to the classified ads.

"Hey, Garnet," I heard from behind the bar.

Marco Grenoble was not a good advertisement for the famous homemade pizzas he concocted in the little kitchen at the back of the restaurant or the tasty Italian pastries displayed in tiers along the bar. Tall, reed thin with a concave abdomen, he wore a T-shirt and an apron stained with pizza sauce.

"Hi, Marco."

"The usual?"

"Sure. Thanks."

"I'll bring it myself."

I went back to the ads for property rentals. It didn't take long to see there was nothing there for me. I'd try some online sources later.

"You lookin' to move away from home?" Marco asked, placing a mug of latte on the table and then, beside it, a plate with three tiny lemon tarts in the middle.

"Thanks, Marco, but I only ordered the coffee."

"You gotta eat somethin'. You're too thin."

I folded up the paper and put it aside. "Well, thanks."

Marco nodded toward the paper. "So . . ."

"I'm trying to find space to rent," I explained. "The shop at the back of our store isn't big enough for the business I hope to start up."

I went on to describe what I was after. I needed room for a few large work and layout tables, machines like saws and planers, a booth for spray staining, and an electricity supply that would take the strain of all that equipment. I didn't have the machines lined up yet, or the money to buy or lease them, but I could at least search for a place.

"Latte okay?" Marco asked when I had finished talking.

"Perfect."

"How big an area d'you need?"

I looked around the restaurant. "About what you have here, give or take."

Marco turned his head from side to side, taking in the room as if seeing it for the first time. "I got this cousin," he said, but didn't finish the thought.

I nodded to encourage him, took a sip of my latte, said, "Uh-huh."

"A distant cousin." He smiled, making creases like parentheses on either side of his mouth, and ran his fingers through greying hair. "Real distant. From the brainy side of the clan—the Corbizzis. Heard of Professor Corbizzi? Never mind. Anyways, the old prof passed away some time ago. I heard that whoever takes care of the estate wants to rent out the coach house. You prob'ly know about the old mansion."

"No, I don't think so."

"It's up the lake a ways. North of town. Sits out there on

its own little peninsula. Course you can't see the house from the water. Too many trees. Anyways, if you're interested I'll try to get you the phone number."

"Sure," I said. "Why not?"

"Might take me a day or so. It's unlisted, and I don't know who inherited the place."

"No problem."

"One thing, though," Marco added, "there might be a string or two attached." He smiled again. "With the Corbizzis, there always is."

II

THE RAIN SHOWER that began as I left Orillia had faded to light drizzle by the time I delivered the chest with the repaired drawer to a house on Big Bay Point. When I pulled into a parking spot across the street from the bus station in Barrie, the afternoon sun was shouldering through the overcast, flooding the street and the whitecapped waves of Kempenfelt Bay with honey-coloured light.

After a while, the Toronto bus turned onto Maple Street, its engine roaring, its brakes hissing, and swung into the station. The doors flapped open and the driver hopped out and heaved up the cargo doors. He began to pass cases and bags to the knot of passengers who had quickly gathered behind him. Raphaella was the last to step off the bus, a tote bag slung over one shoulder.

I stayed in the van for a few minutes, watching her. She would be expecting to see our old white van and wouldn't notice me right away. She looked around as commuters flowed past her, rushing to taxis, the parking lot, or the line of cars in the pickup lane by the curb. Although their bodies were here on Maple Street, their minds were already somewhere else—at home, most likely. Whoever said you couldn't be two places at once was wrong.

Raphaella wasn't like them. She stood under the eaves of the station, beautiful as always in a black leather coat with caramel trim at the collar and cuffs. Her coal black hair, gathered behind her neck, fell to the middle of her back. The afternoon light seemed to highlight the wine-coloured birthmark on her neck and right cheek.

Even from my vantage point across the road I could sense the stillness that she wore like a comfortable cloak, the calm that sheltered her without making her seem vulnerable. Raphaella was the only person I knew who seemed secure in who she was, rooted and at home in the present, totally unlike the frantic passengers schooling past her.

But I couldn't sit and feast my eyes on her forever. I tapped the horn and got out of the van and threaded my way across the street, dodging cars as they scrambled away from the depot. Raphaella caught sight of me and her face lit up. We had been together for about a year, but whenever she smiled at me like that I felt a nerve at the back of my neck wake up and tingle.

She set down her bag, threw her arms around my neck, and kissed me like we'd been apart for a year rather than a couple of days.

"I missed you," she said after breaking the kiss.

"Me, too. How did everything go?"

"Perfectly—almost. They had everything we'll need and the price is right, but the man I had to deal with is a leerer. With an aggressive comb-over."

"Well . . . theatre people," I remarked, earning a punch on the shoulder.

The Orillia Theatre Group was putting on a musical, and Raphaella was stage manager. This time it was *Merrie Olde Orillia*, written by a local author. She had turned Stephen Leacock's *Sunshine Sketches of a Little Town* into a musical comedy. Naturally, I referred to the show as MOO. I hated musicals, but Raphaella loved them—the only defect in her otherwise perfect personality. She had spent the day in Toronto at the costume rental company.

"Let's boogie," I said.

She laughed. "You sound like your dad."

We made our way across the street and climbed into the van.

"So you finally gave in and got a new vehicle," she commented as we headed north. "Or rather, new-ish."

My father had been forced to give up our white rattletrap when it shuddered and died in the driveway like an overworked draught horse. The "new" vehicle, brown this time, was ten years old.

"Yeah. No choice. Um, changing the subject, I may have a line on some rental space for a workshop."

I told Raphaella about Marco's possible connection.

"It may not work out, but it's possible," I said. "Anyway, you're invited for supper at our place tonight."

"Who's cooking?"

"Me. I'm doing cold pasta salad with chopped olives and tuna, barbecued chicken on the side. Nothing complicated."

"Oh, I *am* glad to be home," she said.

Two

I

WICKLOW POINT, north of town, was a peninsula that hooked into the lake and pointed back toward Couchiching Park. At the end of Wicklow Road and occupying the entire peninsula was an estate enclosed by a high stone wall with a wrought-iron gate set into granite pillars. The dense stand of trees beyond the wall was flagged every fifty metres or so with NO TRESPASSING posters, whose message was emphasized by a PRIVATE: NO ENTRY sign on the gate.

I had never been out there before but found it easily enough with the GPS mounted on the handlebar of my motorcycle, a vintage 650 Hawk GT. My dad the traditionalist gave me lots of grief for using the electronic gizmo so much. "Pretty soon you'll need that contraption to find your bedroom," he joked.

I coasted slowly up to the gate and pushed a button below a brass grille. A hollow, tinny voice responded after a few seconds.

"You rang?"

"It's Garnet Havelock. I have an appointment."

"You may enter," said the grille.

There was a click, followed by the hum of an electric motor and the rattle of chains as the gates rolled aside. I heard them closing behind me as I guided the bike slowly up the gravel drive that curved through a grove of maples, birch, and a few conifers, and into a clearing where a big two-storey stone house brooded in the shadows.

It looked like something out of a history book—slate roof with three broad chimneys, flagstone porch, oak double doors adorned with black lion's-head knockers, mullioned windows along the first floor and dagger-shaped windows, their tips glazed with crimson stained glass, on the second. To the right of the mansion, also built of quarried granite, was a three-car garage in a stand of birch, with a concrete apron in front and along the side. This must be the "coach house" Marco had mentioned.

"The phone number I said I'd get for you," he had announced a few days earlier at the Half Moon, slapping a scrap of paper on the table beside my coffee. "You'll be talking to a Mrs. Stoppini about the coach house. Good luck."

It was the same Mrs. Stoppini, I assumed, who was now standing in the doorway at the back of the house, squinting in my direction. I shut off the bike, pulled it up onto the centre stand, and hung my helmet on the handlebar. Already pessimistic that I could afford to rent space in a setup like that, I approached the house.

"Hi," I said.

If the house seemed forbidding, Mrs. Stoppini was worse. She was tall and skeletal, with a long face, pale skin stretched tight over flat cheekbones, intense, bulging eyes, and a wide mouth painted crimson. Her iron grey hair was cut short. Dressed entirely in black, her long-sleeved dress buttoned at the neck, she looked like something from a story told to scare children.

She scrutinized me as if she found my jeans and leather jacket below standard.

"How do you do?" she replied to my greeting. "You must be Mr. Havelock."

"Call me Garnet," I said.

"I am very pleased indeed to meet you, Mr. Havelock. I am Mrs. Stoppini. Do come in."

I followed her into a spacious, well-lit kitchen with a view across the patio to the lake.

"You'll take tea," she informed me, turning to the countertop where a tray holding cups, a sugar bowl, and a jug had been prepared. "Any seat will do."

Mrs. Stoppini's enunciation was correct and formal, her English slightly accented, and she seemed to use her politeness as a shield. I did as I was told and sat at the table, trying to imagine the inside of the coach house. I could tell from the quick glance I got that it contained all the space I'd need. But why was she interested in renting it out in the first place? The stone wall, the gate, the sign—all demanded privacy. The house, the grounds, the silver tea service shouted money. Whatever the answer, the place wouldn't come cheap. The rent would be a lot more than I could afford.

She placed the tea tray on the table, then added a plate of steaming biscuits and a bowl of pale yellow butter. She sat, her erect spine at least ten centimetres from the chair back.

"Are you enjoying this lovely weather?" she enquired woodenly.

I hated small talk. "Yes. Nice riding weather today. Motorcycle, that is—not horse."

"I beg your pardon?"

"I ride a motorcycle. A Honda Hawk 650."

"Indeed." Mrs. Stoppini poured the tea. "Milk? Sugar?"

I said no thanks to both and accepted the cup. Close up, her long face, with its wan complexion, was startling. She had unusually thin lips and had applied her lipstick beyond their borders to make her mouth appear fuller. The effect was both comical and eerie.

She seemed to sense that I wasn't up for a lot of chit-chat and got right to the point. "Mr. Grenoble has informed me that you may wish to lease the coach house," she began.

"I'm interested," I said. "That's the building to the right of the house as I came in?"

She nodded, took a sip of her tea, and whacked the cup back onto the saucer, rattling the spoon.

"But I'll have to take a good look at it before I make up my mind," I added.

"Let us assume for the moment that you find it suitable," she countered.

"And you need to realize that a woodshop can be noisy now and again."

"That will not be a problem."

I didn't have much experience at negotiations. My father was a championship haggler who enjoyed bargaining over antiques at the store. He handled all the sales. I stayed away from that part of the business as much as I could. But if I wanted my own shop, I'd have to learn how to be a businessman. Sooner or later we'd have to talk money. Should I bring it up now? I wondered. I took a sip of tea to stall a little.

"With your permission, Mr. Havelock," she put in, beating me to the punch, "I wish to put to you a proposition."

I nodded, relieved that she'd taken the initiative. "Okay."

"You may find it a trifle unusual."

If it's half as unusual as the person making it, I thought, it's bound to be strange.

"And," she went on, "I am obliged to inform you that I have made certain discreet enquiries."

"Er, I don't follow."

"Concerning your family—and, of course, you. Please don't be offended. What I am about to propose—and I would not have agreed to this meeting had I not received a glowing report on the Havelocks—requires that I place in you a considerable degree of trust."

"You had me and my family *investigated*?" I blurted. "Who do you think—?"

"Do calm yourself, Mr. Havelock, I beg you," she exclaimed, eyes bulging. "I merely enquired of my lawyer, who is well acquainted with the town, whereas I am not. The late professor and I have led an extremely reclusive life here. All it took was a phone call. I say again: please do not take offence. My precaution—you will agree, I am sure, once you hear my ideas—was quite necessary."

I struggled to hold down my anger. Well, you horse-faced, dried-up old stick, I can push too.

"I'll have to look over the coach house before we go any further," I said, setting my cup and saucer on the table and getting to my feet.

Mrs. Stoppini's thick dark brows dived toward the bridge of her nose. She was about to object, but she checked herself. She seemed used to getting her own way. Not this time.

"If you insist," she said.

II

I KEPT MY ENTHUSIASM reined in as I looked the coach house over from the inside. There were three overhead garage doors at the front, with a standard entrance on the side facing the main house. Big windows on three walls provided lots of natural light to supplement the overhead fixtures. The concrete floor looked recently painted and was as clean as a dinner plate. The building was fully insulated, and there were electrical outlets spaced every two metres or so along the walls. The power supply—unusual for a garage—looked adequate for my needs.

When I returned to the kitchen Mrs. Stoppini was at the sink rinsing the tea cups.

"Will it suit, do you think?" she asked, wiping her hands on a tea towel.

"It's perfect," I was tempted to say. But I settled for "I think it might."

"Very well. Shall we sit down again and discuss the details?"

Like an awkward kid assembling a difficult Lego figure, Mrs. Stoppini made what she probably thought was a smile.

"Mr. Havelock, I very much hope that you will permit me to describe my proposal in full before you respond," she began, with her precise enunciation.

"Okay."

"Splendid. The enquiries I made of my lawyer yielded certain information which I found very much to my satisfaction, and which allowed me to hope you could be of considerable assistance to me and to the late Professor Corbizzi." She cleared her throat. "I am prepared to lease the coach house to you, exclusively, for a period of three years, for the sum of one dollar."

"One d—"

She held up a bony hand, palm toward me. "If you please, Mr. Havelock. There is more."

I recalled Marco Grenoble's warning: with the Corbizzis there are always strings attached.

Mrs. Stoppini rolled on. "I must share certain information that I will rely upon you to treat with the utmost confidence."

Meaning, don't tell anybody. I nodded.

"Indeed, as the late Professor Corbizzi was, and I remain, an extremely private person, *everything* I am about to tell you must remain confidential. I have been his housekeeper and companion for the past twenty years, first in Italy and then, for a decade or more, here. Professor Corbizzi was a Renaissance scholar, specializing in Tuscan history. He published several books and many articles. He was always devoted to his studies, but toward the end he became more reclusive, even secretive, spending most of his day behind the closed doors of his library. He passed away suddenly—this is, of course, common knowledge. What is not well known is that there was . . . an incident that immediately preceded his death. An accident. A small fire. These details are my affair, and mine alone."

She paused and looked at her hands folded in her lap. It was the first time since I'd met her that she seemed to soften, even to search for words. But then she looked up, her composure restored.

"That is the first fact that is pertinent to your decision. The second is this: I am the executrix of the late Professor Corbizzi's last will and testament. I now own this estate and most of its contents, but nevertheless I require an inventory of Professor Corbizzi's effects, for legal reasons. A person in my position must conduct matters transparently, so as to satisfy relations who may or may not benefit from the late professor's will. A certain university is also a beneficiary of a number of items. The objects in the rest of the house I can deal with myself, but to note all the contents of the library is too daunting a challenge even for me. Besides, I . . . do not wish to be in the library. At all. The late professor seldom permitted it, and in any case I am not . . . comfortable there.

"This brings me to the third and last item apposite to this discussion, and one that relates directly to your skills and experience. The fire—it was small and easily brought under control—occurred in the library. The authorities concluded that the fireplace was the source, and that the professor, felled by the seizure that ended his life, somehow dislodged a burning log, which then rolled onto the carpet, setting it alight. There is damage to the fireplace mantel, which is of wood, and perhaps the bookshelves on one side, as well as the floor. I trust I have been clear so far?"

"Yes," I answered, my mind darting about, chasing dozens of questions flushed by her story. "Very clear."

"I now come to my proposal. In exchange for the three-year lease on the coach house, I require you to complete two tasks. You will repair all damage done by the fire, and you will make the necessary inventory of the library's contents. You may, within reason, take as long as you deem necessary. I shall provide you with an electronic key to the gate, and you may come and go as you wish. I am always here. I never leave the estate."

The impulsive angel on my right shoulder whispered, "One dollar! Go for it! Now, before she changes her mind! This is a sweet deal!" The logical angel on my left shoulder cautioned, "Maybe this is too good to be true. Remember? The Corbizzis? Strings? Tell her you need a day or so to think about it. Don't rush into something you might regret."

Mrs. Stoppini saved me from being pummelled half to death by two imaginary and opinionated spirits. "I should think you'll want a day or two to think it over," she suggested.

"Yes, thanks."

"Fine. Shall we say two days from today? You may telephone at any time. In the meantime, perhaps you'd care to examine the library?"

I followed the wiry black form of Mrs. Stoppini as she glided along panelled halls, this time to the east wing of the house. Our feet whispered on the oriental rug that covered the central part of the dark hardwood floor. She stopped before a beautifully carved double pocket door sporting a set of brass lion's-head knobs—smaller versions of the ones on the front door. Mrs. Stoppini rolled the doors open.

Stepping back and to the side she said, "Please enter. I shall be in the kitchen."

"But—"

"I don't go in there," she reminded me.
I heard the doors closing behind me.

III

THE LIBRARY WASN'T *in* the east wing of the house, it *was* the east wing—a spacious room full of light, with a view of the lake through wide corner windows, a stone fireplace, antique rugs arranged on the hardwood floor among trestle tables and leather club chairs, floor-to-ceiling bookshelves on every wall. I could easily imagine that it had once been a comfortable, restful place where a scholar might spend the day reading for pleasure, doing research, or writing a thesis.

But it didn't seem that way now. Dozens of books lay scattered on the floor at the end of the room, as if someone had frantically yanked them off the shelves and flung them to the ground. A dark oblong on the hardwood floor indicated that a rug had once lain in front of the hearth between two chairs. One of the chairs lay on its back. Charred wood and blistered varnish scarred the wooden mantel, and tongues of soot streaked the wall and ceiling above the fireplace.

Mrs. Stoppini had said that Professor Corbizzi had suffered some sort of deadly seizure, and the appearance of the room told me it must have been violent. He had probably knocked the heavy chair over when he fell, and when his body hit the rug, the tremor caused a log to roll off the hearth, starting the fire. I shuddered, picturing an old man lying amid smoke and flames, helpless, unable to save himself. I hoped he was dead before the fire got to him.

The professor must have hurled the books to the floor before he fell. Why? What had sparked the kind of rage that made a scholar throw his books around and wreck his own room? Had his anger brought on the fit that killed him? Or had it been panic rather than fury? Had he been searching desperately for something before the seizure came?

The atmosphere of the place was oppressive and vaguely threatening, despite the sunlight streaming through the windows. The heavy air stank from the damp ash and charred logs in the fireplace. The odour of smoke clung to the window curtains. Against my will, I imagined the professor sprawled before the hearth, dying as the rug smouldered around him. Were his sudden attack and the damage to the library the causes of the uneasiness that seeped into me like cold water? Why was I weighed down by the impression that the room didn't want me there?

Unconsciously, I shrank back. Then I swallowed, took a deep breath, and reminded myself that I was there for a reason. I had work to do.

I took a slow tour of the room, moving instinctively away from the fireplace and toward the windows on the south side. To the right of the door was an escritoire with an ancient, clunky-looking black Underwood typewriter on top, along with a small brass lamp and an old-fashioned straight pen and inkwell. A chair was tucked under the desk, and a low filing cabinet stood to one side. There was no computer or printer, not even a telephone.

Trestle tables had been placed along the south and east walls, leaving room to walk between them and the bookshelves.

Set into the northeast corner, where most of the displaced books lay scattered on the floor around a square oak table lying on its side, was an alcove with a small cupboard built into the shelves.

I was anxious to get out of there, but I forced myself to calm down and think. I returned to the fireplace and sat in the upright club chair. Mrs. Stoppini had described two jobs—inventory and repair—as part of the deal. The first would be mostly a catalogue of the books in the room—the contents of the escritoire and cupboard shouldn't take more than a day. I counted the volumes on one shelf, then multiplied by the number of shelves, which, not including the alcove, were pretty much the same length throughout the room. Well over four thousand books—a huge, time-consuming, and phenomenally boring job. But possibly simple, depending on how much detail Mrs. Stoppini wanted catalogued. A list of titles, or titles with authors' names, was easiest because these were printed on the books' spines. I wouldn't have to take the books down from the shelves.

But if Mrs. Stoppini required copyright date, publisher, and edition—the kind of information Dad noted carefully whenever he found an old volume that might be worth something—then every single book would have to be examined. A forever job. I'd be as old as Mrs. Stoppini, and probably just as eccentric, before I finished. I made a mental note to find out exactly what she needed before I committed myself. It seemed strange that an academic wouldn't keep a catalogue of his own books, though. Maybe I'd find one somewhere and knock off one of Mrs. Stoppini's tasks right away.

Feeling more optimistic, I got up and examined the shelves to the left and right of the mantel, looking for signs of heat damage. I couldn't shake the feeling that I was intruding into something that had nothing to do with me, and that I was being watched. I forced myself to concentrate.

The shelves seemed unharmed, but they'd need to be cleared to make sure. The mantel itself was a fussy, old-fashioned design in thickly varnished oak, finished in red mahogany. A little railing, about four centimetres high, with tiny urn-shaped balusters, skirted the outside edge of the shelf. The panels down each side of the fireplace opening had small decorative shelves also bordered by little dowel fences. The mantel was not only charred from the heat of the fire but also warped beyond hope. So, another question for Mrs. Stoppini: replicate the mantel or replace it with a simpler design?

Conscious of the resentment that seemed to seep from every corner of the silent library, I left the room without looking back.

UNLIKE RAPHAELLA, I had always been a two-brained personality. I had a sort of divided and contradictory way of looking at the world. One part of me was scientific and logical, with a love of gadgets and gizmos. The other I didn't know how to describe—spiritual? intuitive? Raphaella called the first one "techno-mode," and until getting to know her I saw things from that perspective most of the time. She brought out the other side of me, the part that realized some of the best things about my life, like love, exhilaration, friendship, couldn't be measured or explained and weren't always predictable. Both of us had learned from experience that spirits and what we called "presences"—the remains of minds or souls who came before us—existed all around us, and that Raphaella had been born with a gift that allowed her to sense them much more deeply than I could. I wasn't New Age, or whatever it was called. I wasn't about to change my name to Prairie Sunburst or something. But the threatening undercurrent in the dead professor's library was as strong—and as real—as the chaos of scattered books and the stink of smoke, and I knew there was no way I could ignore it.

Three

I

"HOUSEKEEPER *AND* COMPANION, she said?"

"Yup. Her very words."

"Hmm."

"Hmm indeed, as Mrs. Stoppini would put it."

"Of course, companion could mean a number of things," Raphaella mused.

"My theory is that they lived common-law because one of them was legally tied to someone else."

"But why describe yourself as a housekeeper if you're partners?"

"Who knows?"

As I set up the rice steamer, chopped vegetables, and arranged spices at the counter in our kitchen, I filled Raphaella in on the offer Mrs. Stoppini had made me earlier that day. Raphaella was sitting at the table with a cup of green tea, watching me work.

I crushed a green and a red chili, a couple of cloves of garlic, some black peppercorns, and a bit of shredded ginger, and put them in a small bowl. In another dish I piled the vegetables—snow peas, whole baby corn, diced red bell pepper, and chopped spring onion. Rice noodles were soaking in a bath of warm water beside a platter of raw shrimp, shelled and de-veined. I hauled a big iron wok out of the cupboard beside the sink and set it on the stove.

"Are you going to accept?" Raphaella asked.

A polished copper ankh hung from her neck on a leather thong. As usual—and, I sometimes thought, only to tempt me—she wore her hair long, caught at the back of her neck with a sterling silver brooch. She was wearing black denims, leather sandals, and a canary yellow T-shirt depicting a street sign in crimson across the curvy front.

WITCHES' PARKING ONLY
ALL OTHERS WILL BE
TOAD

The lame T-shirt joke reminded me of our high school days, when Raphaella's transfer from Park Street Collegiate to my school came with a bundle of unflattering rumours—the tastiest one being that she was a witch. Little did the rumourmongers know, I thought.

"That's what I need to discuss with you," I replied, leaning against the counter. "I told her I wanted to think about it, even though I was tempted to snatch the opportunity on the spot."

"Yeah, it's a bit . . . surprising," Raphaella commented. "Almost too good to be true. You wonder, What's the catch?"

"Marco warned me there'd be one, but I'd like to accept anyway."

"But?"

"Well, it all *sounds* straightforward enough."

Mrs. Stoppini had replied to my two questions very clearly. Yes, the new mantel should be an exact copy of the old one, and yes, some of the books required full notification, but not the majority.

"The woodworking will take time," I continued. "I can replicate the mantel and refinish the floor in front of the hearth. There may be damage to the bookcases that I didn't notice. But cataloguing all those books . . . I'll never get through it."

"Ow!" Raphaella smirked, hands over her ears.

"What's the matter?"

"The loud clang from the hint you just dropped."

"It might be fun, you and I working together."

"Hmm."

"And we could take breaks, go for a swim, smooch."

"Hmm."

"But I guess, with MOO and all . . . And your mother will want you to work in the store as much as you can."

Mrs. Skye owned and operated the Demeter Natural Food and Medicinal Herbs Shop on Peter Street. She didn't like me.

"Don't lay the guilt on too thick," Raphaella said. "How many books did you say?"

"Four thousand, minimum. Maybe five."

"And how many are to be fully catalogued?"

"Fewer than a quarter, I'd guess."

"Hmm."

"That's your third 'Hmm.'"

"It might be interesting."

"That isn't the first word that springs to mind," I admitted. "Working with you, I mean."

"Oh. Well, definitely."

I had been careful to describe the mansion, the eccentric Mrs. Stoppini, and what little I had learned about the tragically dead Professor Corbizzi in a way that I hoped would intrigue Raphaella. But I hadn't mentioned the uncomfortable, oppressive atmosphere of the library or *how* the prof had died.

"I'll talk it over with Mother," Raphaella said. "Maybe I can work away at the books in my spare time."

"As soon as she hears you'll be with me she'll object," I said, turning on the gas under the wok.

Raphaella's mother had never accepted me. She wanted Raphaella to lead a life without males in it. When Raphaella was a little girl her father had humiliated her mother by having affairs and eventually being charged with sexual exploitation of a woman in his firm. Mrs. Skye had learned to dislike and distrust men in general. But in my bumbling manner, without really knowing how I had done it, I had won Raphaella's heart and ruined Mrs. Skye's plans. She wasn't grateful.

"Oh, I don't know. I think she's warming up to you. Give her a few years."

"So you'll help?"

"How could I turn you down?"

"You're an angel," I said with relief.

"But there's one condition."

"Which is?"

"You have to tell me what's bothering you about the Corbizzi place."

Raphaella's ability to tune in to my feelings used to catch me by surprise, but not anymore. She had what her late grandmother had called "the gift," although Raphaella sometimes complained it was more like a curse. She could sense things—emotions and even past happenings. I'd seen her walk into a building or a churchyard and *know* that something horrible had occurred there because she felt the presence of the people who had suffered. Raphaella once told me it was as if she was a string on a musical instrument and vibrated in sympathy with her surroundings. But her powers, her spiritualism, were a secret only she, her mother, and I knew.

"That library is creepy," I replied. "I can't put it into words. It's more than the fact that the professor died there. It's as if the room has . . . an attitude—a negative attitude. It doesn't want strangers."

Raphaella nodded as if everything I said made perfect sense to her. "I see. And that makes you uneasy—and a little scared."

"Yeah."

I poured a dollop of peanut oil into the wok and flipped on the range hood fan. "Hold your breath," I warned. "This may make you cough a little."

Raphaella got up and opened the window that looked out on Mom's flower beds between the house and garage. I dumped the spices into the hot oil. Instantly, the sharp savoury aroma of sizzling chili, garlic, and ginger filled the kitchen. Coughing, I added the shrimp and tossed them with a metal spatula. As soon as the shrimp had turned pink on both sides I scooped them onto a plate and set it aside. Next, in went the vegetables. I stir-fried them for a few minutes, then poured in some chicken broth, sending a cloud of steam into the air, and clapped the wooden lid on the wok.

While the veggies cooked, I drained the noodles. "Okay, here we go," I announced. "The moment of truth."

I removed the lid from the wok, dumped in the shrimp and then the noodles, blending the ingredients quickly, adding fish sauce at the last minute before turning off the stove. Raphaella scooped steamed rice into a bowl. While she set it on the table I poured the stir-fry onto a huge platter, then set it down next to the rice.

"Ready!" I yelled, pulling the strings of my apron.

Mom and Dad came into the kitchen, each with half a glass of red wine, Mom with the bottle. "Smells wonderful," she commented.

Dad waved at the air, wrinkling his nose and pretending to be offended by the spicy aroma. "The fire extinguisher's under the sink," he remarked, grinning at Raphaella. Then he pulled out a chair. "Come on, Annie. No shilly-shallying. Let's strap on the old feed bag."

"Shilly-shallying?" Raphaella said.

As we ate, Raphaella told us about MOO. The cast had had its first run-though and the rehearsal schedule was set. Raphaella would be busy most nights. The dramatic and music directors were married—to each other.

"I hope the rehearsals won't all be like our first meeting," Raphaella said, popping a shrimp into her mouth. "The directors bickered over every point. And the guy playing Josh Smith thinks he knows more than both of them put together.

If by some miracle we can pull the production together and do a good job, there's a chance we'll be invited to perform at a conference opening at Geneva Park on the same weekend. And," she added, giving my father her most winning smile, "the musical ensemble is short one flute player."

Dad shook his head. "Don't even try," he said. "I can't perform in front of people. My mouth gets all dry and I can't pucker."

"But you *teach* flute," Raphaella argued. "Garnet says you're a great player."

Dad looked at me. "You said that?"

"I may have been exaggerating."

Mom got into the mix. "No, you weren't, Garnet. Gareth is a fabulous flautist," she said to Raphaella.

Dad beamed and blushed at the same time. "Well—"

"But he's chicken," Mom said.

II

NEXT MORNING, I paced back and forth in my room, mentally rehearsing what I wanted to say. The more I thought about it, the more I wanted to make the deal. A three-year lease at no cost! The biggest expenses in starting up a business, Dad had advised me more than once, were equipment and plant—the rental or ownership of the workplace. Mrs. Stoppini was offering the second for free, a huge boost to my plans.

But I didn't want to sound too eager, because I had a condition of my own.

Okay, I told myself, it's showtime. I keyed Mrs. Stoppini's number into my cell, took a deep breath, and pushed the Talk button.

She answered with a coldly formal "Good morning. Corbizzi residence."

"Hello, Mrs. Stoppini. It's Garnet Havelock."

Her voice warmed up a degree. "Good morning, Mr. Havelock. How nice to hear from you."

"I said I'd phone and give you my decision about your offer."

"Ah."

"Er, I'm willing to meet your two conditions."

A little more of the frost melted away. "Excellent."

"But I have one of my own."

A pause. "Indeed."

I waited her out, chewing on my lip.

Her voice had iced over again, like a pond in winter. "May I know what you have in mind?"

"I have a friend. She's very reliable. And honest. I want to bring her along from time to time to help with the books."

"Mr. Havelock, I did stress that our business arrangements and all the attendant details, along with information personal to this household, must remain strictly confidential."

"She's very discreet. And I know from experience that she can keep a secret. Forever, if necessary."

"But—"

"I need her help, Mrs. Stoppini."

"Did you say *she*?"

"Raphaella is my girlfriend," I said.

"Indeed," Mrs. Stoppini said again, stuffing as much distaste as she could manage into the two syllables.

Girlfriend. I hated that word. It sounded trivial, as if Raphaella was a buddy I went to the movies with every Saturday afternoon. But how could I explain our relationship to a stranger? And why would I? Especially a cold fish like Mrs. Stoppini. Raphaella and I were soulmates.

"She's my best friend," I added.

Silence.

"My companion."

More silence. Then, when Mrs. Stoppini spoke, her voice took on a neutral tone, as if she had made up her mind.

"Raphaella. An Italian name. It means 'She who heals.' I shall take that as a good omen. What is her surname?"

My turn to hesitate. "You're going to investigate her." It wasn't a question.

"I must, Mr. Havelock. But I shall be just as circumspect as before."

"Skye," I said. "With an 'e.'"

"Fine. Let us agree on the following: provided my lawyer has no objection, I shall consent to your condition and allow your . . . companion to assist you in your work and, to that end, come and go as she pleases."

"Good. Thanks."

"I shall have the contracts drawn up. And one more thing, Mr. Havelock."

"Yes?"

"May I say how pleased I am that you have accepted."

I almost shouted, "Me, too!"

III

When I was in grade nine I went out with a girl named Sandy Mills until I found out I was her reserve boyfriend—the guy she dated as long as her real love interest hadn't asked her out first. Sandy tore away the last shred of my already tattered self-confidence, and I wondered if any girl would ever give me the time of day. I was so desperate for ideas that one evening while my parents and I were washing the dinner dishes—we only used the dishwasher if we had company—I made the mistake of asking them how they met.

They agreed on the first part. Dad was an Orillia boy and Mom met him at the farmers' market one summer Saturday while visiting friends who owned a cottage on Lake St. John and had brought her into town to shop. From that point on, my parents' versions of their relationship story varied.

"She chased me all over town," my father called out from the living room. He had finished washing and left Mom and me to sweep the floor and put the dishes away. "She wouldn't let me alone. It was embarrassing. I'd turn a street corner and there she'd be. I married her just to put her out of her misery."

"Not true!" Mom contradicted, directing her voice toward the living room as she swept. "You were so smitten you phoned me once a day and twice on Sunday. Your phone bill was bankrupting you. I only agreed to your proposal because I felt sorry for you."

"Go on, admit it. I was irresistible. You were head over heels. Obsessed. Besotted."

"You don't even know what besotted means," Mom scoffed, laughing, as Dad came back into the kitchen.

"Yes, I do," he said, taking her in his arms, bending her backwards, and planting a noisy kiss on her mouth. "See?" he said to me over his shoulder. "She still can't leave me alone."

I threw down my dishtowel and left the kitchen. "No wonder I'm immature for my age," I said.

Whatever my father claimed when he and Mom were horsing around, the grin on his beaming face in the wedding photo on the mantel told a different story. He couldn't believe that the young woman holding his arm had agreed to have him.

They were different people—Mom was a journalist whose drive and ambition had made her well known, and had landed her in a few dangerous situations. She would go anywhere to chase down a story. Her favourite drink was adrenaline. Dad was a part-time music teacher—he played flute—and a store owner, and his calm familiar life in the town where he was born was adventurous enough for him. He was, in my mother's words, an old-fashioned stick-in-the-mud, which was why he operated an antique store, preferred the golden oldies station on the radio, and drove a 1966 Chevy pickup truck he had restored himself. Mom had once had dreams that I would go off to university and be a scholar and hold a pen rather than a chisel or screwdriver, but Dad had quietly backed my wish to finish high school and learn cabinetry and furniture design.

But they were as tightly meshed as the strands in a suspension bridge cable, and they made all their big decisions together. Which is why I sat down with them in the living room on the same day I talked to Mrs. Stoppini. I explained what I wanted to do and asked for their support.

"I suppose it wouldn't be the *worst* investment in the world, eh, Annie?" Dad allowed, waggling his eyebrows.

Mom suggested that our family lawyer look over the contract before I signed it, and Dad offered an interest-free loan to get me up and running. We talked about my plans, and I noticed they kept exchanging smiles.

"What's going on?" I demanded.

"Nothing," my mother replied.

"We're proud of you," my father said. "She just won't admit it."

Four

I

WITHIN A COUPLE OF WEEKS the workshop was operational. I had installed a layout table, a drafting board, racks for my tools, and, along the walls, benches equipped with vises. The table, band, and radial arm saws and a power planer were situated on the floor with lots of working room around them. There was also a lathe, only three years old, that I had bought from Norbert for a song. I ordered the wood for the mantel, along with a supply of lumber and specialty woods I'd need to have on hand for occasional work. The vacuum-and-exhaust system would be installed in a day or so.

Meanwhile, I hung sheets over the library shelves, rolled up the rugs, and threw dropcloths over the furniture. I took down the ruined mantel and gingerly carried the pieces out to the shop. Then I power-sanded the burned patches on the library floor. The damage hadn't gone deep, so the sanding took only a couple of hours. It left slight indentations, but not enough to notice, especially if Mrs. Stoppini covered the area in front of the hearth with a new rug.

I spent some time in the paint-and-wallpaper store on Colborne Street discussing the available colours of wood stains with Rachel Pierce, an old high school friend, and comparing colour samples with the digital photo I had taken of the library floor. I left with paint for the wall above the fireplace, half a dozen small tins of stain, a can of urethane, and a few brushes. I figured I would mix the stain right in the library to get the colour match perfect.

When the floor and wall were done and dry, Mrs. Stoppini inspected the job from the hallway outside the library door and pronounced my work "most satisfactory." I concluded that she was pleased, and that those two words were the highest praise I was going to get.

Because soft surfaces absorb smoke much more than wood or leather, the curtains and rugs stank of stale carbon and ash. No one else was permitted in the library except me and Raphaella, so with the work on the floor done, Mrs. Stoppini had me pull down the drapes, remove the rugs, and haul everything to the front door, where a company she had engaged would pick it all up and take it away to be cleaned. I then washed the windows and set about dusting the bookshelves.

All this going to and fro, into and out of the library—careful to follow Mrs. Stoppini's strict instructions and close the doors firmly each time I entered or left—didn't alter my reaction to a room that should have felt homey and inviting. After all, there were the books, the worn, comfortable chairs, the warmth of natural wood and of wool rugs—all bathed by the light streaming in through the big windows. What more was needed to help me relax?

But each time I drew open the double doors and stepped into that silent room I felt something, like the change in air pressure that comes immediately before a storm. Or like a background hum, as if the room was faintly breathing.

I assured myself it was all in my head. But then I had told myself the very same thing in the past, when I had been stranded in a pioneer church during a blizzard and haunted by the frantic, ghostly voices of some men on their way to a murder.

I put much of my uneasiness down to the professor's awful death. At the same time, I had a niggling feeling there was more to it than that. Did all this explain the eccentric behaviour of the crow-like Mrs. Stoppini? She felt the library's strangeness, too. I was certain she did. That was why she refused to enter the room. It was more than grief that I saw in her eyes. It was fear.

II

I FOUND MOM at her desk in her study the next morning, her hair still wet from the shower. She took a run most mornings, summer or winter, before she began her day, and put in a couple of hours' work before lunch. The sun was bright in the window behind her, highlighting the red and pink petunias in the window box.

Except for the tiny crow's feet in the corners of her eyes,

Mom looked young for her age. She was slender and small-boned, easily taken for a frail person—until the fierce energy in her eyes hinted at her iron will. Her determination was one of the ingredients that made her a national-class journalist—and sometimes got her into trouble. Her face glowed with the brightest intelligence of anyone I knew, except Raphaella. Her eyes sparkled with wit and creativeness, and if you paid attention they told you a lot about what she was thinking.

And once in a while, just for a second, they'd lose their focus. At those times I knew she was flashing back to the day about a year before when she had been on assignment in East Timor, reporting on the brutal events of a dirty war in which one side employed so-called militias—gangs of rapists and murderers who used religion as a battering ram. Mom was abducted by a gang of young Islamist men with guns and medieval ideas about women who didn't "know their place." Enraged by a female who had the nerve to be a reporter, they had thrown her into the back of a truck, beaten her, and threatened her with death for hours before dumping her in the dust by the side of a road. She had come home cut and bruised and in a kind of otherworldly shock that kept her numb for weeks.

This morning, she was clicking away on the computer keyboard. I didn't ask what she was working on. She wouldn't tell me until it was almost complete, but it would be either an article for a print or online magazine or an entry on her blog.

She looked up.

"Off to work?" she asked.

I nodded, then said, "Have you ever heard of a Professor Corbizzi? Lived near here?"

Mom was also a magician when it came to research. "Lived? Past tense? Doesn't ring a bell. A professor, you say?"

I nodded again. Her fingers blurred over the keyboard.

"Eduardo Corbizzi?"

"I don't know his first name."

"There's someone here. Wrote a few books. Died recently. It just says he lived somewhere near Orillia."

"Must be him. There can't be more than one professor in the area with an unusual name like that. What are the books about?"

"The Italian Renaissance, all out of print. Wait a minute. That's where your new shop is—that estate up the lake."

"Right."

"It's his library you're working on. Might be interesting."

"It already is," I replied. "Anyway, see you later."

"'Kay," she replied, her hands already in motion, her eyes on the screen.

III

IT WAS A SULTRY MORNING, the heavy air already sweltering when I got to the Corbizzi gate and activated the remote I kept clipped to the inside of the fairing on my motorcycle. I drove up the lane, grateful for the cool shade of the woods, and parked under the birches by the workshop.

I saw Mrs. Stoppini's mannequin-like shape in the kitchen window as she worked at the sink, probably washing her breakfast dishes. I waved, but she didn't seem to notice. I let myself in the side door of the shop and hung my helmet and leather jacket on a hook by the door. Then I flipped on the overhead fans, wound the windows open, and put on my apron, mentally rehearsing my plans for the day.

I clamped one of the new mantel's side panels into the bench vise and began to plane the edges. As usual, I got lost in the work, and when my cell rang I was surprised to hear Mrs. Stoppini announce, without so much as a hello, "I shall be serving a light lunch on the patio in thirty-five minutes."

Even under the patio umbrella the air was sticky and oppressive. The lake gave off a brassy glare under the relentless sun, and the flowers in Mrs. Stoppini's gardens drooped as if they had given up the fight hours ago. For the first time I noticed that there was no dock on the shore, which probably meant that the late professor was not a boater. It also meant that no one could conveniently visit the estate from the water.

Mrs. Stoppini had prepared panini—Italian sandwich rolls—of prosciutto, cheese, and lettuce and arranged them on a platter beside a bowl of olives. When we had made our deal and signed our contract, she hadn't said anything about providing tea and coffee and lunch. But I wasn't going to bring it up.

"I would customarily offer a good Chianti at lunch," she said, looking cool despite her long-sleeved black housedress, "but as you are using machinery I thought mineral water might be best."

"Good thinking," I said, helping myself to a sandwich.

She sat down opposite me, straight-backed and rigid, and proceeded to demolish a panino. I popped an olive into my mouth, savouring the saltiness, and watched an Albacore far out on the water by Chiefs Island, desperately searching for a snatch of wind.

"If I may say, Mr. Havelock, you seem an admirably quiet and serious young man."

I felt myself blush.

"Not like those uncivilized creatures whose animal noises and whoops one hears from the city park when the wind is in an unfavourable direction."

"Raphaella says I'm steady. And reliable. I think she means dull."

Something happened to Mrs. Stoppini's face. I realized she was smiling. Sort of.

"I shall look forward to meeting this Miss Skye of yours."

"I don't think she'd like the 'of yours' part."

"Indeed."

"Do you mind if I ask something?" I said, changing the subject. "Professor Corbizzi—he was a university teacher?"

"He was an eminent historian and author of several books. He held a chair at Ponte Santa Trinita University in Renaissance studies in our native Florence, and his specialty was the San Marco church and monastery. I take it you have not had an opportunity to examine his library."

"Too busy," I said.

"Indeed. Well, he was, some years ago, offered a post at the University of Toronto, and after a few years he retired to this place. I fear he was not happy at Toronto. His work was . . . a trifle unorthodox."

"Oh."

There was something unusual in the way she talked about the man who had been her companion. Raphaella and I assumed that meant they were a couple and had been for years. Yet she seemed impersonal when she spoke of him. "He was not happy," "he retired," "his work was unorthodox." Strange, I thought as I munched on the last olive in the bowl.

"He continued his work here, but I am not aware of its exact nature. He did not share it with me."

I got the message. Don't enquire any further. I drank down the remains of my water and stood.

"Well, thanks for the lunch," I said. "Time to get back to work."

IV

DURING THE AFTERNOON, thunder grumbled on and off in the darkening northwest sky. I wondered if I should pack it in and head home before the rain came. Riding a motorcycle with a face full of windblown water was no fun. But I put it off, intent on what I was doing, and didn't clue in to the weather again until I heard a handful of rain spatter against the window above the bench. I opened one of the garage doors, allowing a gust of cool air to swirl inside, carrying sticks and dust with it. I pushed the bike inside and ran the door back down, hoping that if there was a thundershower, it would be short.

I sat for a while, safe and dry behind the glass, and watched the drama in the sky above the lake, where thick purple clouds roiled over the whitecaps. Here and there bars of sunlight shot through like yellow spotlights, illuminating the emerald green water. But soon the lowering sky formed a dark ceiling. Lightning flashed and crackled. Thunder boomed like artillery. The wind came like a series of punches, bending the tall spruce between me and the water like blades of grass and lifting the skirts of the willows along the shore. Small branches spun past the window. The patio chairs tipped and rolled across the grass. The umbrella, folded and tied, rattled in its mooring, rocketed into the air, touched down briefly in a sea of irises, and somersaulted toward the lake and out of sight.

A roar like an approaching train announced the downpour, and huge raindrops slammed the concrete apron outside the shop like tiny bombs. Puddles appeared almost instantly. Distorted by the curtain of rain running down the kitchen window, Mrs. Stoppini's tall form appeared. My cellphone rang.

"Are you quite all right?" she asked anxiously.

"Snug as a bug, Mrs. Stoppini."

"I beg your pardon?"

"I'm fine," I said. "It'll probably blow by in few minutes."

"I hate storms," she said, and hung up.

The uproar moved on after less than an hour of heavenly mayhem. The violent gusts of wind gave way to a steady breeze. The rain stopped and the sun came out, drawing steam from the apron and the patio, and setting alight the droplets that hung from every leaf. I went back to work, but by suppertime, when I had planned to quit, a sullen downpour had set in.

Mrs. Stoppini offered me supper and a guest room for

the night, "in view of the weather," and when I saw the doleful look on her face I remembered her saying earlier in the day that she hated storms—which meant they scared her. I called home and let my parents know. After supper—pasta with garlic, butter, fresh Parmesan cheese, and asparagus—I put in another hour's work, then called it a day.

"Let me show you your room," Mrs. Stoppini said when I came back into the house holding an umbrella against the rain. She went ahead of me up a wide staircase that gave onto a carpeted landing, turned left, and led me down a wainscotted corridor, past a few doors to the east wing, floating like a wraith ahead of me, her leather lace-ups tapping the floorboards. How does she *do* that? I wondered.

She pushed open a door and gestured toward a large tiled bathroom. Then she showed me into a spacious bedroom with its own fireplace and easy chairs, as well as a four-poster bed with what looked like antique end tables. A bulky dresser took up most of the wall opposite a huge bay window that looked out over the lake. There was no TV, no radio, no clock in the room.

"I trust you will be comfortable here," she said, flipping the light switch beside the door. "There are candles and matches in one of the end tables. Electrical storms often cause power outages here. You will find towels and a bathrobe in the lavatory."

With that, she turned on her heel and left the room, saying "Have a pleasant evening" over her shoulder.

I drew back the window curtains to reveal a view of the side yard and the lake spreading beyond a row of willows, then sat down on the cushioned seat. Darkness flowed across the grounds and rose up the trunks of the trees. The rain hissed in the big blue spruce to the left of the window and gurgled in the gutter over my head. Thunder boomed out over the lake, and lightning flickered. Another cell was moving in. I switched on the crystal lamp that stood on the night table nearest the window and pulled open the drawer to find a half-dozen candles, a box of wooden matches, and a saucer-shaped brass candle holder.

I looked around the room for something to read but had no luck. Then I remembered I was directly above a huge library. I made my way along the dim corridor and down the stairs. At the bottom I noticed the faint smell of smoke. Old, stale smoke. Strange, I thought. The library had been completely cleaned.

The ground floor was sunk in shadow. I considered returning to my room for a candle rather than blundering around looking for light switches, then changed my mind. The notion of visiting that gloomy library with a storm brewing overhead to make a creepy place that much creepier didn't sit well with me.

I climbed back up the stairs The faint sound of weeping floated from the west wing, where Mrs. Stoppini's room was. I crept down the corridor toward her door, cringing at every creak underfoot.

"How could you leave me? How could you?" I heard, followed by pitiful sobs muffled by the door.

I had been so involved in my own projects—setting up the shop, solving the various problems that came with making a replica of the mantel—I had forgotten that Mrs. Stoppini's life companion had suddenly been snatched away from her. I told myself as I turned toward my room that I would try to be more sensitive in my dealings with her.

I took a long shower, towelled off, and pulled on the blue hooded bathrobe I found neatly folded with the towels Mrs. Stoppini had left for me. By the time I closed the bedroom door behind me the sky was black. A brilliant blue-white flash momentarily lit up the spruce branches outside the window, then the thunderclap whacked the house, shaking the glass.

The lights went out.

With thunder banging and crashing on the roof, I felt my way to the bedside table, lit one of the candles, and carried it to the dresser top, the highest flat surface in the room. I crawled under the duvet and settled into a soft mattress. The candle flame reflected by the dresser mirror gave off a comforting yellow glow. I thought about calling Raphaella, then remembered that the power outage would have killed the cell network. She was probably in her room, looking out into the dark. I imagined her profile in her window, sporadically lit by the lightning. I wondered if she was thinking about me.

The commotion in the skies slowly moved east, and the sound and light show faded, leaving the soft thrumming of rain. Out on the water, I thought I heard an outboard motor running roughly and muffled shouts as the sound faded. Wondering what kind of fool would be boating at night in a storm, I drifted off to sleep.

Soon I was in the grip of one of those anxiety dreams. I was alone, cowering in a dark corner of a small cabin. It was stiflingly hot, but I was wearing a heavy overcoat. Someone was trying to break in, howling with malice as he hammered on the door. Someone who I knew was dead. I dashed back and forth, frantically checking the door lock, which never seemed to close properly, and broken window latches that spun uselessly on the sash. The heat was unbearable. I tore open the coat and tried to take it off, but my arms tangled in the sleeves. There was a deafening boom and the cabin door flew off its hinges, and I stood helpless, my arms snared by the coat.

I awoke struggling and thrashing in the bed, one arm snarled in the sleeve of the bathrobe. The bed was hot, the room airless. I sat up, throwing back the duvet. The candle still burned. I got out of bed and opened the window, admitting a draft of fresh, cool air. I returned to the bed and pulled the sheet over me.

Every house has its own night noises, and the older the building the more it seems to creak and groan, like an old dog getting comfortable in his basket. The Corbizzi mansion was no different. And if you had a big enough imagination, every squeak and crack had a sinister cause—a malevolent intruder creeping slowly up the stairs, an evil spirit bent on revenge pushing open a door. What is there about the dark that awakens primitive images and drags them to the surface of your mind? And why will a rational human being—like me—lie awake, telling himself, "That's just branches scraping against the roof slates," or "It's only the floorboards shrinking as the building cools"? And why don't these explanations bring any comfort?

After a while my body sank deeper into the mattress and my eyelids grew heavier. I became aware of a sound emerging from the air around me, muted and faint. It reminded me of two pieces of cloth rubbing together, or a fingertip brushing repeatedly across an open notebook. Soft as a whisper, the sound was rhythmic. Like breathing.

There was someone in the room.

I jerked to a sitting position. Frantically scanned the shadows in the corners of the candle-lit bedroom. The breathing grew louder and rougher. I jumped from the bed and threw open the door. Nothing. The hallway was a silent black cave. The breathing was coming from behind me. The respiration became laboured and coarse—someone struggling to draw air into constricted lungs, fighting for every breath, saliva rattling in his throat as he began to choke.

It stopped.

The room was silent except for the window curtains brushing the sill with the breeze.

I closed the door, crawled into bed, curled up, and dreamed.

V

A BLACK RAT SCUTTLED across the floor of a dripping jail cell, the yellow light of a single candle reflected in each glassy eye. It passed unnoticed beneath a rough-plank trestle table where three men in hooded robes sat deep in shadow, their hands folded on sheaves of documents.

An iron key struck a lock. A heavy oaken door squealed open on rusty hinges. A man clad in only a filthy shift, his face veiled in shadow, was dragged into the room by two burly jailers and dropped on the floor. He moaned, rising to his knees, clasping his hands to his chest as if in prayer. The jailers yanked his arms behind his back and bound his wrists with leather thongs.

One of the three men at the table nodded almost casually. A jailer reached overhead for the rope that hung from a pulley bolted to the ceiling and passed the end between the arms of the groaning victim, tying a stout knot. Both jailers moved away into the murk at the opposite end of the room.

The rope tightened and quivered, the pulley squeaked as it took the strain. The kneeling man's arms were pulled up and behind his body, squeezing an animal-like noise from his collapsing chest. He was hauled up until his feet barely touched the stone and his contorted shoulders took the full weight of his body. Then, in sporadic jerks, he was winched higher and higher until he hung close to the ceiling, like a grotesquely misshapen angel.

He cried out, then his voice fell to a chant. "*Credo in unum deum patrem omnipotentum factorem caeili et terrae. Credo in unum deum . . .*" He paused, choking. "*De profundis clamavi ad te domine, domine esuadi vocem meam.*"

For the second time, one of the men at the table nodded.

The bound man plummeted toward the floor. The rope unspooled, then thrummed viciously when his body jerked to a stop, inches above the ground, the momentum of his fall dislocating his shoulders with a sickening crack. His scream exploded against the stone walls.

The pulley began to creak again.

I WOKE UP PANTING, breathing raggedly, my heart knocking at my ribs, my eyes frantically probing the gloom for faceless men in hooded robes. There was barely enough pre-dawn light in the bedroom to show the outline of the bedposts and the dresser. It was a dream, I told myself, lying back to stare at the ceiling. Just a nightmare. I forced myself to breathe evenly, repeating my words until my heart rate slowed almost to normal. I threw back the sheet and stood by the bedside, closing the bathrobe and tying the belt tightly. I looked around the room. The window curtains lifted and fell in a cool breeze. The house was silent.

I made my way on unsteady legs to the bathroom and gulped down two glasses of water, then splashed more on my face. I held my hand out. It was shaking. Tension knotted my stomach. I hadn't had a nightmare that bad in a long time. I returned to the bedroom and looked out the window. A gold-red line, with a pastel blue band above it, marked the horizon.

"A normal day," I said out loud. "I hope."

On the dresser top a spent wick lay in a pool of wax on the candle holder.

I climbed back into bed. Raphaella had once advised me that you should always confront a nightmare right away. Lie back, tell the dream to yourself, analyze it, ask yourself what the dream is trying to tell you. That way you can put it in perspective. A fear faced is a fear defeated. Show your terror who's boss, she told me. But I wasn't ready to face the horrors I had witnessed. I had seen five men calmly torture a sixth, indifferent to his suffering.

I pushed the images away, reminding myself they were only that—images—and forced myself to concentrate on my plans for the day. I would return home for a change of clothes, call Raphaella, and see if she could come and begin to catalogue the books. I would work on the mantel while she got started in the library.

Fixing on normal, everyday things brought me back to reality. I rolled over, hoping to catch an hour or so of sleep. I dozed. A black rat scuttled into my mind. A candle flame flickered. Suddenly, the room was flooded with light. I jumped up, jolted with adrenaline, looked frantically around the bedroom.

"What the—?" I yelped.

The overhead light had come on, as had the lamp by the bed. The electricity was back. I hadn't switched the lights off when the power failed in the storm.

"Stupid fool," I said into the empty room.

Five

I

MRS. STOPPINI HAD BREAKFAST READY when I came downstairs. She had dark circles under her eyes. For my part, I had managed an hour of fitful half-sleep that hadn't relieved my fatigue one bit. And my head ached.

"Good morning, Mr. Havelock."

"Morning, Mrs. Stoppini."

"I would customarily enquire as to how you slept, but I expect no one for miles around managed a restful sleep last night."

"You can say that again."

The music of robins and starlings trickled in from the yard, and outside the patio door a hummingbird darted and hovered over flowers sagging from the night's onslaught of wind and rain. Mrs. Stoppini rose from her chair and stepped over to the espresso machine on the counter. She wore the same type of long-sleeved black dress that fell past her knees—only this one had a velvet collar—and woollen stockings with black lace-up leather shoes.

"Cappuccino or straight espresso?" she asked. "Or perhaps you'd prefer a caffè macchiato."

"Er . . . a—"

"Espresso marked with a little milk foam," she explained. "It was the late professor's preferred morning drink."

"Sounds good."

There was a plate of small pastries in the centre of the table alongside a bowl of warm rolls. Mrs. Stoppini placed a small cup of deliciously aromatic coffee in front of me and indicated the food with a turn of her hand. "Please," she invited.

As I layered butter on a roll she sat down. "The patio chairs and umbrella seem to have disappeared during the storm. The gardener doesn't come until Wednesday. I wonder if you'd be so kind . . ."

I took a sip of the coffee. It tasted as good as it smelled—hot and strong.

"Sure," I replied. "Be glad to."

Mrs. Stoppini nodded.

"If you'll make me another macchiato," I said.

I FETCHED MY PUSH BROOM from the workshop and swept the leaves, sticks, and dirt from the patio before tracking down the four chairs the storm had tossed across the lawn. I found the umbrella knee-deep in the lake, up the shore a bit, where the sandy beach gives way to gravel and shale. I waded in and hauled it onto the bank and allowed the water to run out of the canopy, still furled around the pole, secured by a bungee cord.

Something glinted at the waterline. Glass. I bent to pick it up, thinking glass on a beach is a danger to bare feet. It was a hand-held GPS with a camo finish, a waterproof variety, the same brand as the GPS on my motorcycle. The display screen was cracked, allowing water and sand in. I pushed the Power button, but the screen didn't light up. Ruined, but too valuable to throw away, I thought, jamming it into my pocket. I'd check it out later. Maybe the batteries were dead.

Back at the house I erected the sodden umbrella and opened it to dry in the sun.

II

AFTER SAYING A TEMPORARY goodbye to Mrs. Stoppini and thanking her for putting me up for the night, I mounted my motorcycle and headed back into town. It was cool in the shaded roads along the lakefront, and the air, washed by the storm, was fresh and fragrant, coaxing the aftermath of my nightmare from my mind. I rode slowly, 650 cc's of power rumbling serenely between my knees, along Bay Street, around the park, and up the hill on Brant to our house. I parked in back by the garage.

Mom was at the kitchen table reading a manuscript, a pencil in her hand, her favourite dictionary close by. She liked to edit her work on hard copy rather than the computer.

"Hi, Mom," I said. "Dad at the store?"

She looked up and smiled. "He has a line on a nineteenth-century pine table. He's trying to persuade Summerhill to sell it now rather than put it up for auction, but so far it's no go. He's as happy as a clam."

"I'm going to change," I said, heading for the stairs.

My room was on what Dad referred to as the third level and I called the attic. Accessed by a steep flight of narrow stairs, it was a good-sized, wainscotted room tucked up under the mansard roof, with two dormers looking out onto Brant Street—one a window and the other a glassed door to a small balcony. Another window overlooked Matchedash Street. It was the kind of place where, in a gothic novel, the family would lock up their mad auntie when company came over. In real life, a century or so ago, in the days when rich people owned the house, my room was where the servants had lived. I liked it. I had the balcony, lots of light, and if I craned my neck a little, a view of the lake.

I showered and changed into fresh jeans and shirt. I pulled a duffle bag out of my closet and tossed in a set of clothes, a flashlight, a novel, and the charger for my cell. I planned to leave the clothes at the shop in case I was ever soaked or stranded again.

In the kitchen I made some sandwiches and raided the fridge for a few cans of juice, making a mental note to find a small used fridge for my workshop, and put the food into my pack. Dropping into a chair, I sat back and keyed Raphaella's number into my cell.

"Hello?" she answered.

"It's your boyfriend."

"You'll have to be more specific."

"The good-looking one."

"That narrows the field to seven."

"The one you love the best."

"Oh. Hi, Steve."

"Very funny," I said. "Listen, can you make it out to the Corbizzi place today?"

I heard the muffled sound of Raphaella holding the phone against her body and telling her mother she'd be there in a minute. "I'm at the store," she said to me. "I have to unpack and shelve a big shipment of Chinese herbs that came in this morning."

Raphaella's mother made up natural medicine prescriptions. Lately she'd been teaching Raphaella to prepare some of the simpler ones.

"Can you mix me up a batch of frogs' teeth and spiders' tails?"

"Not today. I've got to get going."

"How long will you be?"

"Probably all day. Maybe I could come by your place for dinner."

I tried to keep the disappointment out of my voice. "Okay. Give me a call if you get the chance."

"I promise. Gotta go."

"Okay, bye."

"Bye, Steve," she said brightly.

III

BACK AT THE SHOP I cut pieces of dowel to make spindles for the decorative "fence" around the edge of the new mantel top. I fixed the first one between the spurs of the wood lathe, clamped the tool rest into position, and turned on the motor. Using one of the old urn-shaped spindles as a model, I meticulously shaped the wood until I had an accurate replica, finishing it with sandpaper. Then I turned off the motor.

The lathe had a feature that made the rest of the process easier, an electronic gizmo with a stainless-steel tip much like a ballpoint pen. I manoeuvred the tip to rest against the new spindle, turned on the device, and stood back as it silently travelled the length of the spindle, "reading" and memorizing its shape. I had only to remove the spindle, put a blank in its place, fix a cutting tool into the attachment, push a button, and watch as the lathe automatically shaped a new spindle exactly like the first.

It was slow tedious work as the lathe did all the thinking and cutting while I fed it blanks when the time came, but in less than an hour and a half the job was done. At the workbench I laid out the mantel top, the fence rail, and the spindles, then glued and clamped them, careful to keep the fence spindles perpendicular to the top. Then I made the decorative fences for the side panels. I was hanging up my apron when my cell rang. As usual, Mrs. Stoppini got right to the point.

"I shall be serving lunch on the patio in twelve minutes, if you'd care to join me."

"Thanks, Mrs. Stoppini. Perfect timing, as always."

"Indeed."

After eating a plate of cold pasta salad with sparkling

mineral water—a few notches up from the peanut butter sandwiches I had brought with me—I told Mrs. Stoppini I'd be working in the library for the afternoon.

"Splendid," she commented, and began to clear the dishes.

I looked up into a perfect summer sky whose blue deepened as my eyes moved up from the horizon. There was a cool breeze off the lake, just enough to turn the leaves on the maples in the yard to show their pale undersides. I would have preferred to go swimming with Raphaella at Moose Park or lie on a blanket on the grassy shore and read—or doze off to the sound of kids playing in the sand at the edge of the water. I was beginning to feel the loss of sleep the night before, and the prospect of spending time in that unwelcoming room full of old books wasn't exactly inspiring.

But about an hour later I banged the top back onto a paint can and surveyed the newly painted wall above the fireplace. Satisfied, I gathered the roller and brushes, folded the dropcloths, and took the stuff to the workshop. I decided to take a break and go for a ride on the Hawk while the paint in the library dried and the fumes cleared away. It was a soft summer day, and a motorcycle ride along quiet roads outside of town sounded like a good way to relax.

Then I noticed the broken GPS I had found on the shore lying on the workbench, pushed to the side. I had planned to try new batteries in the hope the unit hadn't been destroyed in the lake. I might be able to find the owner's house and return the device—giving me a destination for my ride.

I inserted the fresh batteries and pressed the Power button. Nothing.

"Oh, well," I muttered.

Then a thought sparked. I powered up my laptop, connected the GPS to it, and launched the GPS software.

"Searching for devices" appeared on the laptop screen. "Device found" was my reward.

Because my own GPS was the same brand, my software could talk to the camo GPS and read its files. I searched around for information on the owner but came up empty. Not to worry. I might find his home by deduction.

A GPS like the camo one was pretty basic but powerful. It could memorize positions—longitude and latitude references—called waypoints, create a route linking selected waypoints, lead you to a specific waypoint using a compass rose, and record tracks. A track was a trip memorized and stored by the GPS. The tracks were usually filed in the unit's memory by date, unless the user had given them titles. This unit was useless because the screen was broken, but I could read its files. And copy them.

The software displayed all the waypoints on a map. After a quick search, I found that almost all the activity was in an area northwest of town, and one spot in particular had a lot of tracks leading to and from it. I deduced that this place was the owner's residence.

On my laptop I created a folder, naming it "Found Unit," then uploaded the contents of the camo GPS into the folder. I slipped outside and removed my GPS from the motorcycle's handlebars. I downloaded "Found Unit" into my GPS. I had now duplicated the contents of the camo GPS on my own.

I threw on my leather jacket and pocketed the camo GPS and my cell. I clipped my GPS back onto the Hawk's handlebars and turned it on. Before long I was on Burnside Line at the edge of town. The houses lining the road fell away behind me as I rode away from town and into flat green farmland dotted with cattle and a few small stands of trees.

Motoring along under the speed limit—which was rare for me—I glided past an abandoned limestone quarry, a small herd of horses standing drowsily in the shade of an elm, a field striped with huge rolls of hay lined up under white plastic tarps. The new-mowed hay filled the air with a clean summery scent. The North River meandered lazily across the landscape, making its way to nowhere in particular. The tension from the last couple of days dissolved in the brilliant air.

Beyond the Maple Valley Crossroad the blacktop narrowed, the farmhouses took on a tired defeated look, the fields were blistered by protruding rocks. The road grew even more restricted, then played out completely. I turned onto a gravel side road, following the compass rose on the GPS with growing doubt that I was being taken to the owner's residence. The gravel soon disappeared and I found myself bumping along a dirt track twisting its way over stony, rolling ground toward a forest in the northwest. A couple of pickup trucks hitched to flatbed trailers were parked along the verge. ATVers, I figured.

I stopped. I thought I knew where the track led, but I wanted to be sure. I pressed the zoom-out button on the GPS until the map showed a much wider area. The almost-road twisted and looped for miles and ended at Swift Rapids, a lock on the four-hundred-kilometre Trent canal system linking Lake Ontario to Georgian Bay by connecting dozens of rivers and lakes using humanmade canals and locks.

Did the owner of the camo GPS live around here? It seemed unlikely. And how far did my obligation to return the GPS to him go? I decided to poke along the rocky trail until the Hawk objected—it wasn't a trail bike, and although the clearance was pretty good for a touring motorcycle, it was too unwieldy to handle rough travel.

Within fifteen minutes I had reached the forest, and soon after that the pointer on the compass rose indicated I should leave the track and take one that branched to the right. This one was narrower—but still wide enough for me to ride—fairly flat and covered with leaves that showed few signs of disturbance. I tooled along for a couple of klicks. The trees on either side of the path gradually squeezed in until the track ended.

Now what? I had not reached the destination I had been making for. I looked at my watch, deciding to walk for another few minutes, then give up on what was looking more and more like a wild goose chase. As a precaution, I entered a waypoint into the GPS and labelled it "mc." If I got lost, I'd be able to find the Hawk.

I gulped down half a bottle of juice, then followed the footpath into a thickening forest of second-growth hardwoods. A couple of hundred metres farther, where it seemed that the trail was about to peter out, I found myself at the edge of a clearing.

IV

THE OPEN SPACE was half the size of a football field, sunlit and quiet. A small clapboard cabin sat off to one side, a stovepipe poking at an angle through the tarpapered roof. No doors or windows—I was looking at the back of the place. I watched for a while, standing motionless inside the treeline, but saw no activity beyond a pair of blue jays darting around and a black squirrel that seemed unable to make up its mind where it wanted to go.

I crossed the clearing. Shallow trenches and tent-peg holes made a pattern indicating that a few tents had been pitched opposite the cabin not so long ago. The building itself was a simple structure with one cracked window, a padlocked door, and a roofless verandah across the front. The shiny padlock looked new.

All around the window and door, yellow, red, and blue splotches streaked by rain marbled the bare wood, as if a half-dozen demented kindergarten children had been let loose with brushes and cans of paint. They were paintball hits. I stepped onto the creaking porch and peered through the window, letting my eyes adjust to the dark interior. I saw two bare bunks against the far wall, a wooden table, a few broken rail-back chairs, a small wood stove. Nothing else. No sign—a hat on a peg, a few dishes—that anyone used the place.

But outside, along the east wall, was a metre-high stack of firewood. The ground around the cabin was a mess of boot prints and ATV tracks leading to a trail heading north-east through the dense bush. If the direction held, the track would meet the Trent canal system near Morrison Landing.

I sat on the porch. Whoever used the place had left nothing behind that would identify them. It seemed clear that I had stumbled onto a paintball camp. I knew people in town who enjoyed an afternoon out in the woods, fighting a mock battle using paintball guns rather than the real thing.

War games—and not for kids, either. The broken GPS in my pocket probably belonged to someone who had been out here, likely with a bunch of guys, probably more than once. He had lost the unit on Lake Couchiching—maybe last night, when I had heard a boat—and it had floated to the shore of the Corbizzi estate.

I searched the waypoint file again and displayed them on the map. Sure enough, there were points marked along the Trent waterway toward Lake Couchiching, proving that the owner accessed the camp by water. That explained both the ATV tracks and the fact that the way I had come in had shown no sign of human traffic.

I brought up the waypoint I had been seeking. A lot of tracks led to that spot from different directions. It was off to my right.

I got to my feet, hit the Go button, and followed the compass into the bush, away from the cabin and the ATV trail. The forest was thick, and pushing through it was hard work. After ten minutes of slogging I came upon a huge granite outcropping, like a stone kneecap protruding half a metre above the leaf-mantled ground. A fissure cut across the rock at a jagged angle.

I looked around and saw only the rock surrounded by a wall of trees. Why would the guy come here so often? I wondered. To be alone? Was this a hiding spot during the war games? A place to ambush "enemies" and shoot them with a ball of paint that would explode on impact and mark them as dead?

I circled the granite kneecap, thinking. This was no hiding place. Here, you'd be out in the open, an easy target. My eyes were drawn to the fissure snaking through the rock. Near the crest, juniper branches poked out. I carefully pushed the prickly boughs aside. Something down in the hole reflected the light. I reached deep under the shrub. My hand closed on a plastic bag.

Sealed inside it was a cellphone.

V

BEFORE I COULD OPEN the bag I heard the wavering rumble of small engines in the distance. The noise swelled gradually until I could distinguish four or five motors, their individual rackets rising and falling as the drivers worked the throttles. The clamour seemed to converge on the cabin.

I scrambled off the rock, skinning my palms, and darted into the trees, my heart leaping around behind my ribs. Instinctively I crept deeper into the forest. I called up "mc" on my GPS, punched Go, and began to walk as quietly as I could—the GPS only worked when it was moving. The compass rose appeared on the screen, rotated casually, and pointed toward the Hawk.

As I walked, placing every step cautiously, pushing branches carefully aside and releasing them slowly as I passed, I heard voices in the distance, laughter, and the commotion of a group of men out for sport. Then the motors fell silent. Someone barked an order and the horseplay ceased.

I made my way through the trees as quickly as I could without snapping twigs underfoot or breaking off branches. After what seemed like an hour of fighting the urge to run,

I spotted the glint of sunlight on the polished aluminum frame of my motorcycle through the branches. My knees wobbled with relief.

Then I realized I still held the bagged cellphone in my hand.

I unlocked the saddlebag and tossed the cell inside and swung my leg over the bike, snapping the GPS into its cradle and pulling on my helmet. A few centimetres from the ignition, my hand, holding the key, stopped. Now that I felt safe, my curiosity began to get the better of me. I could sneak back and take a quick peek, I told myself.

"Don't be an idiot," cautioned my logical angel. "A gang of strangers finds you spying on them? Is this a pretty picture?" But I got off the bike, pocketed the key, perched my helmet on the saddle, took the GPS out of its holder, and headed toward the clearing, following the line I'd travelled earlier.

Once I'd made about half the distance I slowed and sneaked, eyes peeled for movement, ears alert for the slightest noise. I stopped when I spied shapes through the screen of leaves, gliding back and forth. Voices in a strange language floated in the warm air. No laughter now. The talk seemed serious and purpose-driven. I peered through the thick foliage. A droplet of sweat trickled down my rib cage.

I bent into a half crouch and crept forward until I reached a spruce tree a couple of metres from the edge of the clearing. Through the fragrant boughs I could make out the cabin and, nearer to me, nine men dressed in camo, right down to the caps and boots. They were erecting tents, also with a camo design, in the same place I had seen the trenches and peg holes. They spoke occasionally but didn't waste words. I couldn't place the language.

A tall man came around the corner of the cabin, a gun slung diagonally across his chest. He snapped off a couple of commands. The men speeded up their movements. Sunlight detailed the tall man's gun, the canteen on his belt, the long knife in a calf-scabbard, his thick moustache. Like all the others he had brown skin, and the black hair under his cap was cut short.

I slipped my cell from my pocket, turned it on, and immediately disabled the ringer. I activated the camera, turning off the flash, then took the commander's picture before I captured a few more snaps at random. Stowing the cell, I turned and, careful to keep the spruce between me and the men, began to creep back to my motorcycle.

When I had made about twenty metres I stood, looked back, saw nothing threatening, and began to walk.

And tripped.

I crashed to the ground, making a racket like a thrashing elephant, and dropped the GPS into the leaves. I scrambled to my knees as a shout rang out behind me. Another shout followed. Boots pounded as bodies crashed through trees. I felt around in the leaves for the GPS. Someone hollered, closer this time. My fingers hit plastic, and I snatched up the unit and got to my feet and began to run.

If "run" is the right word for zigzagging though dense forest, eyes on the GPS, eyes ahead, then back to the little glass screen showing me the right way, heartbeats thudding in my ears.

Shouts, snapping branches, and the thump of boots on the forest floor told me the men in camo were closing in. I burst out of the trees, jammed the GPS into my pocket, pulled on my helmet, fumbled out my key, swung my leg over the saddle.

"Don't drop it, don't drop it," I chanted, my hand shaking as I jammed the key into the ignition and turned it. Shapes approached through the trees. I pushed the bike off the stand, made a painfully slow three-point turn—why hadn't I parked the Hawk facing away from the forest?—hit the Start button, kicked the gear shift into first, and roared away, eyes on the rear-view mirror, just as three or four men in military gear broke out of the bush and skidded to a halt in the cloud of dust I had left behind me.

VI

ALONG BURNSIDE DRIVE I looked down at the speedometer to find I was fifty over the limit. I cut back on the throttle and tried to do the same to the flow of adrenaline racing through my veins.

I rode into Couchiching Park, where I bought an ice cream at French's and took it to a bench by the boardwalk. I watched powerboats come and go from the marina under a blue sky where seagulls scribed lazy circles. People strolled by, kids shrieked and complained on the playground equipment. All was normal.

Sugar wasn't supposed to calm people down, but licking chocolate ice cream helped me coax my heart rate back to normal. I had a bad feeling about those guys in the bush. Their appearance and their air of purpose didn't suggest sport, even though they seemed to enjoy chasing me. They hadn't seemed like a bunch of good old boys out for a bit of fun shooting paintballs at one another and pouring down cold beer between pretend battles. They were organized and disciplined. And that leader was anything but one of the boys.

I remembered that during the thunderstorm at the Corbizzi mansion last night, I thought I heard a motorboat out on the water—a strange place to be when the lake was crazy with wind and wave, when lightning flashed every couple of seconds. This morning I had found the GPS. Which had led me to the cabin. A coincidence? I doubted it. The GPS held waypoints stretching from Morrison Landing to Lake Couchiching. I got to my feet, wiped the sticky remnants of ice cream from my fingers with a tissue, tossed the paper into a bin, and walked back to the parking lot where I'd left the Hawk.

The GPS had probably been lost by one of the camoboys. Simple.

Just as simple was the fact that I felt no obligation now to return it. The last thing I wanted was to have to explain to any of those guys, let alone the leader, how I came to possess it. On my way back to the Hawk, I removed the two good batteries and tossed the GPS into a garbage bin. Then I mounted up and rode home.

The cellphone in my saddlebag had completely slipped my mind.

Raphaella laughed.

I called her that night and related my unintentional visit to paintball heaven.

"I guess it does have its funny side," I said, aware that my voice was a little chilly. She wasn't taking the paintballers as seriously as I was. Maybe she was right.

"Sorry," she apologized. Then she giggled. "I can just picture you charging through the trees, chased by the Testosterone Kids with their blotchy green-and-brown clothes."

"Hardly kids."

"All this because you were too conscientious about trying to return someone's lost property."

"Yeah, well, I misplaced that sense of duty in the bush somewhere," I replied. "The GPS is in the trash down at the park, and the cell is still in the Hawk's saddlebag."

"You're not going to try and return it, I hope."

"No. It can stay where it is for the time being. I'll probably end up tossing it, too."

"Good idea," she said, suddenly serious. "They sound like people worth staying away from."

We talked a bit more and then signed off for the night. I watched a bit of TV and went to bed. Before I fell asleep, my imagination replayed images of the camo-boys flitting through the trees, converging on me.

PART TWO

The Lord has brought me here, and has said to me,
"I have put you here as a watchman in the centre of Italy
that you may hear my words and announce them to the people."

—Girolamo Savonarola

One

I

THE MORNING AFTER my unplanned visit to the paintball camp I returned to the mansion and went immediately to the library. I sat down at the escritoire, thinking. I hadn't abandoned the possibility that Professor Corbizzi already had a catalogue of his collection, and I was determined to search the library thoroughly before I started an inventory from scratch. There was no use asking Mrs. Stoppini—she avoided the room. Besides, she had asked me to do the inventory in the first place.

The absence of a computer or one of those old-style multi-drawer file-card systems like they used to have in public libraries was not encouraging. The filing cabinet yielded nothing but old household bills, tax statements, and other papers, and in the escritoire I found only an old pipe tobacco tin containing a broken pocket knife and a rosary with glass beads and a black wooden cross.

One of the bottom drawers of the escritoire jammed when I tried to close it. Wiggling as I pulled, I removed it and set it on the desk. On my hands and knees, I took a close look at the track. It was worn but seemed true. I checked the drawer's corner joints. Sure enough, they were loose, a common problem with old furniture. It would take only a few minutes to fix.

I emptied the contents—a few loose papers and a package of envelopes—onto the desk beside the typewriter and turned the drawer upside down to examine it more closely. Something rattled, then two small brass keys plopped onto the escritoire. I set the drawer down, intending to repair it later, then looked around, my mind back to the quest for a catalogue. I could see nowhere such a thing might be kept—unless among the books themselves. Finding it would mean taking the books off the shelves and examining them—which Raphaella and I would be doing anyway as we worked on the inventory.

Then I remembered the alcove on the other side of the room, and the cupboard built into the bookshelves.

Quickly, I crossed the floor, the little brass keys in my hand. The volumes flung onto the floor by the professor during his last seconds on earth were now stacked on the table in the alcove. I stepped between the table and the shelves on the north wall. The closely fitted cupboard door had a round wooden pull—and below the pull, a brass cabinet lock.

One of the keys opened the lock. I found a stack of small leather-bound books that would have made my father exclaim "Aha!" as he waggled his eyebrows. He loved old books, and sometimes added them to his collection rather than put them up for sale. I transferred the pile onto the table behind me and opened one book at random. It was a Greek–Latin dictionary, published in London in 1763. Assuming the rest were as valuable—or the professor wouldn't have kept them under lock and key—I made a mental note to tell Mrs. Stoppini she would need the services of a rare books expert at some point.

I lifted out a stack of bundled papers, each bunch secured with ribbons, like a parcel. On closer examination, the paper turned out to be vellum—finely polished animal skin. The manuscripts had been penned by different people, and none was in English. Conscious of their value, I replaced them carefully. As I slid them back into the cupboard, my fingernail caught on something. I moved the manuscripts to the table again.

There was a large round knot in the board that formed the right-hand wall of the cupboard. In an otherwise top-quality bookshelf, why use a flawed piece of wood? Any cabinetmaker knows that knots—especially a big one like this—can come loose and even fall out over time as the wood dries. More important, the old vellum could be snagged just as my finger had been, and damaged. A lapse in cabinetmaking quality like this didn't make sense.

I ran my finger across the surface of the knot. It *was* loose. And it was coated with a waxy substance. I pressed it. As I withdrew my finger, the knot came with it. I probed the hole. I felt something. Metal. I pushed.

And heard a barely audible click.

Then nothing.

Taking a step back, I scanned the shelves and uprights. Everything appeared as it should be—except for a barely noticeable gap that outlined three shelves and their uprights to the right of the cupboard. The gap hadn't been there moments before.

I gripped the edge of a shelf between my finger and thumb and pulled. Silently, a section of the shelf unit, books and all, moved toward me like a hinged door, and I found myself looking at another cupboard set into the wall behind the bookshelves, this one secured by a locked metal roll-up door like you'd find on an old writing desk.

And then I heard a shrill ring.

Like a schoolboy caught with his hand in the teacher's purse, I jumped back and snatched a glance toward the library doors, even though I couldn't see them from the alcove. The ring trilled again.

My cell.

It was a text message: *conf din arr 6 k? rs*

I sent back *k* and closed the phone.

I took a breath and reminded myself that I wasn't snooping. Well, not technically. I wasn't prying into the professor's private life. I was doing what I had agreed to do—make an inventory of the library—wasn't I? The alcove was part of the library, wasn't it?

The second key fit the lock and the door rolled up and behind the cupboard smoothly and silently, revealing two wide, deep shelves. The cupboard was like a strongbox—two layers of metal with insulation between. On the bottom shelf lay a messy pile of papers on top of a file case. The sheaf of paper was as thick as a brick, typed, I was willing to bet, on the old Underwood. The title page bore the word "Fanatics" over "by Professor Eduardo Corbizzi." I set it aside.

A wine-coloured book with *Compendium Revelationem* on the spine in cracked gilt lettering rested on the top shelf beside a small container of inlaid wood. I took up the book, surprised by its heavy weight, and laid it on the table. It smelled of old leather and dust and ancient paper. I flipped through. The language wasn't English. The last page was stained, but the words "Hieronymvs" and "Ferrara" were clear. Closer to the bottom I made out "Firenze" and "MCDXCV," then "Ser Francesco Bonaccorsi."

I turned back to the cupboard and opened the small, finely made box, finding a crudely cast medal, green with age, resting in a silk bed. On one side a pigeon-like bird with rays emanating from its head hung suspended in the sky, at the edge of a cloud. A raised line bisected the medal, separating the strange bird from a hand emerging from a cloud, clutching a dagger, its tip pointing toward a collection of buildings. The flip side showed the profile of a man gripping a crucifix with both hands, staring the haloed Jesus in the face. The man, wearing a cape with a hood that covered his hair and ears, had a prominent hooked nose, and the look in his eyes as he glowered at Jesus was anything but reverent.

Worn, almost illegible block letters in a foreign language followed the outside edge of the medal. I turned it slowly in my hands, squinting at the writing—which, like the lines in the red leather book, appeared at first to be English but wasn't. Small diamond shapes were visible between some of the words.

HIERONYMVS SA followed by something illegible, ◊EER ◊ORD◊FREVIRI, and unclear marks, then ◊DOCTISSIMVS.

Turning the coin over I read,

GLADIVS◊DOMINI◊SUP◊TERRA◊CITO◊ET
VELOCITER◊SPIRITVS◊ONI◊SUP◊TERRA◊COPIOSE SUDAT

"Interesting," I whispered. "'Hieronymvs' appears on both the medal and in the book."

I replaced the medal and carefully fitted the lid, then turned to the last article in the cupboard. It was heavy, wrapped in a black velvet cloth so soft the bulky object it enclosed almost slipped out of my hands. I found myself cradling an ornately tooled cross at least sixty centimetres high and encrusted with jewels. The dusky gold seemed to glow from within. Never in my life had I held something so valuable and beautiful.

On closer inspection, one of the jewels turned out to be a dome of clear but imperfect glass held to the base with clips, like a gem in a ring. The glass seemed to cover something brownish black, a kind of disk with a hole in the middle, that had been set into the gold.

Professor Corbizzi must have been a religious man as well as a secretive one, I thought, pushing the thick manuscript into the file case. I wound the string around the paper button, then replaced each object where I had found it and rolled down the door. I locked the cupboard and swung the bookcase door into position, hearing the solid but faint click of the catch. I placed the knot back in its spot and locked the outside cupboard, then slipped the keys under the rosary in the tobacco tin I had found in the escritoire. Carrying the damaged drawer, I left the library with relief, sliding the door shut and thinking about the strange cupboard's contents and wondering if Mrs. Stoppini knew about them.

II

I STOOD IN THE KITCHEN DOORWAY, the drawer in my hand, watching her crank the handle of a pasta-making machine. She hadn't heard me come into the kitchen. Whatever contrast there was between the two of us, we both liked to cook. There she was, making fresh linguine noodles for her supper, which she would eat alone.

She was a strange woman, with her outdated clothing—which I had assumed was a mourning outfit but now wasn't so sure about—her formal speaking style, her old-fashioned manners which didn't quite succeed in glossing over a stern, unyielding personality. She was lost in concentration, humming a sad tune I didn't recognize.

I cleared my throat, startling her.

"Sorry. I'm just going to reset this drawer and then head off home."

She eyed the drawer, then looked at me.

"It sticks," I explained. "I can fix it in no time."

Her stare didn't waver.

"It's what I do," I added lamely.

Brushing flour from her hands, she said, "That's most kind of you, Mr. Havelock. Perhaps you'd care for a beverage before you leave."

I didn't, but it would have been rude to refuse. Besides, the thought of her drudging away at her pasta machine, alone in a huge house, got to me.

"That would be great," I replied. "I'll just slop a little glue on this. Won't take ten minutes."

An almost-smile moved those strange red lips. "Splendid. What would you like to drink?"

"A cappuccino would be good."

She frowned as if I had tracked cow flop across her kitchen floor. "In civilized countries, cappuccino is never served after twelve o'clock."

Well, pardon me, I thought. What a boor you must think me. Instead I said, "One of your delicious macchiatos?"

"Very well."

When I returned from the shop, the sideboard had been cleared, the pasta hung on a drying rack, and the green light glowed on the espresso machine. Mrs. Stoppini drew a tiny cup of coffee, added a drop of frothed milk, and placed it on the table in front of me along with a half-dozen squares of dark chocolate on a china plate.

She sat down with a glass of red wine.

"Chianti?" I asked.

"Indeed."

"I'm hoping Raphaella will be able to come tomorrow," I told her.

"I shall look forward to it."

"Um, Mrs. Stoppini, I want to ask you something."

She put down her glass, her thick dark eyebrows lifting slightly. She fixed her fish-eyes on me expectantly, her bizarrely made-up lips in a straight line.

"I . . . I hope you won't think I'm prying, or that I'm overstepping the terms of my contract . . ."

The eyebrows dropped into a frown.

"I'm aware that you made a big deal . . . er, point about confidentiality—"

"Excuse my interruption, Mr. Havelock, but what—?"

"But you stressed that you wanted a complete inventory."

"Do feel free to speak, Mr. Havelock," she said impatiently.

"Well, am I right in assuming the inventory is to include the little cupboard behind the secret door?"

"The . . . I'm afraid you've lost me."

"Come with me," I said.

Before she could object, I left the kitchen. When I pulled back the library doors she was right behind me. She stood rooted in the hallway, watching me like a puzzled crow, as if I was a demented stranger teetering on the edge of a full-blown fit. I got the keys from the escritoire, crossed the room, and stopped by the alcove.

"You can't see it from there," I said. "You'll have to come in."

"Very well. If you insist."

She drew herself up and stepped in, like a non-swimmer testing the water.

"Farther," I advised.

Mrs. Stoppini advanced stiffly, craning her neck.

I went through the elaborate process of releasing the lock. "Now watch," I said, a little dramatically.

The section of bookcase swung smoothly open. Behind me I heard her catch her breath. I rolled up the secret inner door. I hadn't thought her eyes could get any bigger or protrude any farther, but they did.

"Good gracious!" she exclaimed.

"Take a look at what I found in here," I said, holding back my excitement.

Mrs. Stoppini had gone pale. She looked like she was about to dash off. "I think not, just at the moment," she said uneasily. "Please add whatever it is to the inventory."

"Well, the thing is, it looks like pretty valuable stuff. Maybe you should hang on to this."

I tried to hand her the key. She shrank back, eyes bulging, as if the key carried a curse.

"No, no, Mr. Havelock, if you please!"

She fled the room as if it was on fire.

Two

I

"Hmm. *Fanatics*, eh? Catchy title. What's the book about?"

"I don't know. Someone with too much zeal and too little common sense, I suppose."

"You didn't read any of it."

"No," I replied sheepishly.

Only a few hours had passed since I discovered Professor Corbizzi's secret hoard of mysteries. Raphaella and I were lounging in the living room of my house, lazy and sluggish after a big dinner with my parents, who had gone out to the bridge club.

"And you only took, quote, 'a quick gander' at that thing under the glass dome on the gold cross, and you can't say what it was."

"Right."

"And the title of the big old leather book published around five hundred years ago was in a language kind of like English but not English."

"Right again."

"Which was sort of like the language on the medal, but you're not sure."

"Go to the head of the class."

"And the word 'Hieronymvs' appears on both the book and the medal, but you don't know what it means."

I nodded.

"Remind me never to hire you as a detective," Raphaella said, lying back lazily with her head propped on the arm of the sofa and her feet in my lap.

"I detected all kinds of stuff. I detected so many things that I almost fainted from detection exhaustion."

She smirked. "Poor boy. But you didn't *delve*, did you?"

"I already told you. The place gives me the shivers. And there's more."

Raphaella sat up. "I knew it."

Beginning slowly so as not to leave out any details—I couldn't forget them even if I wanted to—I told her the dream I had had during the thunderstorm at the Corbizzi place. The dark chamber, the black rat, the terrifying silent men at the table, the horrific torture of the man whose face I couldn't make out in the gloom, his heart-ripping shrieks. Her face blanched when I described how they let him drop from the ceiling and how his shoulders made that sickening crack when they were dislocated.

Raphaella had an interesting theory about dreams. She believed that most were a sort of inner conversation in sounds and images and actions. You were telling yourself something, one part of the mind explaining itself to another, without words. If you paid attention to your dream, analyzed it without expecting it to be logical or "realistic," you could eventually understand what it was about.

Both of us also believed that some dreams weren't like these inner conversations. They originated *outside* the dreamer and came from another realm, as if two different realities intersected momentarily, like the past briefly overlapping the present. When Raphaella had one of her premonitions, she believed they came from outside her in the same way. We knew without saying anything that the dream I had described was this second kind.

"Wow," she said when I had finished my story. "Hmm."

"I know what you're thinking," I said.

"The bedroom was—"

"Directly above the library alcove."

II

THAT NIGHT MY ROOM was like a sauna but with nicer furniture. I had both windows open but not even a breath of air stirred the branches of the maples along the street. I read for a while, sitting up in bed, legs splayed. Eventually I gave in and threw down my novel. I cast my eye to the balcony, thinking.

Why not? I asked myself. I had slept out there before on nights like this. It wasn't very comfortable but it was a few degrees cooler. I swung my feet to the floor just as a car cruised slowly down Brant Street, its tuned exhausts thundering in the spaces between window-rattling thumps of a sub-woofer. I fell back onto the mattress and rolled over, giving in to a few hours of tossing and turning.

Sometime during the night, a cool draft made sleep possible and I drifted off. I heard rusted door hinges groan in protest, the tread of heavy boots echoing off stone walls. I saw the candle on the trestle table wavering in the draft, dimly outlining the six characters in the grim drama I had witnessed in my first nightmare—the hooded men, the two jailers, the torture victim. A seventh man, this one wearing a long coat and a shapeless cap, tentatively entered the chamber, pushed the door closed, and bowed to the figures seated behind the table. He turned toward the collapsed human form on the floor.

The prisoner's anguished cries had ebbed to continuous sobbing. The newcomer knelt next to him, pitilessly gripped his mangled upper arm, made a small adjustment, locked his elbows, and then, deaf to the shrieks of the prisoner, threw the weight of his body behind the thrust, relocating the shoulder. He rolled the victim over and repeated the gruesome procedure on the opposite shoulder, drawing more howls of torment. Rising, he brushed dust off his knees and hands, then turned on his heel and left the cell.

The jailers moved in and trussed up the prisoner the same way they had before. The pulley began its grisly song, halting after the prisoner's bare feet had cleared the floor. One of the jailers left the chamber, returning immediately with a smoking bucket of red-hot coals, which he placed under the victim's filthy, dangling feet. He knelt, took hold of the prisoner's legs, and nodded to his partner, who gripped the rope and leaned backwards against the prisoner's weight. Gradually, he eased off on the rope. The hanging man slowly descended. His feet went down into the bucket. Skin and fat sizzled and smoked.

The pitiful screams and wails, the squeak of the pulley, the thrum of the rope abruptly halting the body's fall, the sickening crack of the dislocating of shoulder joints—all amid the nauseous stench of burned flesh—mingled to form a new definition of hell.

III

DISEMBODIED SCREECHES coming from somewhere above drew me away from my nightmare. I lay in my bed, wincing with each sharp cry. I stared at the ceiling, focused on the cracks in the plaster, willing myself to take hold of reality.

I looked out the window into a blue sky. Seagulls wheeled past, shrieking.

The morning sunlight washed away some of the dread in the wake of the dream. Think about it, I told myself. Don't run away from it this time. But what could I conclude—besides that I had seen a man tortured a second time, and that the dream told me, the way dreams do, it was the same man? I had not seen his face, but I knew. Who was he? Who were the shadowed men behind the table presiding over the atrocity? Who were the jailers who had administered the torture with the detachment of clerks stocking grocery shelves? I had no answers.

All right, then. If not who, when and where? There were no clues as to location other than the stone construction of the damp cell. There was the smoky candle, the table's rough-hewn planks, the men's clothing, barely discernible in the three-quarter darkness. I recalled images of the men. Leather jerkins on the jailers, a long coat and soft hat on the man who reset the victim's shoulders, hooded robes on the silent three. Whatever I had seen, it had happened long ago.

And there was the method of torture.

It was a place to start.

But did I want to start? If I began to investigate the dream, where would it lead? Nowhere good, I was sure. But I was—morbidly, it was true—curious. I felt like a kid sticking his head into a darkened cave just to see how big the dragon is.

MY STOMACH, still knotted by the nightmare, rebelled at the idea of breakfast, but I forced down a piece of toast and took a second cup of tea to my room and powered up my laptop. Before long my tour of online encyclopedias led me into a house of horrors offering lots of gruesomely illustrated techniques human beings have used over the centuries to inflict degradation and pain on each other.

There seemed to be two main reasons for torture—to force a confession or to extract information. "I confess to being a witch—or unbeliever, or terrorist, or heretic" was almost always followed with "Tell us the names of other witches—or unbelievers, or terrorists, or heretics." Politics, war, and religion were the main theatres of torture. I had assumed that torture was a thing of the past, but it was still performed. Everywhere. And, I was shocked to learn, by everyone. Even the good guys. I didn't want to think about where the churches and prisons and army camps recruited their torturers.

There was a grimly realistic pencil drawing of the grisly technique I had seen in my dream. It was called the *strappado*—Italian for "tear" or "rip." The picture showed a woman accused of witchcraft hanging from the ceiling like a damaged moth, her arms up and behind, her feet weighed down by a heavy chain wrapped around her ankles. The *strappado* had been busy for centuries—in the Roman Catholic Inquisition, the Puritan Salem witch trials, the North Vietnamese prison camps in the 1970s, and today in the hunt for terrorists. The references said that the *strappado* was almost as "effective" as waterboarding, where the victim is tied to an inclined plank, head down, and water is poured into his mouth and nostrils, making him think he is drowning.

I logged off in disgust before I lost what faith in humanity I had left, and called Raphaella. Her voice was like spring water on a dry throat.

"I'll pick you up in five," I said. "Bring a smile with you."

IV

WHEN I TURNED THE CORNER of her street, Raphaella was standing on the curb outside her house. Dressed in a mauve T-shirt and sky blue jeans, she was a bright splash of colour in a depressing morning. She climbed into the van and dumped her backpack on the floor. As I pulled away, I felt her eyes on me.

"No good-morning kiss today?" I asked.

"What's happened?" was her reply. "You're giving off vibes like a radar tower."

"I'm fine. Hey, you look great."

"Don't change the subject."

"Mrs. Indeed will be impressed."

She continued to fix me in her gaze. "You've had another dream," she said.

"Yeah."

She nodded. "Okay," she added, as if we had come to some kind of decision. "Anything different this time?"

"A few more details. About the torture."

"Let's stop here for a bit."

I slipped the van into one of the shaded parking spaces near the Champlain monument in the park. We got out and strolled to a bench on a grassy patch by the lake. Across the water to the north, Wicklow Point, densely cloaked in maples and willows, hooked into the bay like a claw.

I told Raphaella the dream and described the research I had done.

"So what do we know?" she began. "To me, the most significant fact is that you can't see anyone's face clearly, especially the four most important characters in the story."

"The prisoner and the three people supervising the torture."

"Men," Raphaella corrected. "They're men. Women don't torture."

I nodded. "I think the victim's male, too, judging by his voice. And the clues point to the past. The *strappado* is still used, but the candle and the clothing go back centuries. Besides, in a dream you just *know* things, without needing a reason."

"*Strappado*. Sounds Italian. That's what this kind of torture is called?"

"Right. It means ripping and tearing—in this case, the shoulders."

"Since nobody says anything, we can't figure out the reason for the torture," Raphaella went on.

"Wait! The victim *does* say something, but it's like words all mixed up with cries and groans. Not in English, though. And it sounds like . . ." I jumped to my feet. "A prayer! I think he was praying."

"Who wouldn't?" Raphaella said. "But that's good. It's not much, but every clue helps."

I sat down again, shaken. "When I feel ready, I'll go over the nightmare again. Maybe a few details will come to the surface, but I'm pretty sure there's much more to remember."

Raphaella put her arm around me and laid her head on my shoulder. Her hair smelled of flowers and soap—fresh, like spring. There was a time I would have rejected the conversation we were having. What's around us, I would have argued—the lake, the sky, those kids on the playground over there—is real. Dreams aren't. Now I knew different.

"I guess I'll just have to wait," I said, "for the third dream."

"You think you'll have another?"

"I know I will."

Three

I

Mrs. Stoppini had tea for three laid out on the kitchen table when Raphaella and I appeared at the back door of the Corbizzi mansion. Stiff and stern, she ushered us inside.

"Good morning, Mr. Havelock," she intoned, then turned to Raphaella. "And you must be Miss Skye. I am very pleased to make your acquaintance." She held out a bony hand.

"Hi," Raphaella replied, throwing me a glance that said "I see what you mean."

"You'll take tea," asserted Mrs. Stoppini, showing us to the table with a turn of her wrist.

We chit-chatted about the weather—the kind of aimless small talk that drove me nuts—then our hostess got down to business. She had begun to impress on Raphaella the need for discretion and confidentiality when I cut in and excused myself.

"If you don't mind, I'll leave you two to discuss details. I need to see about something in the shop."

I went out the door before anyone could object.

In the workshop I turned on the lights and fan, then slipped into my apron. The assembled mantel lay on the workbench, bristling with clamps, pale under the lights. I freed it and carried it to the wall, where I stood it beside the blistered and scorched remains of the original. Stepping back a few paces, I ran my eye over every detail, comparing them. Satisfied, I lifted the new one to a dust-free bench and cleaned it with rags lightly sprinkled with solvent, careful to remove every speck of sawdust. Then I took it to the spray booth and spent twenty minutes or so mixing stains to match the old mantel's red mahogany finish as closely as possible. After trading the apron for a set of coveralls, a hat, gloves, a mask, and goggles, I turned on the sprayer and began to apply the finish.

I returned to the house to find that the two women—whom I wouldn't have been surprised to see facing off like a couple legionaries—were still at the table, their cups empty, their plates sprinkled with crumbs, chatting almost informally about MOO. Raphaella tossed me a "get me out of here!" look.

"That's that done," I said, closing the door behind me.

Raphaella got to her feet. "Thanks for the tea, Mrs. Stoppini. I suppose Garnet and I should be getting to work."

ALTHOUGH SHE HAD HIDDEN it well during our tea, Raphaella was nervous about the library, and as we walked down the corridor to the east wing, her tension grew. When

I rolled the doors aside and stepped into the room, which was bright with morning light, she stopped.

"I see what you meant," she murmured. "Something happened here all right."

"Professor Corbizzi died."

"Something more. Much more. Something bad."

"Like the churchyard on the 3rd Concession?"

On the way home from a delivery to the city one night more than a year before, I had run smack into the worst snowstorm to hit the county in ten years. Barely escaping a huge pileup of cars, buses, and tractor-trailers near Barrie, I had steered off the big highway and taken the 3rd Concession. My luck held for a while, but the darkness and thick, whirling snow reduced visibility to zero and I skidded off the road, smashing into something I couldn't even see. Luckily—I thought at the time—the pioneer church called African Methodist, unused for years, was close by. I slogged through blinding snow and howling wind to take shelter inside. I passed a long, cold, and scary night, haunted by dreams and disembodied voices.

About three months later, Raphaella and I passed the church on our way to the mobile home park where I was about to take up a part-time job as caretaker. We stopped to look around. In the quiet sunlit churchyard Raphaella had immediately sensed something evil.

"The feeling's just as powerful, but different," Raphaella replied now. "I'm not being clear, am I?"

"You don't have to be. I've felt it since the beginning. I hoped it would disappear once the damage from the fire was repaired and the smoke odour removed."

Raphaella walked slowly along the south wall, avoiding

the alcove, the way I had done on my first exploration of the library. Her fingertips brushed the books as she passed.

"What a collection," she said, awed by the sheer number of hardcover volumes. "Show me the secret cupboard."

I fetched the keys from the desk and went through the unlocking ritual.

"It's like an Alexandre Dumas novel, isn't it?" she whispered.

"I've never read a Dumas novel. And why are you whispering?"

She stood behind me as I rolled up the screen, revealing the interior of the hidden cupboard.

"Hmm."

Making a dramatic little show, I lifted the items from the shelves to the table one at a time, then stood back. "Open the big one last."

Raphaella quickly inspected the typed sheets, the big leather-bound volume, the wooden box with the inlaid crucifix design. "Did you record this inscription?" she asked, scrutinizing the medal.

"Not yet."

She put down the medal and removed the velvet cloth from the cross. "Look at this!" she whispered in awe, standing it on the table. The light pouring through the library windows sparkled in the gemwork and set the carved gold aglow, making it seem alive. The cross stood tall and solid, a work of art that seemed anything but holy.

Raphaella picked it up and tilted it this way and that. "It's kind of sinister, isn't it?" she mused. "It's supposed to inspire reverence, but it's a little . . . menacing. And this is the part you told me about," she added, peering into the blown-glass globe.

I went over to the desk and brought back the magnifying glass. She took it from me and squinted through it.

"The glass is wavy and it has tiny bubbles in it. This thing inside, I can't tell what it is. It's shaped like a big washer, with a little projection out each side. Strange."

"I wish that was the only odd thing around here."

II

THAT AFTERNOON, with the secret objects locked away and the weight of the room's disapproval on our shoulders, Raphaella and I discussed the most efficient way to inventory the library. She had established a base at the trestle table nearest the window, setting up her laptop and pulling from her bottomless backpack a couple of notebooks, some pencils, a pencil sharpener, a ruler, and a cellphone with a camera, as well as Internet and email capability and a digital music player. Then she quickly created a database on the computer, ready and waiting for us to fill it with information.

"And you accuse *me* of slipping into techno-mode once in a while," I said, pointing to the cell.

"I'm willing to make an occasional concession," she said, picking up the shiny black button-covered device, which the manufacturer called a PIE—a personal information exchanger. "They come in crabapple, lemon, strawberry, and licorice. This one's licorice."

"In keeping with the food metaphor."

"I guess."

"Anyway, let's start by trying to discover if the professor organized this gigantic book collection according to a system," I proposed.

"Good idea. I'll start with these books behind me and go that way," she replied, pointing to the escritoire.

We began a slow tour of the shelves, moving in opposite directions.

"The most obvious thing is that there are no numbers or letters on the spines, unlike a public library," I pointed out.

"Dewey Decimal or Library of Congress notations."

"And no coloured dots glued on."

"And the shelves aren't labelled."

We continued our slow progress.

"Aha!" I crowed.

"I know, the books are arranged by the author's last name."

"And," I added, brushing my fingertips along the books on a bottom shelf, continuing on to the top shelf of the next unit, "they're organized by topic, if that's the right word."

"I'm in a reference section," Raphaella said. She had reached the wall behind the escritoire.

"I've got philosophy here. Somebody named Aquinas. Plato. More Plato."

"Wait! I've got an idea."

Raphaella went over and rummaged around in her backpack. "Just what we need—removable labels," she said, holding up a small box.

"Okay. I'd say what we should do now is find the professor's starting point. The reference section behind the escritoire is probably it. Things should be easy for you now."

"Wait a second," Raphaella protested. "What do you mean, easy for *me*?"

I sat down at the escritoire and wound a piece of paper into the Underwood. "I didn't bring my laptop today, so I'll start a list of the non-book stuff, beginning with this ancient writing machine," I replied, "and you can transfer it to your database later." I pushed hard on the round black keys, each with a gold letter printed on it. A satisfying clack accompanied every stroke.

We worked for over an hour. Raphaella was humming along with the show tunes serenading her through the ear buds of the PIE. I made a list of the contents of the escritoire and filing cabinet, then noted the furniture and carpets, with a brief description of each item. I left the library to check on the mantel. The deep red finish was drying nicely. When I returned, Raphaella was standing on a three-step riser, sticking a label on the top edge of a bookshelf unit by the window. Bits of yellow, pink, and blue paper adorned the shelves all over the room.

"Good. You're back. Now, take a seat."

I flopped into a leather chair as Raphaella perched on the edge of her working table. Pointing with a pencil, she began.

"We already know the books are arranged by author surname. They are grouped by subject—history, art, et cetera—but that's still too cumbersome when there are so many books. All Mrs. Stoppini needs is an inventory, right? And a way to find a certain book, if necessary. So I've come up with a plan. Each of the bookshelf units will be called a column. Starting to the right of the doors over there we have column one. Beside it is—"

"Column fourteen."

"What? Col—?"

"I thought it might be more interesting if we numbered the columns randomly."

"Garnet, don't be immature."

"But being immature is part of my boyish charm."

"You don't have any charm, boyish or otherwise. May I continue?"

"Indeed."

Raphaella flashed a smile. "To the right of column one is?"

"Two?"

"Excellent. Two. And so on, moving clockwise around the room till we come to the doors again. Got it?"

I nodded.

"Each shelf in a column is called a row," she went on, "and each row is numbered, starting from the top. Each book in each shelf or row is called a slot."

"Brilliant. Your talents are wasted in a health food store."

"Garnet."

"No wonder the Orillia Theatre Group always chooses you to stage-manage their productions."

"Test time. Roman numeral V, baby Roman numeral x, arabic numeral 12 is?"

"Column five, row ten, slot twelve," I answered.

"Which is—" Raphaella slipped off the table and crossed the room to the shelves beside the newly painted wall above the fireplace and placed her index finger on the spine of a book—"*Fresco Techniques of the Italian Renaissance.*"

"I've been meaning to read that, but I never seem to find the time."

Raphaella ignored my remark. "When I enter the titles in the database, every book in this room will be identified and easy to find. For the books that will be listed in more detail—the ones in the alcove—we can put in the particulars afterward."

"It's clever, astute, and brainy," I said. "Really."

Raphaella gave a mock bow, then walked back to her table and picked up her backpack. She consulted her wristwatch.

"I'm glad you're pleased. Now you can take me home."

III

AFTER SAYING GOODBYE to Mrs. Stoppini I locked up the shop, then Raphaella and I drove into town. I dropped her at her mother's store on Peter Street, turned around, and headed for the fresh produce market out by the highway. It was my turn to cook dinner.

When I approached our back door with my groceries, I heard loud voices coming from Mom's office. Angry voices. At first I thought it must be a radio or the TV, but I soon realized it was my mother and father, hammering away at each other in a way I'd never experienced in my life.

I slipped through the kitchen door and quietly placed my grocery bags on the table. I couldn't believe my ears. My parents had never fought like that. They argued once in a while, and not always good-naturedly. They grew impatient with each other—or with me—now and again. But the noises coming out of the next room were shocking.

"No, no, and no again!"

"Gareth, you're shouting. Control yourself, for heaven's sake. I'm trying to explain—"

"There's nothing to explain," Dad insisted.

"The war is in the south. I'll be in the western part of the country, in Herat."

"The war is all over the place! You know that. What's—?"

"Herat is peaceful, I'm telling you!"

"Are you listening to yourself? You know that country! It's a hellhole of macho tribesmen trying to kill each other and every foreigner they see. Not to mention NATO air strikes."

"I'm telling you I'll be safe. I go in, do the research, and leave."

"You of all people ought to know what nonsense you're spouting. You're being ridiculous. Look at that Iranian-Canadian journalist a few years ago. She was beaten to death! By the police!"

"That was in Iran."

"Which is on the western border of Afghanistan. And Afghanistan is even more dangerous! The place is falling apart! And with their attitude toward women—let alone a woman *reporter*, a *foreign* woman reporter asking impertinent questions! Look, Annie," my father said, forcing himself to calm down, "I've never interfered with your career before, even when you went to . . ." His voice hardened as it quieted. "Not this time, Annie. No. When I think of what happened in East Timor . . . Garnet and I—"

Standing there at the edge of the volcano, I quickly pieced together what was happening. My mother had been offered an assignment. Investigative journalism was her strength and—I sometimes thought—the most important thing in her life. In Afghanistan, this time. In the middle of a vicious civil war. And she wanted to accept the job. I knew her. She would sneak into the country if she had to—anything to get the story. Whatever the story was. She thrived on the adventure and, although she'd never admit it, the danger. And she was ambitious. Already well known, she was always afraid that she'd be pushed to the sidelines if she didn't stay in the game.

"Don't bring Garnet into this!" she yelled. "It has nothing—"

"Garnet's already in it," I said, stepping into the room.

My parents fell silent. My father, his face red with anger, and my mother, eyes flashing, features twisted with frustration—they seemed like total strangers, as if, while I was away, two impostors had invaded our home.

"Why should you leave me out of it?" I demanded.

"Because this is my decision," she said quietly but firmly.

"Yeah, I guess it is, Mom. I guess you're the only one who matters."

"Garnet," my father said.

There was a sticky silence in the room.

I didn't mean that, I wanted to tell her. But I *had* meant it.

My father's colour was returning to normal. My mother's face softened a little. My mind was racing. How could I convince her to change her mind? Bullying her wouldn't work. My father had already proved that.

"Can we discuss this calmly?" I asked.

"Not if—"

"Annie, please let him talk," Dad said, throwing himself into a chair.

My mother tilted her head a little, a gesture of agreement.

"I . . . I have an idea," I began, my thoughts forming quickly. "A sort of compromise."

My father bristled. There was not going to be a compromise as far as he was concerned. I held up my hand. "Just let me say something, Dad."

He settled back. My mother sat down slowly at her desk.

"Okay. Now, Mom, if you insist on going, I'd like to come with you. No, really," I added, cutting her off again. "Hear me out. I'd be a help. I could carry your equipment. More important, we know that conservative Muslim men over there, not to mention the Islamists, insist that women should never go out in public unless they're accompanied by a man—"

Mom's face coloured with impatience.

"Their husband, or elder brother, or eldest son. I'm your son, right? So you see, I could go along. I'd always be with you, and you'd be . . . well, legal or whatever the word is. Besides, I've never had much chance to travel, so—"

My mother snapped, "It's out of the question!"

"But why?"

"Because it isn't—"

And she stopped.

"Safe?" my father said quietly, not so much as a hint of triumph in his voice.

The room went still again. After a moment, Mom got up and left the office. My father turned to look as the front door closed quietly.

IV

As IF THE ATMOSPHERE in the sky above the roof was tuned to the squally mood of the Havelock household, thunderstorms began to hit the town early in the evening and rolled overhead like a succession of bowling balls for most of the night.

From my balcony, where I had retreated with a book right after supper, I watched the first storm cell gathering. Dark clouds poured from the sky and a cool wind drove the daylight into hiding. I turned pages, half-concentrating, for as long as I could in the failing light, then gave up and dragged my chair back into my room just as the thunder announced itself. I read in bed for a while, then turned in for the night.

As always, the dream came indirectly, padding into my sleep like a predatory cat, taking shape as if emerging from a dark mist. In the background, thunderclaps and rapid strobe-like flashes of lightning ebbed away, revealing the now familiar prison cell shrouded in darkness barely diluted by points of yellow light. There were two candles on the long table this time. The only sounds were the gasps of the prisoner and the occasional scrape of a leather sandal on the stone floor.

The victim, his back twisted under his filthy shift, his shoulders misshapen, knelt on the floor before the table, forehead on the stone, mumbling repeatedly, "*De profundis clamavi ad te domine, domine esuadi vocem meam.*"

Partially within the glow cast by the candles, their faces in the shadow of their hoods, the three men were at their places behind the table. The one in the centre was shorter than the other two, his shoulders broader, and he was in command. He said something calmly, as if passing the time of day with his colleagues, and the jailers approached the victim. One held the leather thongs for the prisoner's wrists, the other clutched the end of the hoisting rope. Still on his knees, the prisoner placed his elbows on the table's edge, grunting with the pain, his hands together as in prayer.

"*Credo in unum deum . . .*"

The man at the table spoke again. The prisoner looked up, and as he did the candlelight fell upon his face, revealing sunken cheeks, thick lips, and a large hooked nose. There was no mistaking his identity.

He was the man on the medal hidden in Professor Corbizzi's secret cupboard.

Four

I

Rain bucketed down for half the night, then slackened as the storm rampaged off to the east and beyond the lake. When morning light rose in my window I was able to sleep.

But not for long. Mom called me for breakfast at the usual time. When I slouched into the kitchen, yawning and knuckling sleep from my eyes, I found my parents at the table, their faces blank and cold. I poured a coffee and dropped two slices of bread into the toaster.

The only sounds in the room were the clink of cutlery on a plate or a jam pot and me slurping down hot coffee to kick-start my brain. Mom had the local paper open to the city page. I laid my hand on her shoulder and leaned over to scan the dramatic headline shouting that the city's third drowning victim had been found at the north end of Cumberland Beach, near Greyshott Drive. The unidentified man was wearing sporting gear, the article said, and was unknown to locals.

"Any chance you'll be assigned to cover that?" I asked, just to make conversation.

Mom shook her head. She didn't do accidents. She did wars, conspiracies, naughty politicians. I took my toast to the table, sat, and spooned a dollop of Dad's homemade strawberry jam onto my barely singed bread.

"Um," I began, hoping to break the ice that held my parents in its grip, "do either of you know anything about Roman numerals?"

"Does," Mom said.

"Pardon?"

"It's '*Does* either of you know.'"

"Oh, sorry. Okay, I tries again. Does youse guys can reads Roman numerals any good?"

My father's eyes twinkled. "Garnet, please doesn't be sarcastic. We all gots to talk good, or people will think we ain't been edjimicated."

Mom let out a theatrical sigh. "I'm living with a couple of boors. Who always gang up on me."

"I can," Dad said. "Read Roman numerals, that is."

"Good. I know numbers one, five, and ten, but that's all. What's MCDXCV?"

"Let's see . . ." he mused, scrutinizing the ceiling. "It's a lot."

"It's 1495," Mom cut in.

"Exactly what I was going to say," Dad added, nodding wisely.

"And one more question—Was the Italian language in 1495 pretty much the same as now?"

It was my mother who replied. "Back then, Italy wasn't a unified nation as it is today. It was a group of small republics, duchies, and kingdoms—Venice, Milan, Naples, for example. And each area had its own dialect. Books were usually written in Latin, the language of those your father would call edjimicated. It was sort of the universal language of Europe."

"And of the Roman Catholic Church," Dad put in. "Which, at that time, was *the* Church."

I had a thought. "So prayers would be said in Latin."

Both of them nodded at once. "The mass was said in Latin, too," Dad said.

My sleep-deprived brain was suddenly energized. I felt my excitement growing, but I did my best to sound casual.

"If I gave you a few sentences in Latin, could you translate them?"

Dad shook his head.

Mom replied, "No, but we know someone who could."

Dad gave a look of mock confusion. "We does?"

II

BEFORE I LEFT for the estate and the thousands of books waiting to be catalogued I phoned Raphaella, but the call went immediately to her voicemail. I wanted to let her know that I had discovered the identity of the torture victim in my dream. "I'm pursuing a lead," I said, "just like a detective. It has to do with language," I added mysteriously.

I disconnected and sat down to compose a letter to Marshall Northrop, my parents' friend in the classical studies department at York University. Mom had called him after breakfast and left a message asking for help and telling him I'd be in contact.

I had noted the title of Professor Corbizzi's antique book on my laptop, along with the inscription on the medal, so it was a simple matter to paste the information into a letter. I explained to the prof that the medal's words were very hard to read, but I had done my best to copy them accurately. Last, I asked him to call my cell at his convenience because there were some oral expressions I wanted to ask him to translate. I didn't say that the words had been uttered by a man who was being tortured. In a jail cell somewhere back in history. In a dream.

I sent off the email, then walked down Matchedash Street to Mississauga and over to the Half Moon Cafe. Nodding to Marco, I took a table near the bar. The mid-morning crowd was thin, the cafe fairly quiet, except for a table of women who were chirping away enthusiastically, coloured shopping bags at their feet and crumb-sprinkled plates next to their empty cups and mugs. Beside a trio of men in suits, their table strewn with pamphlets and papers, Evvie McFadden was reading a book, on her break, I guessed, from the Magus Bookstore a few doors down. I waved when she raised her head. I had known Evvie since grade one, when I had been in love with her for a week or so.

Marco appeared with my latte and two tiny pastries, each dusted with powdered sugar and topped with a dab of chocolate.

"How did you know what I was going to order?"

The parentheses appeared briefly at the corners of his smile. "I took a wild guess," he said, wiping his hands on a rag.

"Thanks, Marco." I nodded toward the back. "Who are the suits? I don't recognize any of them."

"Dunno. They're with Geneva Park, they said. Some conference or other."

"I think I heard about that. Raphaella mentioned her production might get to perform out there. By the way, thanks for connecting me with Mrs. Stoppini."

Marco waved his hand as if swatting a fly. "Don't mention it. Everything workin' out okay?"

"Couldn't be better. I have the shop set up and operational." I kept in mind my promise to Mrs. Stoppini not to disclose any details about my contract and didn't say anymore.

"Great," he replied.

"Marco, you said the professor was a distant cousin. Can you tell me anything about him?"

Marco settled back in his chair and rested an ankle on the opposite knee. "When I asked around the clan for his phone number I ran into a few road blocks. Nobody had much to say about him, which is rare in our family, where everybody butts into everybody else's business, and where a dinner party is like a football match with everybody talking at once. But my aunt Isabella, she was married to . . . well, never mind the details. Anyways, she seemed to know a lot about the prof and was happy to talk to me."

I sipped my latte and waited. Marco's pause was my cue to prompt him for details. He loved to gossip, and he passed on information with a storyteller's gift for drama and a comedian's sense of timing. I popped one of the pastries into my mouth, chewed, swallowed, and raised my eyebrows to encourage him.

"See," he went on, "our family has two lines, the Bianchis and the Corbizzis. How they mingled up with each other I got no idea. Nobody seems to know when it happened. Prob'ly a love affair somewhere along the road. Who can say? The Bianchis were Calabrian farmers, dirt poor and rough around the edges. The Corbizzis were Florentine merchants, minor nobility—they think they still are—and naturally they're snobs. Look down on the Bianchis like a queen looks at the maid who cleans her bathroom. During World War II the Corbizzis sided with the Fascists. But Aunt Isabella says Eduardo Corbizzi—that's the prof—wasn't like the rest of them. He broke from his clan. He also refused the family money, struck off on his own, got an education, and became a scholar. Then he left Italy—a mortal sin among the Corbizzis. He was a real radical. Quit the Church at fifteen, didn't believe in marriage. That's what Isabella said."

I thought about what Marco had told me. Whatever embellishments he or his aunt might have added, it fit with the little I had learned from Mrs. Stoppini. It explained her relationship with the prof, for one thing. She and the prof had been a couple but had never married in a church or at city hall. The prof was estranged from his family, a recluse, a man who held unusual opinions. Mrs. Stoppini had hinted as much when she explained that he hadn't fit in very well at the University of Toronto. She had also indicated that he had become obsessed with his work toward the end of his life.

"Interesting guy," I commented.

Marco leaned forward, elbows on the table, and dropped his voice. "Aunt Isabella said the prof was into some pretty weird stuff."

"Like what?"

"Something to do with religion. She wouldn't go into detail. I don't know—maybe she was exaggerating. She's a Bianchi, after all. Thinks the Corbizzis haven't noticed that the world has changed. Funny thing is, from what she said, the prof prob'ly would've agreed with her."

"So, Marco," I said mischievously, "you're a Grenoble, not a Corbizzi or a Bianchi. How did that happen?"

He got up and waved his hand. "Don't ask."

III

WHEN I GOT TO WICKLOW POINT the estate gate was blocked by a panel van with BRADLEY SUMMERHILL & SON, AUCTIONEERS painted on the side. Brad Summerhill, the son, was heaving his bulk from the driver's seat. I pulled my motorcycle around the van and activated the remote.

"Follow me," I said, and steered through the opening gate.

Brad backed the van up to the coach house door. I helped him lug the table into the shop.

Brad handed me a clipboard. "Sign here," he said in his usual barely civilized manner.

I initialled the hand-printed form and passed the clipboard back.

"Your father was lucky," Brad remarked.

"Oh?"

"He should never have gotten the table so cheap."

Brad always seemed as if he'd sucked half a dozen lemons before he began his day.

"He bought it at auction, didn't he?"

"Yeah."

"Your auction."

"So?"

"So how does an auction work? Remind me."

"Forget it," Brad growled. He squeezed himself behind the wheel and drove off.

"YOU'LL TAKE SOME refreshment before you begin your work," Mrs. Stoppini informed me.

"Love to."

"Tea?"

"I guess it's too late for a cappuccino," I said, "even for an uncivilized guy like me."

Mrs. Stoppini checked the kitchen clock. "Most assuredly not."

She went to the coffee machine and began to froth the milk. Over her shoulder and in a voice that suggested a major crime had occurred, she protested, "Your friend left without saying hello."

"Brad was delivering a table my father bought. It needs to be refinished. Brad was in a hurry. He's not a friend, really. More of a business, er . . ."

"Associate?"

"Right. More that than friend. He's a little abrupt at times."

"Then he has missed out on a homemade brioche."

"Serves him right."

Mrs. Stoppini made the espresso in a wide cup, then poured the foamy milk on top and set the cup on the table.

"May I enquire how your work is progressing?" she asked, sitting down and pushing the plate of pastries toward me.

"Well," I said after swallowing a piece of bread roll as light as a fairy's wing, "as you know, the repairs, the painting, and the mantel are finished. I've made an inventory of the furniture and everything else that isn't a book, including the items in the, er . . . well, as I said, everything. Raphaella has worked out an efficient way of cataloguing the books. Which reminds me, I'll need to know which ones you want noted in detail."

"There are a number of volumes that he valued more than the others. They are all to be found in the alcove," Mrs. Stoppini replied.

I should have known. "Okay" was all I said.

"Splendid progress, Mr. Havelock."

"I have work to do in the shop this morning—the table I mentioned—then I'll put in a few hours with the books."

"Excellent. And I do think your young lady will prove to be an asset."

I left the house smiling, picturing the look on Raphaella's face when I informed her that she was not only a young lady but an asset.

Nourished by the cappuccino and brioches, I crossed the yard to the shop and began to inspect the table—a plain, functional piece of pine furniture, still sound but showing its age through scratches, dents, flaking paint, cigarette burns, and one wobbly leg. Dad wanted it refinished as original, which meant seeing to the leg and then stripping off the old finish and sanding the table before repainting it.

I set to work, and after a few hours the piece stood clean and ready for sanding. I hung up my apron, washed my hands, and went to the house. I wanted to acquaint myself with the books in the alcove before Raphaella and I began to catalogue them in detail. On the day we had worked out the professor's method of organizing his collection and Raphaella had stuck her labels on the "columns," we had avoided that part of the room.

I entered the library and shut the doors behind me. I felt as if I had closed myself off from the world. Since the first day I had come through those pocket doors with their lion's-head knobs the alcove had seemed like a sinister space all its own, a special niche that was physically part of the larger room but at the same time a separate area. Most of the books scattered across the hardwood and rugs had been found in or around the alcove, and the table there had been knocked over, as if the professor's final struggle had begun there. But it was more than that. The room's menacing atmosphere intensified as I neared the alcove. The occasional whiff of smoke I often detected in the library was stronger there. My discovery of the keys and the secret cupboard with its weird contents seemed to intensify the mystery and malevolence.

Once again I wondered if I was letting my imagination carry me away. Could the whole mystery surrounding the professor's death and the fire be explained by a simple break-in gone wrong? Had someone known about the cross, the vellum manuscripts, the medal—all worth who knew how many thousands or millions of dollars—and entered the house bent on theft? Could a violent struggle with a burglar explain the condition of the room the night the professor died—even the death itself, and the fire?

The theory was attractive. It explained things logically, in a real-world way, and it pushed thoughts of the supernatural and of sinister presences back into the land of superstition, where they belonged.

But it didn't account for my dreams, which I *knew* were connected in some way to the Corbizzi house and the medal, although I hadn't discovered how. It didn't clarify the premonitions felt by both me and Raphaella. I trusted Raphaella's insight more than I would a compass or an adding machine. And once more I reminded myself that my own experience had proved that presences and the supernatural were as real as the hardwood floor under my feet.

So I stood there in the alcove, leaning back on the table, and let my eye wander at random over some of the titles. *The Pazzi Family of Renaissance Florence*, *Savonarola and Il Magnifico*, *The Renaissance Popes*, *The Siege of San Marco*, *Blood in the Cathedral: The Pazzi–Medici Feud*, *Savonarolan Theocracy*—the last by none other than Eduardo Corbizzi.

The prof had been a scholar of Renaissance Italy, which I knew—after I looked it up—was the period from 1300 CE to 1600 CE. But that was all I knew, besides the fact that I couldn't have found Florence on a map. I went to the reference shelves behind the escritoire and took down an atlas, looked up the city's name in the index. Florence was in Tuscany, a region in central Italy, just like Marco had said.

My cell trilled. A city number I didn't recognize.

"Hello?"

"Garnet Havelock?"

"That's me."

"Hello, this is Marshall Northrop."

My parents' friend, the professor from the classical studies department at York University.

"Thanks for calling," I said.

We traded pleasantries for a few minutes, then Northrop got down to business. "You needed some translations. Got a pen handy?"

I sat down at Raphaella's work station by the window and pulled a writing tablet to hand.

"Ready," I said.

"First, let's talk about the book. The title, *Compendium Revelationem*, is easy. The English is 'Collection of Revelations.'"

"Okay."

"Hieronymvs is a given or what used to be called a Christian name," he went on. "You may not have known that in Latin a *v* is an English *u*. The modern spelling would be Hieronymus, like the artist Hieronymus Bosch."

"Ah, I see," I said knowingly. I had no idea who the prof was referring to.

"In English the name would be Jerome."

"Got it."

"Ferrara is, of course, the Italian city."

"Uh-huh."

"Firenze is the Italian for Florence."

"Right."

"You have the date already—1495. The rest is a name—the printer and/or publisher of the book, Signore Francesco—that's Francis, like the saint—Bonaccorsi. With me so far?"

"I'm with you," I replied, scribbling.

"Now to the words imprinted around the circumference of the medal. As you said in your email, some of the words are indecipherable."

I didn't remember writing a six-syllable word in my letter. But I said, "Understood."

"Remember that the *v* in Latin is a *u* in English. Also relevant is this: it was customary when putting Latin inscriptions on buildings, statues, medallions, and so on to compress words where space demanded. *Sup* is 'super' or 'above,' for example. Add this fact to the poor quality of the inscription and I have quite a challenge. All I can be sure about for the one side of the medal is 'Hieronymus' and 'Doctissimus'—Most Learned Jerome—a formal title for an academic or churchman.

"On the reverse side of the medal we have better luck. I find 'The sword of the Lord above the earth' and 'speedily and rapidly' and 'the spirit copiously advises.' That might also be 'amply warns.' But here's a loose translation: 'Behold, bold and swift shall be the sword of the Lord upon the land.'"

"Got it," I said, jotting furiously.

"Good. I'm not sure how helpful that is to you."

"It's very useful," I said. "Thanks a lot. You've cleared up a few things. Um, if you have a minute or two more, there's something I heard that I'm almost certain is Latin. I'm not sure how accurately I can repeat it."

"Go ahead."

I recited the words spoken by the torture victim in my dream.

And the professor laughed.

"I guess I didn't say it very well," I said, disappointed.

"Sorry, I wasn't laughing at you. What you said is taken from two very well-known works. Well, if you're Catholic and know Latin, that is. The part beginning with *Credo* is from a statement of belief, the Nicene Creed. It goes, 'I believe in one God, the Father almighty, maker of heaven and earth.' And so on. Want me to repeat that?"

"I'm writing it down. Go on."

"The second bit is a prayer. 'Out of the depths I have cried to thee, oh Lord. Lord hear my voice.' It's from the Psalms and has been widely recited since medieval times."

"Oh."

"I believe it was Oscar Wilde who wrote a book while in prison. He titled it *De Profundis*, or 'From the Depths.'"

"Prison, you said?"

"That's right. They locked Oscar up for being gay. It was against the law in those days. What a world, eh? Anything else I can do for you?"

"No. This is great," I said. "I really appreciate it."

"Any time, Garnet. My best to your parents."

And he was gone.

With swelling excitement I opened my laptop and brought up the page of words I had copied from the medal and the professor's old copy of *Compendium Revelationem*. My eyes darted back and forth between the computer screen and the scribbles I had made during the phone call.

The man in my dream was the man on the medal and his name was Hieronymus.

One of the names on the *Compendium* was Hieronymus. Northrop had said that Bonaccorsi was probably the publisher. So Hieronymus was probably the author.

I had the names of two cities in Italy, Ferrara and Firenze, or Florence. How they fit the puzzle was anybody's guess.

I sat back and stretched. Puzzles. Conundrums. Riddles. Enigmas. Fun? Sometimes, but not this time. Frustrating?

Definitely. Dangerous? I looked around. Maybe. Probably.

My gaze was drawn to the alcove. "Well, Professor Eduardo Corbizzi," I said out loud, "maybe I should ask you."

I crossed the room and took his *Savonarolan Theocracy* from the shelf and carried it to one of the comfy leather club chairs in front of the hearth and the new mantel. Wondering what "savonarolan" meant, I began to read. The first chapter took me to Renaissance Florence. After half an hour or so of dry academic paragraphs I sat back and stared at the ceiling, the book open on my lap.

It couldn't be this easy, I thought.

Savonarola. A surname. First name, Girolamo. Born and educated in Ferrara. Lived and preached in Florence. A Dominican monk and a priest. A writer and renowned orator. One of his most famous books was *Compendium Revelationem*, in which he recounted visions of the future he claimed were revealed to him by God.

He was the subject of Professor Corbizzi's book.

His name, Girolamo, meant Hieronymus in Latin and Jerome in English.

He was the face on the medal, the author of the "Collection of Revelations," the subject of Professor Corbizzi's book, and the tortured prisoner in my dream. And according to Professor Eduardo Corbizzi, he was a fanatic.

PART THREE

I am the hailstorm that's going to smash
the heads of those who don't take cover.

—Girolamo Savonarola

One

I

I CALLED RAPHAELLA to fill her in on my discoveries and deductions. She didn't answer her cell, so I left her a message. "I've been detecting some more. And *delving* deeply. Call you later."

With the new information spinning around in my head, I left the library behind and went to the shop. Working at my trade always took my mind off other things—a welcome relief at that point. I had too many new bits of information and a host of questions spinning in my mind.

Outside, the air had cooled and slate-coloured cloud had rolled in. I flicked the shop lights on, then, wearing apron, gloves, and mask, opened a can of primer. I flipped the table upside down onto a bench and brushed primer onto the underside and legs. A gentle drizzle misted the window, and before I had finished the table a punishing downpour had set in. As I was cleaning up, my cell rang. Raphaella, I hoped.

"Shall I assume you will remain for the night once again, Mr. Havelock? The weather is terrible and the forecast indicates that it will continue until past midnight."

I looked at the rain beating against the window. "Thanks, Mrs. Stoppini. That sounds like a good idea."

"Aperitifs will be served in exactly forty-four minutes."

AFTER A DINNER of grilled lamb chops with roast potato, carrot, and fennel I went back to the shop under an umbrella hammered by rain and sat down at a bench with a carpenter's pencil, ruler, and graph paper. I scribbled calculations and drafted plans for about twenty minutes. Then I turned on the band saw.

Two hours later I wheeled my invention into the library. It was a chest-high stand, like a flat-topped lectern, on wheels. I placed my laptop on it, powered it up, pushed the lectern to the reference section behind the escritoire, and launched Raphaella's database. As a trial run I noted a few book titles and authors—mostly editors of reference books—then shut down the computer again. The lectern would be handy for cataloguing books when I was on my own. I could work right next to the shelves.

I dropped into the chair by the library windows and phoned Raphaella.

"It's your lover," I said.

"No way. My lover left the house five minutes ago."

"Hah."

"So you've been delving."

"Yup." I described my research, pausing after I had connected the medal and the antique book. She was silent.

"You didn't say, 'Hmm,'" I pointed out.

"Curious. The man who wrote the book is the man whose face is on the medal is the man who is tortured in your nightmare. Why are you dreaming about him? What does he want from you?"

"I wish I knew. I'll bet he's mentioned in Professor Corbizzi's manuscript."

"We need to read it."

"And we'll have to learn more about this Friar Savonarola guy."

"Want to flip a coin?" Raphaella asked.

"No," I replied, my eyes trained on the alcove. "I want the whole story. You take the manuscript."

"Good."

"Are you coming out tomorrow?"

"I can probably make it for a few hours in the morning. I'll call you."

II

I LEFT THE LIBRARY and returned to the shop to collect my duffle bag of clothes and toiletries, my phone charger, and my book. I locked up the coach house and secured the deadbolt on the kitchen door, then made my way up the staircase, which always reminded me of a suspense movie. On my way to my room, I heard Mrs. Stoppini calling me. I turned on my heel and approached her open door and knocked on the frame.

"Do come in, Mr. Havelock."

Mrs. Stoppini's suite consisted of a good-sized bedroom, which I glimpsed through an open door, and a small sitting room with two upholstered chairs arranged in front of a fireplace. One wall of the sitting room was a large open bookshelf bursting at the seams. There was also a small desk and a cabinet. Mrs. Stoppini occupied one of the chairs, and a wine bottle with two glasses sat on the table beside her. She wore a silk dressing gown—not black, but almost—and dark slippers. It was the first time I had seen her in anything but her black outfit. She held a thick book in one hand, a finger between the pages.

"I hoped you would join me in a glass of sherry before you retire," she said.

I reminded myself that she appreciated company, although she seldom said as much. "Sure," I replied.

"If you'd care to pour."

I followed her suggestion, then sat down. The windows were open, and the cool evening air freshened the homey little room.

"*A votre santé*," said Mrs. Stoppini, offering her glass to be clinked.

"Cheers."

"The late professor used to say," Mrs. Stoppini mused, "that properly prepared food and things like caffè macchiato and sherry make us civilized."

"You must miss him a lot."

She looked down into her glass and said nothing.

"Sorry. That was a stupid thing to say."

"Not at all, Mr. Havelock. You are quite right, of course."

"He certainly was a scholar," I said lamely. "I've had a

chance to take a closer look at parts of his collection."

"He was indeed," Mrs. Stoppini said wistfully. "A true scholar is a rare thing in today's world. One sees . . ." She didn't complete her thought.

"I was wondering if it would be all right if I—and Raphaella—read a few of the books in the library. Especially the ones the professor wrote."

"Provided nothing is removed from the library, I cannot think of an objection."

I wished my mother was there. I was dying—wrong word—*eager* to dig more information about the prof from Mrs. Stoppini, but I was no good at wording questions that would tease out facts the way Mom could. So far, Mrs. Stoppini had volunteered almost nothing about the prof, but I knew there was something strange about the circumstances surrounding his death. All she had said was that he had become more private—almost paranoid it seemed—especially about his work, which he kept from her. I had concluded that the manuscript titled *Fanatic* was what had occupied him.

But why be secretive about it? He was a professor of Italian Renaissance studies. In the library there were lots of books on the period. He had written a few. *Fanatic* was probably one more. What was there about *that* book that demanded secrecy?

Raphaella and I now had permission to try and find out.

"Interesting book?" I asked, nodding at the volume Mrs. Stoppini had been reading when I came into the sitting room.

"Enough to pass the time, that is all."

She didn't mention the title. Why was I not surprised?

III

I HAD BROUGHT a novel with me, but with all the drama of the last couple of days I had forgotten that I was almost finished it, and not long after I had settled into the chair by the guest-room window on the second floor I closed *Captain Alatriste* and set it down. It was eleven o'clock, but I wasn't sleepy. I looked out the window across the yard. The rain had stopped and the clouds had broken up, revealing a few stars and allowing moonlight to form patterns on the lawn.

Mrs. Stoppini's door was still ajar and her light was on when I slipped along the corridor to the stairs, barefoot, wearing only pajama bottoms. The downstairs hall was shadowy, but enough moonlight came through the windows of the front foyer that I made my way easily along the hall to the library without turning on the light. I found myself thinking about Mrs. Stoppini's irrational attitude to the place. She had respected the professor's wish for privacy while he was working—and even that seemed a little extreme, but what did I know?—but with him gone, what difference did it make if she left the doors open and went in and out as she pleased? She was a reader—the bookshelves in her sitting room made that clear. Why avoid the library? Her behaviour when I showed her the secret cupboard was extreme. She was afraid of the place.

To her, the library was taboo. But why? Was it because her companion had died there? Or was there more? I couldn't fully understand her reaction to the room any more than I could make sense of my own.

I rolled the doors aside and stepped in, reaching for the light switch—and froze.

The acrid stink of stale smoke, burnt paper, and singed cloth and rotten wood hung in the air. Maybe Mrs. Stoppini had lit a small fire in her bedroom for comfort, and the smoke had curled over the roof, pushed into the library by the night breeze. No, her windows had been open, the fireplace cold. Besides, I had closed and locked the casements in the library earlier, hadn't I?

On the other side of the room something stirred. In the far corner, the table and chair by the window, as well as a section of books and a patch of floor, were brushed with moonlight.

Thoughts flitted across my mind like bats. Whatever had caught my eye could have drifted past the window on the outside of the house. Or it could be with me, here in the room. I took a breath and slapped at the switch, flooding the room with light and dissolving the shadows.

There was no one there. I saw no trace of smoke, but the smell remained. Curbing my uneasiness, I walked quickly to the window. It *was* closed and locked. So much for my theory about the source of the smoke. I looked out, but the brightness behind me made it difficult to see anything in the yard except shadows cast by tree branches shifting randomly with the wind. Probably a moving shadow was what I had seen. I took a deep breath and let it out slowly, willing my heart to slow down.

I went over to the fireplace. The hearth was cold, its tiles swept clean, just as I had left it. I made a slow circuit of the room, sniffing like a spaniel as I went, and detected nothing that could have produced the odour of smoke.

"Smarten up, Garnet," I said out loud. "It's your imagination again."

When I got to the section of shelves that held the professor's fiction collection, I stopped and forced myself not to rush, to scan the titles slowly. I selected *The Name of the Rose* only because I had heard of it somewhere.

Before I left the library, I turned out the light and walked back to the window. I stood for a few minutes, looking out across the yard. The gardens, the trees, the patio furniture were all silvered by the moon, and bright lines rippled on the surface of the lake. At the shore the willows stood in pools of darkness cast by their drooping branches. Between two willows, visible against the lighter backdrop of the lake, stood a human figure wearing an ankle-length hooded cape.

A figure that cast no shadow.

Only his outline was visible. A silhouette the size and shape of a smaller-than-average man standing as still as the earth, facing the window where I stood.

I knew who it was.

I dashed out of the library and through the kitchen and into the yard. The patio stones were cold and damp on my bare feet, the grass cool and dewy. I made my way along the edge of the flower garden and stopped at the corner of the house, my irrational burst of courage pouring away like water through a grate. I saw nothing on the shore. I craned my neck around the house, my cheek brushing the cold stone. Shades streaked the moonlit ground, criss-crossed by the shadows of branches. A light wind whispered. The lake murmured. There was a faint smell of smoke.

I stood in Mrs. Stoppini's flower bed, the damp earth pushing between my toes, the novel still in my hand.

I RINSED MY FEET in the kitchen sink, feeling foolish and terror-struck at the same time. After checking the deadbolt for the fourth time, I crept back upstairs. Mrs. Stoppini's door was closed, the corridor a tunnel of darkness. I went into my room and shut the door behind me without turning on the light. I pulled on a T-shirt, then padded over to the window, keeping to one side, and peered around the curtain.

He was there.

He stood on the shore in full view, motionless, looking up at my room. He knew I was there. An icy chill inched up my spine and through my limbs.

Focused intently on my window, the man in the hooded cape floated slowly toward me, an otherworldly motion, like lava flowing across the grass. My heart battered against my ribs. My breathing was so ragged I felt I was suffocating.

He stopped by the broad skirts of the spruce tree below my window, his head tilted sharply upward, a pool of dark where his face should be. I could feel his malign hostility fixated on me, his will as strong as the granite wall between us.

The strain was unbearable. I couldn't take anymore. I threw open the window, shrieked, "Why are you here? What do you want from me?"

The shadow didn't react. My pulse pounded in my ears. Then, almost unaware of what I was saying, I spoke again. "*De profundis clamavi ad te domine, domine esuadi vocem meam.*"

Still no response. There was only the night breeze, the reek of smoke.

But gradually, the high-voltage hostility that pulsed against the window began to recede. The spectre stood a moment longer, then withdrew in that same slow flowing movement until he reached the shore, where he faded, a shadow into shadow.

I slammed down the sash, locked it, jerked the curtains closed, then collapsed into the chair. I got up and stumbled to the night table, switched on the lamp, and snatched up my cell, falling to my knees and leaning crookedly back against the bed.

"Raphaella," I gasped as soon as she picked up, "it's a haunting. It's happening again."

Two

I

I SAT ALONE at the table in the Corbizzi kitchen, watching grey pre-dawn light flow into the landscape, giving definition to trees and gardens, the dew-pearled furniture on the patio, the glass-flat water beyond the indistinct shoreline. I was still shaking from the disorientation that comes when an experience shatters your version of reality like a rock smashes a window.

After the spirit's visitation I had spent the rest of the night in the chair by the guest-room window, startling at every sound, unable to prevent myself from leaping up every few minutes and stealing a glance through the crack between the curtains. Every light in the room was on. I had been caught in the classic dilemma of a haunt's victim. The bedroom, with door locked, window secured, curtains closed, was a sanctuary, a cave. At the same time it was a trap that cocooned me from sight and sound but made me vulnerable to stealth.

During the night I had spoken to Raphaella for a long time on the phone, but after a while we began to cover the same ground. There was no doubt now, no denial possible. The Corbizzi mansion was being haunted by the spirit of Girolamo Savonarola. And the apparition had chosen me, approaching at first through my dreams, showing me how he had suffered during his life, tortured in a rat-infested cell by men who went about their job as calmly and unperturbed as a janitor sweeping a hall.

But what was my connection to a Roman Catholic Dominican friar who had lived half a world away, more than five hundred years in the past? Nothing, probably, beyond my coincidental presence at the Corbizzi estate. Was it fate that had brought us together? Why was he showing me how he had suffered? Why had he slipped away when I repeated the line from the Latin prayer?

Before Raphaella and I ended the call, we had agreed to keep our minds open about the spirit, while allowing for the possibility that this haunting was evil. It had certainly *seemed* that way.

"But," Raphaella had reminded me, "ghosts are frightening by nature. Their otherworldliness seems threatening even if it's not."

"Okay," I had conceded. "Point taken. But I still think this apparition caused the prof's seizure, even if he scared the poor old man to death without intending to. And there's the fire and smoke. The smell seems to come and go, but it's associated with the spirit. There was fire when the prof died."

We agreed that she'd come over in the morning, and in daylight, we'd think of a plan.

"Good," I said as we ended the call. "I like plans."

Raphaella had once thought that haunts were "neutral"—the spirit neither harmed nor helped the person receiving the visitation. But our personal experience had proved her wrong when we had been chased through the forest near the African Methodist Church by eight spirits intent on stoning us to death. Only Raphaella's quick wits had saved us.

I got up from the kitchen table and put the kettle on to boil. In my jeans pocket, my cell vibrated.

eta 9 rs.

I replied, then made a cup of tea. When it was ready I carried it outside and down to the shore.

II

RAPHAELLA ARRIVED just as Mrs. Stoppini was removing a tray of homemade croissants from the oven. The sight of the buttery golden brown crescents and the fragrance of freshly ground coffee improved my mood, but not nearly as much as Raphaella did when she burst through the door, dropped her backpack on a chair, and bowled me over with a bear hug and a deep passionate kiss.

"My hero," she said, kissing me again, longer this time. "My brave knight."

"Ahem." Mrs. Stoppini stood stiffly by the counter, a jug of steamed milk in her hand.

"Morning, Mrs. Stoppini," Raphaella said, smiling. "Sorry. I lose control when I'm near him. He's magnetic."

Mrs. Stoppini scowled at me.

"It's a gift," I said. "I can't help it."

"Indeed."

Raphaella was wearing a white silk blouse, jeans, and leather sandals. She had swept her hair up onto her head and secured it with two plastic barrettes shaped like butterflies—her "let's get down to work" look.

The three of us sat down and sipped espresso, munched croissants, and chatted. Raphaella told Mrs. Stoppini about the Demeter Natural Food and Medicinal Herbs Shop and described the lessons her mother was giving her on how to mix herbal remedies. Mrs. Stoppini actually looked interested. After breakfast, Raphaella and I excused ourselves and went to the library. I dragged a chair to Raphaella's table by the window.

"I think Mrs. S. has a streak of kindness under that severe exterior," Raphaella commented.

"She does."

"And I believe she's lonely."

"Yup, no question."

"And she thinks you're a fine man."

"She's an excellent judge of character, and very perceptive."

"Mind you, she could be wrong."

"That's true."

"Do you think she knows?" Raphaella asked, switching tracks.

"I've been wondering since the day I met her just how much she knows. All along she's been careful about what she tells me. She doesn't talk about him much. At first I thought she was protecting the prof's reputation or something, because of the fire—you know, gossip, scandal, questions, his seizure and so on. All I know is he was a prof, wrote some books, left the university because he was dissatisfied with his department and vice versa. Not that I expect her to tell me more. It's none of my business, after all."

Raphaella nodded.

"But," I went on, "her paranoia about this room is something else."

"So she's aware of *something* going on around here."

"Exactly. All she'd say was that the prof had been working on some project that he kept from her for some reason. He wouldn't allow her into the library. What could he have been keeping from her? His new book, the manuscript in the secret cupboard? She didn't know about the cupboard either, and when I showed it to her she didn't want to hear anything about the contents."

Raphaella played with her pencil, standing it point down on the writing pad, sliding her fingers down the length, reversing it, jabbing the eraser end down, repeating the motion.

"She's in denial. Unless . . ." she said mysteriously, beginning to doodle.

"Unless what?"

"Maybe the professor kept her away not to hide a secret but to protect her."

"That could be it. If somebody knows you don't know, you're safe. If they know you know, you're a threat."

Raphaella gave me a look. "I *think* I followed that."

"Mrs. Stoppini still won't come in here," I continued, "even though the prof is dead and everything here belongs to her now—or is under her control, since she's the executor of his will."

"Hmm. So what's our next step? Confront her with what we know? Ask her if she's seen or heard anything . . . out of the ordinary?"

"Better to let things develop," I answered. "Until we learn more."

I got the keys from the desk and opened the secret cupboard, then laid out the *Compendium Revelationem*, the file folder, the box containing the medal, and the cross on the square table. For a moment my eyes rested on the *Compendium*—the ancient book that had been written by the man whose spirit was haunting me—and I shivered. The book was like a weapon with a dark history.

I picked up the file containing the professor's manuscript and carried it to Raphaella at the table. "Enjoy," I said, setting it down.

She unwound the string, opened the stiff paper file, and slid out the stack of sheets.

"It's typewritten," she observed, leafing through the pile.

"Yeah, on the Underwood over there on the escritoire." I looked closer. "He'd been editing with a pencil, just like Mom does."

"You realize," Raphaella said, "this is probably the only copy."

"I never thought about it. If he had word-processed the book, why bother to make a copy by banging away on an ancient typewriter? He wrote this here, in this room."

I fetched the professor's magnifying glass from the escritoire and examined the back of a sheet, talking as I peered through the glass. "People used to make carbon copies as they typed, by putting carbon paper between two sheets of stock before typing. But I don't see any evidence of that."

"How do you know all that stuff?"

"I work in an antiques store. And my father is at least a century behind the times. He'd fit right in around here."

Raphaella smiled, then her eyes returned to the manuscript. "I guess we can't take it away with us and get it photocopied."

"Nope. I'm—we're—not supposed to remove anything from this room."

"Where can we get hold of a portable photocopy machine or a scanner?"

"I don't—"

"Wait!"

Raphaella pulled her new phone from her backpack. "I've got one right here! The PIE has a camera! I can shoot the pages and email them to myself."

She then put down the PIE, placed the manuscript pages back on the stack, and straightened it. She picked up her pencil and slid the writing pad closer.

"In the meantime," she said, "let's do some reading."

AS RAPHAELLA DIVED into her work, I crossed over to the alcove and took down *Savonarolan Theocracy*, holding it as I slowly scanned the shelves for more volumes written by Professor Corbizzi. Mom told me she had found four titles—all of them out of print—on the web, listed with his bio. The books in the alcove were not shelved in order of each author's surname because many of them had been pulled down and flung on the floor the night the prof had died, and I had replaced them haphazardly. But eventually I located three of the books I was seeking—*Lorenzo and the Friar*, *San Marco's Hounds of God*, and *Puritanism, Fundamentalism, and Theocracy*.

"All thrilling reads, I'm sure," I muttered, stacking the books beside the cross. But I was interested in works about Savonarola, so I searched the shelves some more and came up with two other books devoted to the friar, then settled down at the table, across from Raphaella.

Under different circumstances it would have been a golden morning, a quiet interlude with Raphaella in a beautiful room, with a perfect summer day as a backdrop. Raphaella had sunk deep into her reading. Her powers of concentration were amazing. Mine were okay, as long as I was interested in the topic. When I was in elementary school my dad used to say I had excellent powers of concentration—but only for five or ten seconds at a time. Take me fishing, though, and I was a different boy.

I opened a book and began to read more about the life of the man who was tormenting my dreams.

Three

I

THE LIBRARY WAS CALM and quiet, except for the whisper of pages being turned and the hiss of pencil lead crossing paper. Birdsong trickled through the open windows. As the hours passed and the morning slipped by, the heat rose, making me drowsy, and I began to feel the effects of my lost night's sleep. But Girolamo Savonarola was a fascinating man—not necessarily, I was learning, for good reasons—and his powerful personality and the violent times he lived in drew me through the chapters as if I was reading a mystery novel.

The ringing of my cell broke the spell. I opened it, listened for a couple of seconds, closed it. Raphaella raised her head from her book.

"Mrs. Stoppini will be serving a light lunch on the patio in exactly nine minutes," I announced.

Raphaella and I cheerfully obeyed the summons, taking our notes with us. Mrs. Stoppini had made panini stuffed with chopped plum tomatoes, fresh basil, and grated Parmesan cheese. A tall bottle of Italian mineral water beaded with condensation stood in the centre of the patio table. Mrs. Stoppini would not be joining us for lunch, she had said. She had to "attend to some overdue correspondence"—which probably meant write some letters.

Raphaella bit into a roll and pushed a bit of tomato into the corner of her mouth with the tip of her little finger.

"Want to share discoveries?" she asked after swallowing.

I nodded as I chewed.

"You first," Raphaella suggested.

I took a few gulps of sparkling water, said, "I'm really glad I wasn't born in the fifteenth century," and bit into my panino.

Raphaella sighed theatrically. "That's it? A whole morning's reading and all you can say is that fifteenth-century Florence isn't your cup of tea?"

"I haven't got to Florence yet. I started in Ferrara and now I'm in Bologna."

"Whatever."

"That was only my intro," I continued. "There's more."

"Give," Raphaella commanded, then took a modest bite of her tomato roll.

I opened my notebook but didn't consult it. I could usually remember what I had read. "Girolamo—Jerome in English, Hieronymus in Latin, spelled with *V*s—"

"Stop showing off."

"Savonarola, born Ferrara, Italy, an independent duchy, September 21, 1452. Son of a medical doctor well connected with the ruling d'Este family, hence loaded with money and privilege and favour. Girolamo was one of seven children. Extremely bright, academically gifted, went to Ferrara University. Physical characteristics: small, even by the standards of those days, thin, ugly, with thick lips, a big, hooked nose, and green eyes. Don't let *your* eyes glaze over. I'm getting to the interesting part."

Raphaella dabbed her luscious lips with a napkin.

"And stop doing that," I said. "You're distracting me. From early on it was clear that Girolamo wanted to lead the life of an ascetic. That's a person who subjects himself to severe self-discipline and abstains from all forms of pleasure, like this delicious panino on my plate or the even more delicious woman sitting across from me. Like fine clothing, paintings, jewellery—"

"I get the picture."

"This guy grew up surrounded by finery, waste, money, luxury, but he saw it all as corrupt and unholy. He ate plain food, insisted on sleeping on a straw mattress, wore a shift of coarse wool next to his skin to make himself uncomfortable and remind himself that the world was a corrupt place full of temptation."

Raphaella's voice hardened. "Something tells me you're about to say he hated women."

"Apparently their charms were lost on him."

"Because they were the origin of all sin, and they enticed men to do wrong with their weaknesses and sexual looseness, et cetera, et cetera."

"Young Girolamo would hardly speak to women, and when he did he preached at them."

"And he probably preferred that they hide themselves under a dozen square metres of cheap cloth and cover their faces and submit totally to the rule of men."

"There's more," I pointed out, waving my notebook.

"Go on."

"He ranted on against corruption and moral decadence at the court, in society in general, even in the Church establishment. He rejected his family, left home at twenty-three, and went to Bologna to join the Dominicans. He left behind a nasty, bitter essay called . . ." I checked my notes to get the pronunciation right . . . "*Dispregio del Mondo*, 'Contempt for the World.' I think the title says it all."

"Wow. Give you a morning in with some old books and you're quoting Latin."

"Glad you're impressed. The Dominicans were a preaching order of monks, defenders of correct Roman Catholic doctrine, and—get this—they were the boys who conducted the Holy Inquisition, torturing and burning people all over Europe. There was a play on words I'd like to tell you about if you don't mind a bit more Latin."

"I think I'm up to it."

"Do-mi-ni-can," I enunciated. "*Do-mi-ne Ca-ne*. Latin for 'the dogs of God.' Nice fellas if you could catch them in the right mood. Anyway, that's what I've learned so far. Savonarola is in Bologna, studying to be a good Dominican preacher."

"It sounds like this Girolamo didn't get enough attention as a child."

"People at the time thought he was holy."

Raphaella scoffed.

"Anyway, the food's all gone," I pointed out. "Want to take a walk?"

"Let's take the dishes inside first."

II

We didn't get far—just along the shore a ways, near the spot where I'd found the GPS—before we sprawled on the grass in the shade of a willow at the edge of the water. White butterflies fluttered in the hot air, and the lake lay calm and green under a cloudless sky. Raphaella reclined on her back, and I lounged beside her, propped up on one elbow.

"How's the prof's manuscript?" I asked lazily.

"Not as academic as I thought it would be."

"That's a surprise."

"Yeah. He says in the preface it's for a general audience. But it's a little dry."

"As in 'boring'?"

"Not at all. It's slow going, though. Very intellectual. And theoretical. His central thesis is—"

"In just a few hours you've read enough to work out his *thesis*?"

"It was pretty easy," Raphaella replied nonchalantly. "I just read the paragraph in his preface that begins, 'The thesis I hope to demonstrate in this book is . . .'"

"Oh."

"The prof says that two similar trends in the modern world have led to a number of theocratic governments, and that this type of regime is the enemy of democracy and tolerance."

"Ah."

"Or words to that effect."

"I see." I didn't see at all.

"Not exactly light reading," Raphaella remarked, "even if the book is for the general public."

"Speaking as a member of that public, I'd say there are quite a few heavy-duty polysyllabics in that thesis."

"The key one is theocracy—government by priests or ayatollahs or the equivalent who claim to rule according to God's laws. The prof claims theocracies are dangerous. It works like this: God wants us to live according to his laws, which have been written down as Holy Scripture like the Qur'an, the Torah, the New Testament, whatever. God inspired the Scriptures, so what they say is true."

"But people have been arguing for centuries over interpretations of those books."

"Exactly. In a theocratic government there's always someone, or a small number of men—and it's *always* men—who claim special knowledge. They're usually priests, or the equivalent—imams, rabbis, the Council of Seven. They—and only they—have the correct interpretation. So *they* say. To go against them is therefore to go against the will of God. There's no room for disagreement by ordinary people."

"So there's no real democracy," I said. "The average citizen is left out."

Raphaella nodded. "And no tolerance. If there's only one divinely inspired holy book, there's only one 'true' religion. And if the laws are based on the book, they're infallible."

I stated the logical conclusion. "And if you oppose the government, you're going against God. I can see why the prof was worried enough to write a big thick book."

"He was distressed, that's for sure."

"I'm reading one of the prof's books. It's called *Savonarolan Theocracy.*"

Raphaella sat up. "In the manuscript, the prof devotes

a whole section, which I haven't read yet, to your Dog of God monk."

"I think I can guess what he'll say."

"Ready for a couple more polysyllabics?" Raphaella asked.

"Fire away."

"Okay. Throughout history two related movements occur, then fade, then emerge again, in a sort of cycle—puritanism and fundamentalism."

"Aha! That fits with another of the prof's books, *Puritanism, Fundamentalism, and Theocracy*. I'm familiar with both terms. Puritans are the American Thanksgiving guys in their black suits and funny hats, right? And fundamentalists are the ones who rant against movies and books that have too much sex."

"Um, not exactly."

"I knew it couldn't be that simple."

"Originally, 'puritan' meant someone who thought his religion had wandered off track. Puritans wanted to go back to the basics in their worship and doctrines. There was the feeling that this purity had been lost somewhere along the way. A fundamentalist was very similar. He was afraid his religion had become watered down or corrupted, and he wanted to get back to the fundamentals of his faith. In both cases, these people take their holy books literally. They tighten up on the so-called interpretations and say there's nothing to interpret. It's the words of God coming through the prophets, or the Prophet. It means what it says. Period.

"The prof wrote that history shows these movements usually shift toward theocracy. What started off as an attempt to improve the religion ends as an intolerant and undemocratic form of government, like in Salem, Massachusetts, where witches were burned, or like today's Islamist political movements or governments."

"Everything I've read about Savonarola so far suggests he was a puritan."

We were silent for a moment, each of us fitting ideas together, attempting to make a clear picture from the bits we had discovered so far. Raphaella's eyes suddenly widened.

"Do you get the impression that the Corbizzi mansion is a battleground between the long-dead monk and the recently dead professor?"

I nodded. "And we're standing between them."

I looked out over the lake, suddenly overwhelmed by what I had gotten us into.

"Raphaella, I wish I had never gone to the Half Moon that morning and talked to Marco. I wish I hadn't come to this place and made that agreement with Mrs. Stoppini."

"If wishes were horses, beggars would ride."

"I'm sorry I dragged you into all this," I said.

Raphaella lifted her face to the sky, removed her barrettes, and shook her hair free, allowing it to tumble over her shoulders and down her back, as if she was preparing herself for a challenge. Then she turned to me and smiled.

"I go where you go, Garnet."

Four

I

WE STROLLED SLOWLY back to the house, our energy drained by the soft summer afternoon, the drone of bees in the flower beds and the gloom that followed in the wake of our reading. We had been dragged into an otherworldly conflict, like swimmers in a riptide, and we knew our only defence was to go with the current until it lost some of its strength, then strike off in another direction. Not a cheerful thought on a beautiful summer's day far removed from the world of Professor Eduardo Corbizzi—and that of the cranky Italian friar who had been linked to him by events or forces Raphaella and I could so far only vaguely understand.

As we turned the corner of the mansion, I stopped. And groaned. Something had flickered behind the library window.

"Not again," I muttered.

Raphaella looked at me, eyebrows raised.

"Did you see that?" I asked.

"What? Where?"

"In the library. Something moved."

At that time of day, with sunlight slanting across the yard, throwing shadows over the lawn, the window glass was a pattern of reflected sky and treetops so deceiving that birds might fly directly into the glass thinking they were winging through the trees. But I could have sworn I had caught sight of someone moving inside the library.

"I can feel something, but I didn't see anything," Raphaella whispered. "Are you sure?"

"No. Yes. I don't know."

"Well, I feel better now that you've cleared that up. And why am I whispering again?" she added, annoyed with herself.

"We're both on edge."

"The edge of sanity, I'd say. Let's go in."

Any doubts I had held about my vision disappeared as soon as we closed the library doors behind us. The acrid odour of smoke was so strong it stung my nostrils. Raphaella stood still beside me, sniffing the air. A cold fingernail of dread scratched the back of my neck.

"Where there's smoke there's—"

"A ghost," Raphaella cut in, drawing air through her nose like a professional wine taster, analyzing the ingredients of the invisible smoke the way I had seen her nasally exploring the medicines in the Demeter. Dealing with herbal remedies required a finely tuned olfactory organ, she had often told me.

"This is what you've been telling me about?"

"It's him again," I said. "But the smell is stronger this time."

"I see—smell—what you mean." Raphaella wrinkled her

nose. "Burnt wood, cloth," she murmured, as if taking inventory, "leather, hot iron, paper. And—ugh—underneath it all, something fetid. But why smoke?"

"What do you mean?"

"Why would this presence leave behind the smell of burning?"

"I assume because he caused the fire that led to the professor's . . ."

"Maybe," Raphaella mused. "But you'd think—"

"Look," I exclaimed, leading the way across the room. "Something's disturbed the manuscript."

"I left it in two neat stacks."

The bitter stink was more pronounced here. The books I had been using lay open where I had left them, but the manuscript had been tampered with. Several pages were askew. I checked the window. It was closed and locked as it always was when I left the library, so no breeze had moved the pages.

I looked around, alert for any more signs of the spirit's presence. Was he here now, I wondered, keeping himself invisible? My eyes probed the alcove. The bookcase door hung open, exposing the secret cupboard with its rolled-up door and empty shelves. The cross gleamed on the tabletop, untouched, with the small wooden box beside it.

"There's a page on the floor," Raphaella said, bending to retrieve the sheet. Between trembling hands she clutched it, with its lines of neatly typed letters and pencilled scribbles here and there, and sniffed it.

"Smoky," she murmured.

"Look at the edges," I pointed out.

Along one margin and across the top of the typed page, the thick white paper showed a faint brown stain. I had seen marks like that on lots of old books. Books that had been near a fire.

II

"I'D BETTER PHOTOGRAPH the pages now," Raphaella cautioned. "Just to be safe."

We worked fast. Raphaella leaned over the stack, snapped a picture, I removed the page, the camera clicked again, and so on. When the PIE's memory was full, she emailed the images to her address at the Demeter, cleared the memory, and started shooting once more. It was a tedious process, but we got it done.

Raphaella tidied up the manuscript and tucked it back into its file case, securing the flap with a stouter than necessary knot. She tossed the PIE into her backpack. I returned the *Compendium* and cross, box, and manuscript to the cupboard and locked up.

"We have to make sure we do this—return everything to the cupboard—whenever we leave the library," I said.

"Right. Well, I'm ready," she said, looking around nervously.

"Let's get out of here."

Tucking the little brass keys into their place under the rosary in the box and closing the escritoire drawer, I was unable to shake the feeling that the spirit was watching every move.

We found Mrs. Stoppini sitting at a small desk in the main-floor room she called the parlour, writing letters on thick creamy paper with a fountain pen as if she was still in the last century. She insisted on seeing us to the door.

"See you soon," I said.

"I shall look forward to it."

Outside, Raphaella kissed me goodbye and slid behind the steering wheel of her mother's car. She waved out the window as she drove off down the shady lane. She had a few hours' work to do at the Demeter.

I went into the shop, gave the refinished table a quick final inspection. It looked great. Dad will be pleased, I thought as I locked up. I pulled on my jacket and helmet, mounted up, and piloted the motorcycle through the estate gates, glad to be leaving the place and wondering once again how Mrs. Stoppini could live in that house without contact with the spirit that I was more and more sure was full of dark intentions.

And not for the first time I felt guilty leaving her alone there. I reminded myself that she had been by herself in that big house when I met her, and beyond her fear of the library—which I could now fully relate to—she had showed no signs of knowing about any spiritual visitations.

I rode straight into town, heading for the public library across the road from the Olde Gold. The beginnings of a plan were moving around in my mind, like puzzle bits scattered across a tabletop.

An hour or so later I walked in the back door of my house with two books on Savonarola under my arm—the same titles I had been reading in the prof's library. In our kitchen I listened for signs of activity from Mom's study. All was quiet except for the ticking of the clock above the kitchen sink.

"Anybody home?" I called out.

Things had been tense since Dad and I had ganged up on my mother about the Afghanistan assignment. For a day or so it had seemed she had given up on the idea, but she had never said so in so many words. All three of us avoided the subject altogether—which made it one of those "elephant in the living room" things that just kept everybody on edge.

So I was kind of glad to have the house to myself for a while. Tension was one thing I didn't need right then. My nerves were tight as piano wires as it was. I fixed a mug of tea and took it up to my room, dumping the books on the desk.

I set up my recliner on the balcony beside a small table, then took my notebook, library books, and tea outside. There was just enough breeze to stir the leaves on the maples along Brant Street and to bend the column of steam rising from the mug. I picked up the book I had been reading at the mansion, found the page where I had left off, and settled back in the chair.

III

WITH HIS FIERY ZEAL and deep intelligence, Savonarola quickly established himself among the Dominicans at Bologna, gaining a reputation far and wide as a fiercely intense, repent-or-burn-in-hell preacher. He had lost none of his hatred of the world, his disgust with the Church and its riches and corruption, his puritanical opposition to art, literature, costly garments—anything that in his sour view would lead a person away from religious devotion. He still wore his scratchy hair shirt under his clothing, and had added a spiked belt to punish his flesh even more. According to my reading, that kind of "mortification of the flesh" was widely practised at the time. After seven years he was sent in 1482 to San Marco's priory in the most important city in all Italy.

The friar from Ferrara was thirty years old when he walked through one of Florence's twelve gates, bound for the Dominican convent at San Marco Church and bursting with zeal to clean up a republic with a reputation—among fundamentalists like him—as one of the most sinful in Europe, a cesspool stained by every shade of wickedness. One of the largest centres in Europe, enclosed by a high wall and divided in two by the Arno River, Florence contained almost 42,000 "souls," sixty parish churches—one for every 680 inhabitants—and dozens of friaries, convents, and religious brotherhoods. You couldn't walk down one of the narrow streets without bumping into priests, nuns, or monks. Religion—and only one religion—coloured every part of a person's life.

Florence was also one of the richest cities, but most of the coins were tucked away in the pockets of a few fabulously rich banker/merchant families or in the strongboxes of the Church, whose high offices were filled by men from those same families. It was a dangerous place, where sometimes blood ran in the streets and mutilated bodies littered the city squares because of conspiracies and power struggles between families.

As time passed, Savonarola honed his preaching skills and was soon in such demand he delivered his frightening sermons in the cathedral of Santa Maria del Fiore. By now he was claiming that God spoke directly to him. He made prophesies. His visions of doomsday, he ranted, had been revealed to him by God, and he recorded them in his *Compendium Revelationem.* He began to interfere in the government, criticizing it for ignoring the poor and underfed. But most of his energy went into forcing his brand of strict morality down people's throats.

Savonarola urged the passing of laws to burn homosexuals alive, to publicly beat prostitutes, whom he called "pieces of meat with eyes." He sent bands of youths through the city to harass men and women who dressed too richly, to force their way into houses and confiscate "vanities"—books, sculpture, fine clothing, paintings, jewels—and to burn them in great bonfires.

In his sermons he attacked the Medici family, calling Lorenzo, the top man, a tyrant—which he was. He railed against Pope Alexander VI, saying he was corrupt—which he was—and unfit to be God's representative on earth. In this way, Savonarola pitted himself against two of the most powerful tyrants in Europe. There was no discussion with Girolamo Savonarola. To oppose him was to stand against the will of God.

Some Florentines saw the friar as an enemy of their power and wealth. Many became his followers, but just as many considered him a puritan and fundamentalist who claimed he spoke in the name of God when he censored or destroyed literature, art, music, and all ideas that were not in agreement with his. He had become, they said, a fanatic.

IV

I TOOK A BREAK from my reading when my eyelids threatened to close permanently.

My parents had come home, and supper was almost ready. Mom sat at the kitchen table, her plate shoved aside to make room for the newspaper. Bowls of steaming vegetables waited in the centre of the table.

Dad pushed through the door. He gave me a look, then set a platter of barbecued steaks beside the bowl of carrots. The look meant things were still a little tense on the homefront. I knew the cause: Mom hadn't turned down the Afghanistan assignment yet.

"Ready," Dad said with forced enthusiasm.

We ate without much conversation, and after dessert all three of us seemed to have pressing things to do. My parents went to bridge club. I watched TV for a while, but the sitcoms seemed inane and childish, completely divorced from the real world. Turning off the TV, I laughed out loud.

"A TV comedy is make-believe, but a ghost in a loony library is real?" I asked myself.

I returned to my room and got into bed, the last light of evening fading from the sky. I yawned, picking up the history book.

The last chapter described how Savonarola had made so many enemies that after only three years or so at the height of his influence the city turned against him, including many of its priests and monks. The pope, who was Savonarola's boss, wanted him dead. The Medici wanted him dead.

So he was kicked out of the church, excommunicated, and commanded to cease preaching. He ignored the pope's orders. He was arrested—charged with, of all things, crimes against the church—and executed in 1498. The order to torture and hang him was signed by Pope Alexander VI.

I tossed the book down in disgust. Images from my dream swirled into my mind. The dark damp cell, the victim kneeling in agony, the candle illuminating papers bearing the pope's seal.

"The pope," I muttered. "God's representative on earth."

I lay back and dropped off to sleep.

IN MY DREAM I saw three nooses dangling from a gibbet, swinging lazily to and fro in the morning breeze, their shadows flickering across piles of brushwood stacked around the base of the gallows platform. Around me was a vast city square enclosed by six-storey stone buildings and densely packed with spectators. Their collective gaze was fixed on the closed doors of a stone fortress whose soaring bell tower pierced the clear morning sky. From the crenellated fortress roof, guards watched the crowd, pikes in hand, the pale morning light gleaming on breastplates and helmets.

A marble terrace fronted the building, and from the north end a wooden walkway stretched into the square to a gallows resembling a cross.

The crowd seethed and shifted. The air trembled with anticipation. The wide oaken doors of the fortress swung open and a hooded man emerged, followed by three monks in manacles and ankle chains, then a number of other men, some in long coats, some in clerical habits. The chained men were stripped of their black cloaks and white habits before the hangman led them along the walkway, their leg irons clanking on the new boards just above the heads of the spectators.

The hangman lifted a ladder from the platform and leaned it against the gibbet, then pushed the first prisoner up the ladder ahead of him, snugged the noose around the prisoner's neck, tied a chain around his waist, and shoved him off the ladder as if he were a sack of grain. The crowd groaned, all eyes on the dying monk twisting and jerking at the end of the rope. The hangman moved the ladder to the opposite end of the gallows' crossbar, then prepared and dispatched the second prisoner, whose neck could be heard breaking.

I saw the crowd lean forward when the ladder was moved again. I felt the morbid excitement, the fear, the fascination. What would happen when Savonarola was flung off the ladder to his death? Some whispered that he would take wing, like an angel. Others claimed the devil's hand would reach up from hell and drag him down. Still others said that when the firewood was set alight the famous friar would learn what hell was like.

The hangman mockingly swept his hand up, inviting Savonarola to mount the ladder. The friar, his body twisted by the *strappado*, awkwardly climbed onto the lowest rung, his leg irons hindering ascent to the top. The hangman fixed the noose in place and looped the chain around the friar's waist.

"Oh, prophet," a voice rang out from the crowd, "now is the time for you to work one of your miracles!"

Was it a sneer or a prayer?

The hangman heaved the famous preacher off the ladder, and the spectators uttered a collective gasp. Savonarola's bare feet kicked and jerked as the quivering rope throttled him. The hangman descended and walked to the marble terrace, then took the stairs to ground level. The crowd parted as he made his way to the foot of the gallows, an unlit torch in his hand.

Spasms of nausea seized my gut. The three men twisting and wriggling above the platform were to be burned alive. Savonarola struggled, writhing and kicking as if he could somehow free himself from the choking noose.

The hangman had lit his torch, but before he could shove it into the brushwood someone burst from the crowd clutching a burning brand. "Now," he shouted, his eyes on the friar, "I can burn the man who wanted to burn me!"

And he thrust the flaming brand into the brushwood.

As smoke curled upwards the flames spread quickly, snapping and popping, but not loudly enough to smother the friar's screams. Some in the mob tossed small bags of gunpowder into the fire. The sacks sparked and burst, feeding and spreading the flames, the conflagration forcing the onlookers back. The bodies on the gibbet blackened and blistered and smoked.

After a time, the burnt arms dropped into the fire, followed soon after by the charred, twisted legs, sending showers of sparks into a sky darkened by smoke. The hangman chopped down the gallows and it crashed into the fire in a shower of burning embers.

I saw a trio of men off to the side, two leaning against a cart, the third holding the halter of a sway-backed horse whose eyes had been covered with a piece of cloth. One of the men never took his eyes off the gallows, and when he was called in by the hangman to pile more wood on the fire, he carefully noted the position of the friar's charred body parts before he heaped brushwood on them.

"Let there be no remains to tempt the relic hunters," the hangman commanded. "You know what to do."

Later that day, when the fire had cooled to a heap of smoking ash, the trio prepared to shovel the debris into the cart. But the vigilant one called a halt. Wading into the smouldering ash, he dug out the three hot chains and tossed them behind him, urging the others not to waste valuable iron. While his companions were occupied, he quickly sifted through the ashes at his feet, stooped, and slipped something into his pocket.

In short order the debris of execution had been shovelled into the cart and transported to the river nearby. At the foot of a covered bridge, the three men dumped the ashes into the swirling brown water, careful to sweep the last speck from the cart.

"That's done, then," said one.

"To be sure," said the other.

The third brushed his hand over his trouser pocket and nodded.

Five

I

Like a bubble rising sluggishly through dark liquid, I slowly freed myself from sleep, and from the horrifying spectacle in the city square.

There was no doubt in my mind that I had witnessed the gruesome death of Girolamo Savonarola, along with that of two fellow Dominicans. When I felt up to it I would check the details later in the prof's books, but only for formality's sake. I knew what I'd find.

My bedroom window was full of cheery morning light that mocked the aura of gloom and dread surrounding me. I forced myself to get out of bed, almost tripping on something. Cursing, I tossed the book I had dropped on the floor the night before onto the bed. I staggered down to the bathroom one floor below, scooped water from the tap into my mouth, then stepped under a lukewarm shower. I returned to my room, pulled on my clothes, and made my way to the kitchen.

My father was at the table. Hearing the scrape of my chair legs on the floor, he peered over the top of his newspaper and looked me over.

"Up late last night?" he asked.

"In a manner of speaking."

"You look like you been rode hard and put up wet, as they say in the cowboy movies."

"Right."

"There's some scrambled eggs and grilled bacon in the oven," Dad offered. "The bacon's nice and crisp."

My stomach lurched.

"And there's toast," he added cheerily. "But I'm afraid it's burnt."

I barely made it through the back door before I retched violently into the flower bed.

AFTER FORCING DOWN a cup of clear tea I walked down the hill to the Demeter, hoping to find Raphaella alone in the store. No such luck. I pushed through the door, setting off a discreet buzz, and was bathed in the odour of yeast, vitamins, dried legumes, medicinal herbs, and peanut butter from the machine at the end of the counter. Mrs. Skye stood behind the pine counter in her usual green smock, fitting a new roll of paper into the cash register. She looked up.

"May I help you?" she enquired impersonally.

"Fine, thank you, Mrs. Skye. And how are you?"

She hated it when I referred to her as Mrs., but sometimes I got fed up with her attitude. She'd known me for over a year but always treated me like a stranger, hoping, I guessed, that if she was rude enough I'd abandon Raphaella.

"My parents are well, too," I pushed on. "They send their best."

Mrs. Skye made a *psh!* noise and turned her back. She stepped over to the table under a bank of little drawers that contained the herbal medicines she combined into prescriptions, picked up a pestle, and began to grind furiously.

Raphaella came through from the back room wearing a green smock with HEALTH IS WEALTH across the front, a caption not up to her usual witty standard. Or maybe I just wasn't in the mood. When she saw me she stopped.

"Uh-oh, another dream," she stated, eyes boring into mine. "Come on."

She took my hand and led me into the back room, a large space jammed to the ceiling with shelves holding boxes, jars, bottles, clear plastic bags of beans, nuts, grains, and other foods, and furnished with a small table and two chairs. A few cartons with Chinese writing on them sat on the floor by the alley door.

I grabbed her and held her tightly. Raphaella kissed me, then pried herself free and filled the kettle and plugged it in. I pulled her to me again.

"I'm kind of glad to see you," I said.

She pushed me into a chair. I watched as she bustled around, preparing some kind of drink and searching out just the right nutrition bar for someone who had witnessed a legal murder.

"I saw his execution," I said. "Him and two other monks."

"Tell me everything," Raphaella said, plunking a steaming mug onto the table. "And drink this slowly."

I did as she asked. By the time I had finished describing

my vision, I had eaten the bar and drunk two cups of the weird this-will-be-good-for-you tea.

"Now we know the answer to the question you asked me yesterday in the library."

Raphaella nodded. "'Why does the spirit leave the odour of smoke behind?'"

"Right. It's ironic in a gory way," I mused, folding the nutrition-bar wrapper into increasingly tiny squares and pretending my hands weren't shaking. "The preacher who wanted to burn certain so-called sinners ended up being burned himself." I looked up at Raphaella. "But that's not really justice, is it? Nobody deserves to die like that."

"No."

"Are people who design executions so the maximum amount of suffering is inflicted sick? Is something inside them broken, like a cracked microchip or a stripped gear? I mean, just *seeing* it scared the hell out of me.

"I used to think atrocities were a thing of the past. They happened way back in the fog of history. And I thought that the past was like another country, far away, and that things are different now. After I saw Savonarola being tortured I read up on the *strappado* and found out it's *still* being used, but the information didn't sink in. I guess I tried to deny it. But that vision last night—the fire, the way the crowd joined in, enjoying the hanging and burning—"

"You've been thinking about Hannah," Raphaella said quietly.

I nodded.

"And what those men did to her."

Mention of Hannah's name took me back to a windy starless night more than a year ago, when I had been dragged from sleep long after midnight by the mournful cries of a woman walking in the forest behind the mobile home park where I was living during my stint as caretaker there. I followed Hannah Duvalier along a path to a grave at the edge of the African Methodist Church burial ground, and later to the ruins of a log cabin where a terrible killing had taken place. Hannah made that same walk every night. She had been dead for 150 years.

"That was in the past, too. But do you know what Mom told me? A few months ago she was researching an execution in Afghanistan in 2005. A woman was stoned to death in front of dozens of witnesses. Legally. According to Islamic law. This was *after* the Taliban were kicked out. And Mom said stoning is still part of the penal code in Iran. It's promoted by Islamist militants in other countries. Execution by stoning takes half an hour. It's like being clubbed to death, slowly."

Raphaella was standing beside my chair now, and she laid her arm on my shoulder. "Garnet, calm down."

"I don't get it. How could a crowd of men who knew the woman tie her up, cover her face, and throw rocks at her head, hitting her again and again, until she was dead? What's *wrong* with people like that?" I looked up at Raphaella and tried to smile. "I'm repeating myself aren't I? I'm babbling."

She smiled back at me and said nothing.

Another thought burst in my brain, like those little packets of gunpowder the crowd flung onto the fire in my vision.

"It's religious law that allows—hell, demands—stoning as punishment. For adultery. The regulations even specify what size of stone to be used. And by the way, a male adulterer gets a lashing and goes home.

"It was the Church that helped execute Savonarola. The Church's Inquisition burned Jews and heretics. Religious leaders burned the witches in Salem."

"I've always wondered," Raphaella mused, "is it the religion that's evil, or the people practising it? Is the religious law an excuse for committing acts they would have carried out anyway? A way to dress up viciousness as holiness?"

I felt suddenly exhausted, as if my mainspring had wound down. "I'm sick of it," I whispered. "All of it."

Raphaella crouched in front of me and took one of my hands. "But we have to see it through. We have to make him go away."

I kept silent.

"Which means finding out why he's still haunting the Corbizzi place," she added.

I drew in some of Raphaella's energy, the way a sponge absorbs water.

"So we go back . . . when?" I asked her.

"Tomorrow. I believe the answer's in the prof's unpublished book."

I completed her thought. "Which is why the spirit was messing with it yesterday while we were lounging around outside."

"I think we're close, Garnet. I really do."

11

MY STEP WAS A LITTLE lighter as I strolled back up the hill under the canopy of old maple trees in full summer leaf, but I still had a lot of thinking to do. I was so deep in thought when I got home that as soon as Mom hinted it was time the lawn was mowed I said yes without argument and marched straight from her office to the garage to get the electric mower.

An hour and a half later, hot and sweaty, I took my second shower of the day, stuffed my clothes into the laundry hamper, and put on a clean T-shirt and jeans. As I was heading downstairs something caught my eye. The history book I had chucked onto the blankets that morning had fallen open to a page near the back. I picked up the book and was about to slap it shut when I noticed the words "Appendix: The Arrabbiati." Strange phrase, I thought.

Curious, I took a closer look. The *Arrabbiati*, or "Angry Ones," were Savonarola's opponents, the offended citizens who saw him as an intolerant puritanical tyrant. They included people from all walks of life, many from well-known families. The author of the book had listed these families alphabetically.

I ran my finger down the column of names, suddenly knowing what I was about to find.

And there it was, in black and white.

Corbizzi.

PART FOUR

Cut off his head,
although he may be head of his family,
cut off his head!

—Girolamo Savonarola

One

1

I HAD A LOT to think about.

With the discovery that the Corbizzi family had been opponents of Savonarola in the fifteenth century I had found another link between the estate on the shore of Lake Couchiching and an Italian city thousands of kilometres away across the Atlantic Ocean. This was no coincidence. The professor was an expert on the Italian Renaissance, had lived and taught in Florence, and had made Savonarola the centre of his studies, especially the friar's attempts to set up a government that would rule according to Christian morality, as interpreted by him. The prof had written a new book warning against theocracy, a book that devoted a whole chapter to Savonarola, using the friar's career as an alarm bell—the chapter Raphaella would be reading next.

Savonarola had contacted me through my dreams, had shown me how much he had suffered. He had made me watch his inhumane execution. Was he trying to win my sympathy? Who wouldn't have compassion for a man who had undergone imprisonment, torture, hanging, and burning? The trouble was, he had urged that others get the same cruel treatment. And yet he had genuinely wanted Florence to take better care of its poor and underprivileged.

He seemed a brilliant but complex man, one minute inspiring admiration and sympathy, the next contempt. I was no theologian like Savonarola, but I believed that you should treat other people the way you wanted them to behave toward you. I had sympathy for him, but I was revolted by his contradictions—the willingness to torture and burn others, the hatred that soaked his words when he talked about his opponents. It was all symbolized on the medal in the secret cupboard—the friar's profile on one side, on the other the Lord's sword jabbing from heaven, warning of swift, certain punishment. When it came right down to it, I saw the friar as a dangerous man who, if you crossed him, would toss you into the fire without blinking, then tell himself he was doing God's will. For him, that was the ultimate excuse. That was what made him so lethal. And that was what Professor Corbizzi had understood.

Long ago the Corbizzi family had crossed Savonarola by standing against him. For his entire life Professor Corbizzi had opposed what the friar stood for. It seemed clear to me that this visitation by Savonarola's spirit was revenge, pure and simple. The professor had died under mysterious circumstances that involved a fire. His new book was a focal point of the visitation. The medal was, I thought, just that—a "souvenir" of sorts. The cross? Maybe there was something there, something Raphaella and I had missed.

But with the professor dead, why did the spirit hang around? Why involve me? That was the part of the puzzle that just wouldn't fit. That was why I needed to take a break from the estate and its library, so I could think things through.

II

MOM WAS SITTING on the sun-splashed steps of the verandah lacing up her trainers when I sauntered out the door next morning.

"You're up early," she said, turning and squinting up at me.

"Lots to do," I replied vaguely. "See you later."

In the kitchen I prepared ingredients for a Spanish omelette and set them aside to await Mom's return, then poured a second coffee and carried it outside to the driveway. I collected my toolbox, an old Dutch oven, some rags, and a few litres of motor oil from the garage, then rolled out the Hawk and pulled it up onto the centre stand. I set a low stool beside the bike, took a sip of coffee, and set the mug on the bike's saddle.

Working on the Hawk was a little like cabinetmaking. It took my mind away. It required some knowledge and skill, asking me to think and remember. I puttered away in the shade of the ancient maple that stood beside the driveway, entertained by rustling leaves and the conversations of robins and sparrows.

I drained and replaced the crankcase oil, then spent half an hour or so adjusting and lubricating the chain, the clutch, and the brake cables. I wiped the bike down from front to back, taking extra time to polish the aluminum frame and swing arm. A motorcycle was like any machine—it liked to be clean, lubricated, and properly adjusted—but more so, because it operated outdoors in all weather, under conditions like yesterday's, with dirt and dust and a certain amount of abuse.

Some people liked hard saddlebags on a motorcycle, but I preferred my old black leather bags with their chrome-plated lockable buckles. I polished them once in a while and cleaned them out with every oil change. Fetching the portable vacuum cleaner from its rack on the kitchen wall, I opened the right-side bag, half-surprised at what I found there. With everything that had been going on lately I had forgotten the bagged cellphone I had tossed inside in a panic to get away from the paintball camp.

I set it on the saddle beside my coffee and finished what I was doing. Up in my room, I took the phone from the bag and looked it over. It was a common, slightly upscale model you'd see anywhere. It was Internet-capable, but a quick look for emails or a search engine history proved that function had been unused. The call list contained a lot of city exchange numbers, but there were no photos stored in the unit.

What to do? Arriving at a decision took less than a second. I rejected calling a random number from the list and reporting that I'd found the cell. How would I explain my snooping around the paintball camp, trespassing, and discovering the phone? No, the phone would share the same fate as the GPS and end up in a garbage bin.

It was then that I remembered I hadn't erased the photos I'd snapped out at the camp from my own cell. I turned it on and activated the camera and reviewed the few images I had of the camo-boys in the clearing. There was something about the picture of the leader that intrigued me.

I hooked the phone to my laptop and uploaded the pictures. On the bigger screen the details were much clearer. I focused on the leader, standing in the clearing, the cabin off his left shoulder, the tents to the side, his paintball gun hanging from a strap diagonally across his chest.

"Wait a minute," I heard myself say.

I looked closely. I wasn't an expert, but I could see that was no paintball marker. It was a machine pistol. A real gun. A lethal—and illegal—weapon.

I sat back in my chair, thinking, wondering what I had stumbled into out there in the bush. Downstairs, the front door opened and closed. Mom was back after her run.

"Anybody home?" she called out.

And then, like the pins and tails of a dovetail joint slipping into place, interlocking smoothly, a plan came together in my devious little mind.

III

BY THE TIME MOM padded into the kitchen on bare feet, a towel at her neck, I was placing her omelette on a plate beside a slab of toast. She poured a coffee and sat down.

I slipped her plate in front of her and sat opposite, steeling myself for the conversation ahead.

"You're not eating?" she asked.

I shook my head. "I ate earlier."

"Umm."

"Dad's off giving a music lesson?" I asked.

Mom eyed me with suspicion. "You know he is."

"Yeah, true. Guess I forgot. Temporarily."

I lost the offensive after that. I was up against a pro. A pro journalist and—what's even more intimidating—a pro mother.

She carved a wedge out of her omelette and chewed it slowly. "So," she said, "what is it? You smashed up the car?"

"What? Smashed the—?"

"Emptied our bank account and sent the money to the Cayman Islands?"

"I—"

"You were arrested for peddling drugs to the kids down at the skateboard park?"

"Mom, I—"

"Because if this carefully staged intimate mother-and-son tête-à-tête is about me going to Herat . . ."

She raised her eyebrows inquiringly, her eyes boring into mine, then broke contact, pushed another bite of omelette into her mouth, and chewed silently.

"Mom, how could you? I just thought . . . no, it's nothing to do with Herat. Not directly. Maybe *mar*ginally."

"Very articulate," she said, spooning blueberry jam onto her toast.

"What I mean is—" I tried again, but she cut me off.

"Not that I'm complaining about this wonderful breakfast

and the rare opportunity to share it with my eldest son—"

"Mom, I'm your *only* son."

"But I get the sense that there's an ulterior motive at work here. An agenda."

She popped a bit of toast into her mouth.

"There may be . . . there is. Sort of. An agenda, I mean. But not about Herat."

"Umm-hmm."

"At least, not directly."

"Umm-hmm. You're beginning to repeat yourself."

"Mom, just let me talk, okay? You're making me nervous."

Mom leaned back in her chair, hooking one arm over the back. "I'm all ears."

"I think you're going to like this."

"No sales pitch, okay? Just spit it out."

"But first you have to promise to keep what I'm about to tell you secret."

"Oh, please."

"Listen," I tried again, "you're a reporter—er, journalist. I've got information that I know will interest you, but I have to be a whatchamacallit—an unidentified anonymous reliable source."

"Fine. I promise."

She wasn't taking me seriously, but she would in a few minutes if I could lay out my information temptingly and clearly. Gaining confidence as I went along, I described finding the GPS on the shore. I reminded her about the drowned man we had read about in the morning paper a couple of days before. I told her about my visit to the hunt camp or whatever it was. The paintball splatters on the cabin. I fed her the facts without speculating. I knew she'd put it all together in a fraction of the time I had taken. And I kept something back—the two aces up my sleeve.

When I was done, I watched her face. She would have been a good poker player. Her features gave away nothing—another reason she was a killer interviewer. But I was her son. I'd been looking into that face since my cradle days. I paid attention to her eyes.

And I knew I had her.

"Let's go into my study," she said.

IV

I GOT THE FULL-BORE professional interview. Mom opened her pad, leaned forward, and fired questions like nails, fixing times, places, facts, with no invitations to guess or suggest hypotheses. She took notes in her personal shorthand, which nobody else could decipher.

"Let's talk about these men you saw," she said after we'd exhausted the basics. "You said there were ten."

"Yup."

"About ten or exactly ten?"

"Exactly. I counted them."

"All dressed alike?"

I nodded. "And the clothing seemed, if not new, certainly not well used."

"And they spoke a language you couldn't identify. So we

can rule out French, German, Italian—most of the European languages. Any others?"

"Latin."

She almost smiled, but the poker face slipped back into place. "Polish, Ukrainian, Russian?"

"I don't think so."

"Okay, let's leave it at that. Now, don't take this the wrong way but . . . skin colour?"

"Dark, but not black. Brownish."

"All of them?"

"Yup."

"Age?"

"The leader thirty-ish, or a little under. The others in their early twenties, a couple not even that old."

"Teenagers. Maybe minors."

I nodded.

She closed her pad. "Well, this looks like it's worth a couple of hours' investigation."

That wasn't quite the reaction I was hoping for, but I still had my aces.

"Speaking of Latin . . ." I began.

Mom nodded, and this time she allowed a smile. "Go on."

"You've heard of *quid pro quo*?"

"Of course. Something for something. You want something in return."

"Yup."

"Let me guess. I turn down the Herat assignment and work on this instead."

I nodded. "The assignment you haven't agreed to accept, yet. Or have you?"

Mom shook her head slowly.

"So it's not like you're cancelling a commitment."

"Maybe not, but let's be realistic. You don't have much."

"What I've given you is promising, though. Admit it."

"Yes, it is. But it isn't enough. It may all come to nothing."

I reached into my pocket, then placed my cellphone on the desk beside her notepad.

"I have pictures. One of them shows the leader. And you'll see it's not a paintball gun hanging around his neck. I checked it out on the net. It's definitely a machine pistol."

Her eyes widened, then immediately returned to normal. "But I don't get the pictures unless I take your deal."

"You don't get anything. I clam up."

Mom looked over my head. A shadow crossed her face.

"What?" I asked.

"I'm trying to decide if this is a dirty trick," she said sadly.

"It is a dirty trick. And I hate what I'm doing. But I have no choice."

She threw down her ballpoint and watched it bounce off the desk.

"Mom," I pleaded. "Listen, will you? This isn't about Dad and me telling you what to do. He doesn't even know about this, and I'll never tell him no matter what you decide. Dad and I *know* how brave you are, Mom. More than the two of us put together. And we know you're committed to showing the world what's going on in the places you go to—especially what's happening to the women. It's your vocation. Mine is designing furniture. Dad's is . . . well, old stuff. And you and me. If something happened to you, people would admire you. But Dad and I would have to live the rest of our lives in a different world, without you in it."

She moved her gaze to the kitchen doorway.

"Do you know what I'm afraid of, Mom? I'm terrified that if you go there and get killed, I'll spend the rest of my life hating you. So, yes, I'm bribing you."

Slowly I took the cellphone, still in the sealed plastic bag, from my pocket and laid it beside my own. Mom's eyes fixed on it.

For a few minutes, we sat as if someone had sprinkled fairy dust on us and frozen us in time. Mom thought her thoughts; I prepared myself to make the final pitch.

"See, Mom, I think your confidential source—me—stumbled on some kind of para-military group, or a militia, or whatever it's called. I think I discovered their training camp. I've got a few photos. I've got a cellphone here that one of the soldier boys kept hidden from the others. I'll bet it's full of phone numbers and email addresses and other stuff that a renowned journalist could easily track down and use to flesh out a story. And *you've* got a whatchamacallit—an exclusive."

She turned her face toward me. I focused on her eyes. They had softened. She leaned back in her chair, linked her fingers behind her head, and gazed up at the ceiling, puffing her cheeks and letting the air out slowly.

"My own son," she said.

"Don't try the guilt thing on me, Mom. I'm too old for that. Besides, Dad's better at it than you."

She tried not to, but she smiled.

"And you're better at it than both of us," she said.

V

MOM AND I SPENT the next hour discussing the implications of what I had told her. With her experience, she mentally hunted down what she called "ramifications" like a fox after chickens.

"The phone's a bit of a problem," she said. "If these guys are up to something deeply illegal, especially activity that touches on national security, then it's evidence and our possession of it is a crime—even for a journalist. Withholding information is a crime. We could both end up in jail."

"But we don't need the phone or GPS after today."

"Explain," she demanded.

"I copied the GPS files onto my laptop and my own GPS before I junked it. Do you have software that will copy the data card in the phone I found?"

"No, but I can get it."

"Okay. Problem solved. Download the data card onto your computer. I'll take the phone back where I found it and leave it there."

I would rather have stuck my hand into a blender than go back to the camp, but I had to persuade her.

"No, that's too dangerous, especially if you're right about the machine pistol."

"Not really," I argued, not quite honestly. "I can go out there, and if there's anyone around I'll take off and try another day. If there isn't, I'll replace the phone." Recalling some of the crime movies I'd seen, I added, "After wiping it clean of prints, of course. And remember, those guys probably don't even know about the phone. It had been hidden."

"All this assumes that the GPS belonged to the drowned man, and that the phone was his, too."

"True. But it's a solid assumption. Whoever owned the GPS made a lot of visits to the place where the phone was stashed."

"In any case, I need to have a long gab with Mabel Ayers, a lawyer I've worked with in the past. She's up on all the national security implications for journalists. I may need to protect myself, and you. I'll get back to you. In the meantime, let me download your pictures, then I'll erase them from your phone and give it back to you. The mystery phone stays here. Okay?"

"Okay, Mom."

"And let's keep this between the two of us for now."

"The two of us?" I repeated, meaning I shouldn't even mention it to Dad.

"Yup."

As I was leaving her study, she called me back.

"Thanks, Garnet," she said.

When I walked outside I felt like I was floating.

Two

I

I TOOK ONE LOOK out the window the next morning and groaned.

The sun was off somewhere in a sulk. Drizzle seeped from the sullen grey sky and dripped off the limp leaves of trees and bushes. It was the kind of day that made me grumpy and tempted me to crawl back under the blankets.

But I forced myself through my morning rituals. Dad was out somewhere and Mom had been self-exiled behind her office door since yesterday afternoon, researching, writing, making calls, and recording interviews—a good sign that what I thought of as the "paintball gang" story had pushed Herat off her agenda. While I was making toast, she called me into her office.

"I've finished with the phone," she said, nodding to the cell, back in its plastic bag. "I'd like you to take it to your workshop and leave it there."

"Okay, sure."

"Do you have a place where you can lock it up?"

"Yeah. Well, I can improvise something."

"And for the next little while," she added mysteriously, tucking her hair behind her ear in a transparent effort at nonchalance, "you should leave your laptop there as well, okay? Keep them away from here."

"Um, sure. What's this all about?"

"I'll let you know."

After breakfast I drove through wet streets toward Raphaella's house, wondering what—if anything—was waiting for us in the Corbizzi library. I couldn't shake off a sense of foreboding as gloomy as the sky over my head. I hoped the rain that began to lash the windshield wasn't an omen.

When she climbed into the van, Raphaella's forced smile did little to brighten my mood.

"Lovely day," she muttered, shoving her pack between the seats. "How did things go with your mom?"

I had updated Raphaella on my trip to paintball heaven and shared my plan to tempt Mom with the story.

"So far, so good. I think she's hooked."

Raphaella nodded. We drove in silence to Wicklow Point and exchanged a worried glance as the estate gates closed behind us. I parked by the coach house. The grounds looked as if some bad-tempered sprite had crept around during the night, draining the colour from leaves, lake, and grass. Even the flower beds looked bleached. The mansion's dagger-shaped upper windows reflected the grey light, like blank eyes squinting at nothing. I went inside the shop and put the phone in my toolbox and spun the dial on the combination lock.

Mrs. Stoppini opened the kitchen door to us and I saw my second strained smile of the day. Her haggard features and more-than-customarily pale skin suggested that she had had a rough night.

"Good morning, Miss Skye, Mr. Havelock. You'll take tea before you begin your day's work."

The kitchen was warm and fragrant, a welcome contrast to the outside. I smelled biscuits baking in the oven and there was a stockpot on the stove giving off a savoury aroma. A cup of tea around the kitchen table sounded good to me. Before long Raphaella and I were spreading butter on hot steaming biscuits and sipping strong tea.

"How are you feeling today, Mrs. Stoppini?" I enquired.

The protruding eyes widened. Her teacup clunked into its saucer. "Why do you ask?"

Raphaella's hand on my knee under the table stopped me from answering.

"It's just that you look a little tired," she replied for me. "It must be difficult at times, running a big house like this alone."

"To tell the truth, Miss Skye, my sleep has not been very restful of late," she said, dropping her eyes as if she'd just confessed to a crime.

"This weather . . ." Raphaella suggested.

But our hostess sidestepped the invitation to explain further.

"Indeed" was all she said.

We ate and sipped in silence for a little while, then I got to my feet. "Well, hi-ho, hi-ho," I said.

"It's off to work we go," Raphaella finished.

Mrs. Stoppini looked confused. We collected our packs,

thanked Mrs. Stoppini for the tea, and headed for the library. As soon as we turned into the hallway, Raphaella stopped in her tracks. She looked at me, an unasked question in her wide eyes. I nodded. I had felt it, too. As if the atmospheric pressure had suddenly dropped, the air felt heavy and menacing. Raphaella's shoulders tightened as we pressed forward, side by side, the floor creaking under our reluctant feet. We stopped at the pocket doors. The odour of smoke was powerful and repellent.

"He's in there now," Raphaella murmured, wrapping her hand around her ankh.

My heart drumming, I placed my hands on the brass lion's heads, then hesitated for a moment before opening the doors. In a way, I was relieved. Everything Raphaella and I had experienced since I first set foot in the Corbizzi mansion pointed to a confrontation between me and the spectre of the man who had invaded my dreams like a virus, infected my waking life and then spread to Raphaella's. I had known this moment would come, and now it was here.

I felt Raphaella's hand on my shoulder. I rolled the doors aside.

I may have thought I was ready for a showdown, but nothing could have prepared me for what was waiting on the far side of the room.

Covered from head to foot in a tattered black robe whose hood kept his face in shadow, Girolamo Savonarola stood before the alcove, his attention fixed ahead of him. He was as unsubstantial as a shade, but he gave off a frightening aura of willpower, malevolence, and dark purpose made even stronger by the nauseating stench of scorched wood, singed cloth, and decayed flesh.

I closed the doors firmly behind us without taking my eyes off the creature across the room. When the doors thumped together, the monk in black turned slowly in our direction.

How can I describe the indescribable? The pitiful, horrifying face framed by the heavy black wool of the hood. The hawkish nose protruding like a blade between eyes swollen and bulging, each pupil a black marble in the centre of an ash-coloured egg. The charred skin of his cheeks and forehead, seamed with cracks, blistered and withered. The fractured yellow teeth showing where the flesh of his lips had burned away.

He fixed his grotesque bloated eyes on us and raised his arms like a dark angel, the crisped skin of his skeletal hands and forearms cratered and ravaged by fire, exposing charred bones. His hideous mouth opened in a prolonged, silent howl more terrifying than any noise.

Raphaella and I shrank back. I felt the door against my shoulders, heard Raphaella's rapid gasps and my heart battering my rib cage, fought the urge to fling the doors open and run.

I realized we were seeing him as he was the moment he died, choking and gagging as he twisted at the end of the hangman's rope, his windpipe smashed closed, his feet and lower legs already beginning to burn. But he wore the white tunic and black cape of the Dominicans' daily life. The power of his presence was like rocks piled on my chest. Now I understood the spell he had been able to cast over his audiences in church and cathedral. He stood with his arms raised in command, as if delivering one of his prophesies.

He had sent those he called sinners to the torture chamber or the fire. What would he do to us?

"Don't take your eyes off him," Raphaella whispered, her voice shaking. "Don't back down."

His attention bored into her, the freakish eyes radiating hostility as they focused on the ankh around her neck. It wasn't until then I realized that to him she was an unbeliever and no better than an adulteress. Like Mrs. Stoppini, she was not married to the man she loved and shared her life with. They were women he would have had publicly thrashed, or worse.

I stepped toward him, arms chest high, palms facing him.

"Stay away," I said, my mouth dry with fear. "Leave us!"

Savonarola stopped. He lowered his arms. Then he began to . . . dissolve, like salt in warm water, into the air around him.

And he was gone.

II

My knees were shaking so badly I dropped into the nearest chair, certain that the spectre had disappeared but not left. Raphaella did the same. I looked over at her. Her eyebrows rose and fell in silent comment.

"You don't look so hot," she said.

"Bad choice of words."

She giggled, releasing pent-up tension, and I laughed with her. I went over to the windows, winding the casements open as far as possible to ease the overpowering stench. Then I crossed the room toward the escritoire. As I passed her chair, Raphaella grabbed my hand, pressed it to her cheek, let go again. I bent over and kissed her on the mouth.

"Hey, admit it. I really know how to show a girl a good time," I joked.

She smiled. "Were you as scared as I was?"

"More. But it was too easy, wasn't it? I told him to go and he went."

Still trembling, I dug the keys from their hiding place and went through the elaborate process of getting into the secret cupboard. The objects—which I was beginning to consider a curse—seemed in place and intact. I hauled them out onto the table.

Raphaella came to stand beside me. "One of these is the reason he's haunting this house," she said.

She took the medal out of the box, held it on its edge against the tabletop, and flicked it. It spun for a moment, wobbled, and quivered to a stop. She picked up the heavy cross and set it down again, turning it toward the window so the sombre light dimly illuminated the jewels. Brushed the leather cover of the *Compendium* with her fingertips. Untied the string on the manuscript file, took out the stack of pages, and carried it to her work station. She had touched each of those things as if she was receiving a secret message from it.

"I feel like I know less and less each day," I commented.

"It was this manuscript that seemed to attract all his attention last time he dropped in to say hello," she said from her seat, holding up the scorched sheet we had found on the floor. "But . . . well, I just don't know either."

She sighed and pulled open her backpack.

Before long we were hard at work—Raphaella reading and taking notes on the Savonarola chapter of the professor's book, me cataloguing volume after volume of history books, my computer on the wheeled stand I had made in the shop. I had copied and synched Raphaella's database so that any addition either of us made would show up on the other's file. As I pushed forward with the tedious job of recording the author and title of each book, reading the spine and tapping keys, occasionally taking down an old book and checking the title page because the words on the spine were illegible, I tried to put the image of the friar's ravaged face out of my mind. But it kept slipping back, insisting that I note every macabre, loathsome detail.

At the same time my typically divided mind was telling me this was nuts. I was in a room lit by electric lights, not torches or candles, typing on a computer, not writing with a quill pen. It was the twenty-first century! How could I also be thinking about a ghost?

I gave up, my concentration shattered. I saved my work and wandered over to the alcove table, idly picked up the medal, with its image of a fist wielding the dagger of heavenly anger and punishment, its profile of Savonarola, whose revolting smell still lingered on the damp air in the room. I put the medal in its box and closed the lid, running my thumb over the cross.

I rested my hand idly on it, rotated it this way and that, watching the flat light wink in and out of the jewels and make patterns on the gold. On the heavy base of the cross the light seemed to form a little sphere inside the blown-glass dome. Tiny jeweller's clips fit tightly into indentations around the dome, holding it in place. The wavy nature of the glass with its tiny bubbles almost obscured whatever it was meant to protect.

By the window, Raphaella turned a page, looked over and smiled, went back to her reading. I fished my penknife out of my pocket and opened the smaller of the two blades. Working slowly and cautiously I pried up the six clips until the dome came free. The bent clips poked up into the air like little cranes. It was easy to slide the dome out from under them.

I got the magnifying glass from Raphaella's table and examined the object that had lain under the globe for who knew how many years. It was medium brown in colour, blackened a little along the outside edge, roughly circular, with a protruding bit on each side, and hollow in the centre.

It rested loosely in an indentation that had been carved into the gold alloy of the cross's base. With the help of the magnifying glass I could make out the marks left by a carving tool.

"Raphaella?"

"Mmm?"

"Can you come over here and look at this?"

I handed her the magnifying glass. She bent and squinted at the mysterious article.

"Recognize it?"

"Nope."

"Wait," I said.

I slid the knife blade under the object and lifted it out of its place and set it down on the table.

Raphaella inspected it again. "Could it be some kind of shell or animal bone?"

"It isn't wood. Or stone. Or plastic. So, yeah, maybe. Coral? No—wrong colour."

Raphaella was thinking. "Why does the shape look familiar? Hmm. Something tells me I've seen this before."

"If you can't remember, it doesn't matter if you've seen it before."

"Don't be technical," Raphaella replied, taking a page of the manuscript she had been reading, turning it print side down on the table, and sliding the object onto the paper with her fingertip. Using the PIE, she took a picture of the thing, pressed a few buttons, and waited, eyes on the screen. She shut off the phone and put it down.

"I emailed the photo to Mother. If it's animal or human, she'll probably know. What are you doing?"

"Putting this thing back where it came from. Have you noticed a change in here during the last few minutes?"

"Yeah, it's warmer all of a sudden," Raphaella said. She sniffed. "And—"

"Right."

Fighting the urge to hurry, I set the object back into its resting place in the base of the cross, fitted the dome into place, and bent the clips into their seats. The dome was tightly held again.

"Okay," I said. "That should—"

My cell vibrated in my pocket.

"I shall serve lunch indoors today. In eight minutes."

Raphaella and I locked away the artifacts, closed and locked the windows, and gratefully left the library.

III

LUNCH WAS MINESTRONE SOUP, thick and deep red, with beans, vegetables, little chunks of beef, shell pasta—all topped with freshly grated Parmesan cheese and sending off a mouthwatering aroma so wonderful that I held my face over the bowl, inhaling, for so long I upset our hostess.

"Is the *zuppa* quite all right?" Mrs. Stoppini asked in alarm.

"It's great," I replied. "Smells heavenly."

"A nice change," Raphaella put in, aiming a meaningful glance in my direction.

I almost choked on my soup, spluttering and holding off a laugh. Mrs. Stoppini looked confused.

"Don't mind us," Raphaella said. "We're just being silly."

"Indeed."

"Mrs. Stoppini, you ought to open a restaurant," I said in admiration. "Your cooking is fantastic."

Her lipsticked-in lips betrayed the beginnings of a smile. "One does one's best."

Since I met her I had been trying to find a way to pump Mrs. Stoppini for information. Up to now she'd been a dry well. On the few times she'd looked as if she might share something of her life, she seemed to catch herself and hide behind a stern demeanour. Confidentiality was important to her. I had no argument with that, but her attitude didn't help Raphaella and me with the central question: how much did she know about the goings-on in the library?

She had thawed out a bit in the short time I'd known her. She was still formal, if not flinty, most of the time, but I had learned that was a kind of defence that came from living alone after her "companion's" death. Under the black wrapping beat a kind heart. I knew she was growing fond of Raphaella, so I thought this might be a good time to ask her a few things.

"It's sure nice here on the estate," I began, pretty subtly, I thought.

Nothing. Raphaella looked at me as if I had a geranium growing out of my head. Mrs. Stoppini merely nodded and ate some more soup in her ceremonial way, pushing her spoon away from her across the bowl, raising it at right angles to her mouth, and delicately sipping the soup off the spoon.

"It's really quiet here at night," I said to Raphaella.

Sip, from Mrs. Stoppini. An eye-roll from Raphaella, which told me what she thought of my disarming questioning technique. She took a different tack.

"Mrs. Stoppini, do you mind if I ask what will happen to the library collection when Garnet and I have finished our work?"

"Not at all, Miss Skye. The more valuable volumes, the late professor's academic papers and the manuscripts of his published works, are bequeathed to his former employer, Ponte Santa Trinita University in Florence. The balance will, I suppose, be sold to a dealer. Mr. Havelock has already kindly advised me to have them appraised first."

I saw my opening. "You said 'manuscripts of his published works.' What will happen to any *un*published manuscripts?"

"I have read no such papers. But should something be discovered, it will go to the university. They may do with it as they see fit."

"So," Raphaella said, "eventually the library won't be a library anymore. It will just be a room."

Mrs. Stoppini replied firmly, "That is correct. It will be an empty chamber, closed up and unused."

Abruptly, she stood and began to gather our empty bowls. I wanted to ask her if she knew about the cross and medal, but I let it go. Our hostess had obviously had enough chit-chat for now.

Before getting back to work, Raphaella and I went for a walk along Wicklow Point Road. The trees on either side were wreathed in mist so thick it obscured their tops, forming a clammy tunnel. We walked silently, holding hands, putting off our return to the mansion.

"Do you still think we're close?" I asked.

"Yes. Soon—maybe even this afternoon—everything will be clear."

WITH ONLY TWENTY PAGES or so left to read, Raphaella went back to the Savonarola chapter in the prof's manuscript. I started on a new column of books. We had opened the windows again to freshen the room as much as possible, but no breeze crossed the foggy grounds of the estate.

I was replacing a thick old volume on somebody named Dante Something when I heard Raphaella sigh behind me. I turned to see her slumped in her chair, her arms dangling, like a rag doll. I went over to her, not sure if I wanted to hear what she had discovered. I stood beside her and put my hand on her shoulder. She looked up at me, her eyes tired.

"The cross," she said, tapping the manuscript. "It's mentioned in here."

I pulled a chair close to hers and sat down.

"What do you mean?"

"He talks about it."

An insistent buzz broke into our thoughts. The tabletop vibrated.

I started. "What the—?"

Raphaella suppressed a smile. "My cell," she said, pushing books and papers aside and picking up the PIE.

"It's Mother," she said, thumbing a button to activate the speakerphone. "Hello, Mother."

Mrs. Skye's voice was curt and hurried. "I'm reasonably certain it's an atlas. The bone, not the book. But the transverse processes—the projections on each side—are missing. Broken or maybe worn off. Got to go. Mr. Tremblay is waiting for his arthritis prescription."

"Thanks, Mother," Raphaella said, but the connection had already been cut.

"Hmm," Raphaella mused.

"I didn't really follow what your mom was saying," I told Raphaella.

"Hang on a second."

She thumbed more buttons, and after a few moments she handed me the PIE.

"Take a look."

There was a photo on the screen. "It's like the picture you took," I said after a quick glance. "The thing I took off the cross. But different."

Raphaella nodded. "I went online to an encyclopedia site and looked up 'atlas bone.' You're looking a picture of one."

I paid more attention to the image. This one was lighter in colour and there was no black along the edges. And as Mrs. Skye had said, there was a bump, like an ear, on each side.

"Never heard of an atlas *bone*. A book of maps, yes. A god from Greek mythology, certainly. Atlas holds up the world. But a bone?"

"Scroll down a bit."

I read the brief description below the illustration. The atlas is the topmost bone in a human spine, the one that cradles the skull. I handed the PIE to Raphaella and sat back.

"Why is this bone embedded in the base of that cross?" I wondered.

"It's a relic."

"We know it's old, an artifact, but—"

"Not relic as in 'artifact.' A holy relic is something owned or maybe worn by a dead holy person. Or a part of the person's body. It's an object of veneration. People pray to it."

"You're kidding."

"Nope."

"Pray to a fingertip or a scrap of cloth?"

"Or to an atlas."

"Wow."

"And the place where the relic is kept is called a reliquary," Raphaella continued.

"Which is what the cross is. But what did the prof want with it? He wasn't religious in the formal sense. We know that."

"It's all in his book. And your old pal Savonarola is at the centre of it."

"Somehow I'm not surprised."

"Get comfortable. I need to tell you a few things."

I settled back in my chair. "Okay, shoot."

IV

"IN HIS RESEARCH into the after-affects of Savonarola's life and death," Raphaella began, "the prof discovered the existence of a sort of underground cult that started right after the friar's execution. A few of Savonarola's supporters continued to meet secretly and to work toward putting his ideas into practice by influencing the government through whatever means they could. This cult kept going for over five hundred years, and still exists. From then until now, one thing bound the cult together and ensured its continuation—a relic."

"'Let there be no remains to tempt the relic hunters,'" I murmured.

"Pardon?"

"In my vision-dream of Savonarola's execution three men shovelled the burned remains of the gallows and the dead Dominicans into a cart and dumped them into the river. At least, that was what was supposed to happen. But I saw one of the men sift through the ashes and pick something up before they got to work. I didn't realize until now what I had witnessed. The hangman had specifically ordered the men, 'Let there be no remains to tempt the relic hunters.' His bosses in the government and the Church were afraid that Savonarola would become a martyr. That's why they dumped the ashes in the river—no grave, nothing to dig up and worship. But they missed a piece! The atlas!"

"Of course!" Raphaella exclaimed, energized again. "Everything you've said jibes with what the prof wrote."

"Finish the story," I said, pointing to the manuscript.

"The cult continued down the years, held together by the belief that the friar was an unacknowledged martyr who had died for a Christian theocracy—Savonarola-style, of course. They continued the commitment to influence government in that direction whenever and however they could. The prof wrote that he couldn't pinpoint when the cross was made, but it's been dated by experts to within a hundred years of Savonarola's death, which makes it more than four hundred years old. How he got his hands on it, he doesn't say."

Raphaella paused and pulled her backpack toward her, rummaged around, and came up with a bottle of apple juice. She offered it to me.

"You first," I said.

She took a long drink and handed the bottle over. I finished it as Raphaella took up the story.

"Anyway, the prof's book is a warning that there are always people at work, in democratic countries as well as undemocratic ones, pushing to set up a theocracy of one kind or another. He calls these people fanatics, hence the title of his book, because they only see one side of things and close their eyes to other viewpoints, and that leads to intolerance and persecution of any who disagree. A theocracy is an enemy of democracy.

"He uses the Savonarola cult as one of his strongest arguments. The reliquary is physical proof that the cult exists, which is important because there's very little documentary evidence of it."

"This," I put in, "is beginning to sound like one of those conspiracy novels with secret religious brotherhoods and paintings with hidden messages."

"The prof wrote that the Savonarola cult is always small—no more than a dozen or so extremely religious Catholic men. Needless to say, women weren't allowed—and still aren't. It's not like he thinks these guys will take over the world. It's more like he uses the cult as an example of a trend he sees all through history, in more than one religion—various denominations of Christianity, Islam, and others."

We fell silent for a while, slumped in our chairs. I looked around the library. The thousands of books resting on their shelves seemed to mock me. The professor's learning seemed to have been as deep as an ocean.

"It's the cross—or rather the relic—that brought the spectre," Raphaella replied. "It's part of him, part of his body. And until the prof's death, it was in the hands of an unbeliever."

"It still is."

Raphaella looked terrible—pale, her shoulders stiff with stress, her eyes with that otherworldly brightness I had seen before. She was tuned to the spirit world, felt the vibrations rattle through her, shaking her to the core. Until today I hadn't worried too much about her—not as much as she did about me—but today we were stumbling toward a fierce reckoning, and it was taking a toll on her.

After listening to her, I believed that now I saw things clearly.

"The spirit probably tormented the prof without mercy, glad to get revenge on the descendant of his old enemy, Corbizzi," I began. "It definitely came after Professor Corbizzi on the night of his death. What you've read and told me explains why. He was a descendant of the Arrabbiato Corbizzi who stood against Savonarola all those years ago in Florence. In a way, the professor inherited a mission from his Renaissance ancestor. He lived in Florence for most of his life, taught university there, wrote books. But he hadn't yet written the book that would expose the Savonarola cult and what it represents. He wrote that book here, in this library."

"And at the same time he knew the spectre was after him."

"Right. The professor acquired the cross somehow and brought it to this house. The ghost comes with the reliquary. Move the cross and the ghost must go with it. Maybe the spirit appeared to the professor and maybe it didn't—we don't know. But he was at risk, especially once he began to write the book. That's what raised the stakes. That's what the spectre couldn't accept—the anti-theocracy book. Savonarola's reaction fits with his life. He was a book-burner. He torched hundreds of books he considered immoral when he was alive. Like all book-burners, he couldn't tolerate a different point of view."

Raphaella nodded wearily. "It all fits," she said. "It all makes sense. Savonarola had two reasons to haunt Professor Corbizzi—to silence him by burning his book, and to wreak revenge on him."

"I think the fire in this room that night started *before* the prof died—and guess who started it? The official explanation of the events was that the prof had a seizure and the force of his body hitting the floor dislodged a log from the fireplace, starting the blaze. That's what Mrs. Stoppini believes. But that doesn't explain the books hurled all over the place, the upturned table, the knocked-over chair. No, what happened was that the spectre appeared, maybe not for the first time. But because the prof had finished the book, it came with furious vengeance. The prof got up from the table where he was editing the manuscript. He knew what was about to happen. Flames broke out near the fireplace—maybe that's where Savonarola was standing. The prof's terror brought on the beginnings of the seizure. He experienced dizziness. Loss of control, loss of strength. He gathered up the manuscript, struggled toward the open secret cupboard, clutching at the walls as he lurched along, displacing books. He got to the fire-proof cupboard—which, remember, is insulated metal—and shoved the manuscript inside and locked the door. When I found it the pages were loose, piled on top of the file folder. With the manuscript safe he staggered toward the spectre and fell to the floor, knocking over the chair. And he died."

We were silent for a little while, picturing Professor Corbizzi's last moments of life.

"What an incredibly courageous man," Raphaella said.

"He sure was."

"But there's one thing that isn't explained," Raphaella said, her brow wrinkled.

"The keys."

"Right. How could Professor Corbizzi have had time to lock the cupboard, cross the room, and drop the keys into the desk drawer?"

"He didn't."

Raphaella smiled. "Mrs. Stoppini?"

"Indeed."

Three

I

AFTER LOCKING THE CUPBOARD and windows, Raphaella and I dragged ourselves along the hall and into the kitchen. Mrs. Stoppini stood at the table, her hands and forearms white with flour, kneading a fat roll of bread dough, her narrow body leaning into the task. I saw her in a different light now. She knew a lot more than she pretended, but how much she was aware of was still an open question.

We said our goodbyes and I remembered to leave my laptop in the shop. Then, under a sky that still refused to brighten, we climbed wearily into the van. I started the engine, turned around, and drove down the foggy lane.

"I feel like I've been dragged behind a train for an hour," Raphaella sighed, stifling a yawn.

"Me, too."

And I meant it. We were both emotionally beaten up, brain-whacked, and mauled by fear.

"But you have to admit, life with me isn't boring," I added as the gates closed behind the van.

"Should we have left Mrs. Stoppini there alone?"

"I was thinking the same thing—and not for the first time. But I think that if anything was going to happen to her, it would have by now."

"I guess."

"The only way to be sure she's safe is to get the spectre to leave the mansion permanently. And that means moving the reliquary to another location. If we're right in thinking that he's bound to the cross, shifting it should solve the problem temporarily."

"The bigger problem being to have him move on permanently," Raphaella added. "But where could we put the cross? The workshop? Maybe the friar could help you repair antiques."

I laughed.

"But you'd have to keep him away from flammable liquids."

"Lame joke. Do you know that 'edible' and 'inedible' are opposites but 'flammable' and 'inflammable' mean the same thing?"

"You're being evasive."

"Okay. There's too much fire hazard in the shop to take the risk of having a firebug Dominican in there. Unless . . ."

Raphaella turned toward me in her seat. "What?"

"If we remove the manuscript, maybe we accomplish the same thing. He wants to incinerate it. That's his goal. No manuscript means he's stuck in the library with the reliquary."

"But then we'd have a totally infuriated murderous spirit in the house."

"Well, there is that."

"Incandescent with rage," Raphaella added.

"Inflamed with anger."

"Hot under the collar."

"Fuming."

I turned on to Raphaella's street.

"How did we get into this mess?" she asked, her exhaustion colouring every word.

"I went to the Half Moon for a coffee one morning—what?—three weeks ago? But the truth is, I fell for a business deal that was too good to be true. I signed a contract with a very strange old lady who is a mystery cloaked in another mystery. And I talked you into helping me."

"My normally excellent judgment was undermined by your magnetic charm."

"Hah."

"Or it could have been the Thai stir-fry that got to me."

"You know what? I think it's time Mrs. Stoppini came clean. I think I need to confront her."

"I should go with you."

"That would help. Mrs. Stoppini likes you. But I got us into this mess."

"Will you go back and talk to her now?"

"No hurry," I said.

11

For the first time in a long while I got a good night's sleep, and the cloudless blue sky that greeted me when I got out of bed gave me a welcome lift.

Dad was at the breakfast table when I entered the kitchen, reading the paper and drinking a cup of coffee. A bowl sticky with the streaky remains of porridge sat beside his cup. Dad made it the old-fashioned way, with real rolled oats. No instant stuff for him.

"How you can eat that glop is a mystery to me," I greeted him.

He lowered the paper and folded it, putting it aside. "Like most things nowadays, it's a lost art."

"Hah."

"Porridge is the food of the gods. It sticks to your ribs."

"And the pot, your spoon, and anything else it comes into contact with."

"Did I tell you the joke about the Englishman and the Scotsman arguing over the benefits of oatmeal?"

"Not this week. Interested in a grilled cheese sandwich?"

"No, thanks. By the way, my customer was very pleased with the job you did on that pine table."

"I'm glad," I said, searching the fridge for a block of cheddar.

"And there was a young couple in the store looking over the walnut cabinet you made. Spent twenty minutes there. They said they'd be back."

"Let's hope," I replied. "I could use the money."

I turned on the broiler and grated cheese onto two buttered baguette halves, sprinkled them with pepper, and popped them onto the broiling pan. Sitting down opposite my father, I nodded toward the newspaper.

"Anything in there about that dead guy they found up the shore a few days ago?"

Dad shook his head, then got up and topped up his coffee and tilted his head in the direction of Mom's study. "I think she's given up on the Herat assignment," he said, taking his seat again.

"Really? That's great."

"She hasn't actually said so, but she's working away on something big. She told me last night. It's very hush-hush. It could be huge—international, even. She didn't even *mention* Afghanistan."

"That's a relief," I replied, keeping up the pretense that I knew nothing about it. I got up and turned off the broiler, then slid my breakfast onto a plate.

"So what's on your agenda today?" Dad asked.

"Back to the estate, I guess. More inventory to do."

He checked the clock on the wall above the sink. "Well, I'd better skedaddle. See you later, alligator," he said, pulling open the back door.

"Skedaddle?" I could almost hear Raphaella ask.

III

I HAD RUMMAGED THROUGH my brain and couldn't come up with a good reason why Mom or I should hang on to paintballer's cellphone. Mom had copied all the data from the cell's memory card and backed it up, so she had call lists, messages, the whole works. We had the information. The device itself was a liability.

Being the son of a journalist I was familiar with a few cases over the past couple of years where vindictive cops had hassled uncooperative reporters with search-and-seizures, carrying off files, computers, cellphones, and anything else they thought would cause grief to men or women forced to stand by while the law combed through their lives. The spies, as Mom called the Mounties' security branch and the Canadian Security Intelligence Service types, were worse. I wasn't sure what progress Mom was making with her investigation or with her lawyer, but I decided on my own to get rid of the evidence, as they say in the crime movies.

But first the little electronic instrument needed to be sanitized. Wearing rubber dishwashing gloves, I took it apart and wiped down every component—battery, data card, the casing—with a mild cleaning solvent, then reassembled it before dropping it into a fresh sealable plastic bag.

I had concluded that the cell belonged to the drowned man, and that nobody in the paintballer crowd knew about it. Mom had agreed with my deduction. But just in case, why not put it back where I'd found it? Mom had thought about turning it on and waiting to find out if anyone called, but she decided that would not be wise. Phone signals could be traced or monitored. Why invite cops or spies or criminals to our house? No, if the phone was dropped back into the hole under the juniper, we'd be free of it.

I got into my jacket and helmet and fired up the Hawk, already nagged by second thoughts.

IV

BUMPING ALONG the Swift Rapids Road—if a narrow, rock-strewn track can be called that—I followed the dust cloud thrown up by two ATVs, grateful for the rise and fall of their engine noise, like two furious bees in a can, which would make the Hawk's low rumble less conspicuous on an otherwise quiet sunny afternoon.

After I parted with the ATVs I rode into the cool green woods and turned off on the leaf-covered path, torn up now by my panicky escape last time, and stopped a hundred metres or so from the end, just in case the paintballers had a lookout posted there. Struggling against the Hawk's dead weight, I pushed it backwards into a patch of saplings alongside the path. I remembered to save the location on my GPS, then took off my helmet. Before calling up the waypoint for my destination I stood motionless for a short while, listening for any sign of the boys in camo, but heard only birdsong and the wind in the treetops.

It was rough going and I made slow progress, but I reached the rock outcropping after twenty minutes or so. I scanned the little clearing from the safety of the trees before I ventured into the open, then climbed onto the granite cap, followed the fissure to the juniper, and took the bagged cell from my pocket. To avoid any possibility of fingerprints—Mom's caution about the cops hassling her had sunk in—I had wrapped it in a supermarket sack. Careful to touch only the sack, I dropped the sealed cell into the hole, exactly where I'd found it a few days before. I rolled up the sack and stuffed it into my pocket. Mission accomplished. I slipped back into the trees, eager to return to my motorcycle.

But once again curiosity inspired the impulsive angel on my right shoulder to nudge into my consciousness. "Why not just take a quick look at the cabin?" it whispered innocently. "Just to see if anything's changed. Come on. It's not far."

True, I told myself. And I could take more photos for Mom. The more info, the more she'd be hooked by this camo-boy story.

With my stomach doing the jitters, my ears tuned to pick up the slightest human sound besides mine, every nerve tingling, I crept toward the cabin until I could make out the open space through the foliage, flooded with morning sunlight. The pile of cordwood along the cabin wall was lower now. Three three-man tents—I guessed that the leader slept apart in the cabin—stood in their places, their flies undulating in the fitful breeze that swept the clearing, the weather flaps on the front entrances tied closed. Good, I thought. The paintballers have gone off somewhere. Fire rings, one for each tent, had been set at a safe distance, each with a grate laid across the stones and a blackened tripod over it for cooking.

I got out my cell, checked that the ringer and camera flash were disabled, and snapped a couple of photos. I kept to the cover of the trees and crept farther around the perimeter of the clearing until I had a clear view of the cabin's front, with its verandah and cracked window. The door was padlocked, the weathered frame and wall stained by fresh paintball hits. The boys had been making pretend attacks again. I shot a few more pictures.

Aware that I was pressing my luck, I made my way toward the place off to the side of the cabin where the chewed-up ground indicated they parked their ATVs. It was empty. Or so I thought at first glance. Streaked with dried mud that blended perfectly with its camo finish, one ATV stood nose-in to the trees. And I could just barely make out the little licence plate. I took a picture of the machine, zoomed in, and captured the plate. I pocketed my cell.

And froze when I heard the sound of water striking dry leaves.

I held my breath, scanned the trees around the ATV for movement. I finally saw it. Sparkling with captured sunlight, a stream of water arched from the leafy ground to the camo trousers of a figure standing near the ATV, legs splayed, hands at his crotch. A two-way radio hung from his belt. Little wires connected his ears to the lump in his shirt pocket, and his head bobbed as he played the stream of water back and forth on the ground.

"Can you write your name in the dirt?" I almost shouted. If this character was the camo-boys' idea of a sentry I figured I didn't have much to worry about. But then I remembered the chase a few days before, when I could taste my fear at the back of my throat. I began to retrace my steps, stopping every few metres to look back and listen. When I was fairly sure I'd gotten away unnoticed I walked more confidently, sweeping the forest with my eyes as I walked as silently as I could. The sentry's presence proved the paintballers were out and about, and I couldn't let down my guard.

Time to boogie.

Four

I

Sometimes I wondered if Mrs. Stoppini ever left her kitchen for anything other than writing letters or sleeping. When I got back to the mansion, she was making fettuccini noodles.

"Mrs. Stoppini, I need to have an important conversation with you," I announced as soon as I had come in the door.

She turned and regarded me with a mixture of severity and curiosity.

"Indeed? And what is it about?"

"I guess it's about my job here. And our contract."

She searched my face for a moment, her dark brows forming a V, her mouth pursed, and seemed to come to a decision. Brushing flour from her hands and pulling her apron strings, she replied, "If this is to be a business meeting, perhaps we should hold it in the parlour. I shall join you presently."

I walked through to the formally furnished parlour and dropped into an armchair. Sheer curtains on the north window muted the light, making the room feel cool, although a thermometer might say otherwise. There were paintings on the walls—landscapes with rolling hills, stone villas, and spear-like cypresses pinning the earth to clear blue skies.

I psyched myself up for my task. I had confidently persuaded Raphaella that I should do this on my own, but now I didn't feel so sure. The stork-like Mrs. Stoppini could be intimidating at times. Because I wasn't sure how much she knew, I was worried about upsetting her. I might blunder into territory that was none of my business, or trample on her grief.

She glided into the room with a silver tray holding a bottle of clear liquid and two small stemmed glasses. For a split second she reminded me of the spectre, the way her dark form seemed to cover ground without touching it.

"We shall talk over a glass of grappa," she said in her don't-contradict-me tone, setting down the tray and pouring from the bottle. "It was the late professor's favourite aperitif." She sat, perching her angular frame in the centre of the green leather couch opposite me.

"Now, Mr. Havelock, it appears you have something significant to impart. Please go ahead."

I did my best to use a businesslike tone. "Mrs. Stoppini, the lease I signed for the workshop required that I do a full inventory of the library."

Her eyes squinted slightly. Her posture straightened a little, if that was possible. *What are you up to?* her body language demanded.

"And, um, I would feel better if I was confident that you are aware of . . . well, everything."

"Everything?" she repeated in a wintery voice.

"Not long ago I showed you a hidden cupboard—no, please let me go on," I said hastily when she showed signs of bolting, "so skilfully built into the bookshelf that it was invisible. The workmanship was top-notch."

"The late professor never did things by halves," she stated, reluctantly staying put.

"I want you to know, Mrs. Stoppini, that I discovered it without intending to. I was taking out the things in the, er, visible cupboard when one of the vellum sheets caught on the edge of the recess where the release catch is."

"You haven't touched your aperitif."

I lifted the little glass to my mouth and barely allowed it to touch my lips. An unusual fragrance, an unexpected taste.

"Once I found the cupboard and saw what was inside, I tried to show you. But I failed. I think it's important that you know about the . . . er, contents. Or are you already familiar with the items? No?" I asked when she didn't respond. "Then I think I ought to tell you. Raphaella agrees," I quickly added, hoping that would persuade her. "Okay?"

She nodded and finished off her drink without confirming or denying that she knew about the exotic objects in the professor's secret cupboard.

"There are some very old manuscripts on vellum," I began. "I can't read them, so I can't tell you what they are. There is a small handmade wooden box containing a medal with Girolamo Savonarola's image on it."

Her frown deepened.

"You've heard of him?"

"Every Florentine has heard of him," she replied, shakily refilling her glass and clutching it in both hands, as if afraid it would fly away.

"There is a large cross of gold with gems set into it. I don't know anything about jewellery, so I can't say what they are. They might even be glass, but I doubt it."

I had decided to leave out the glass dome and the atlas for the time being.

"Mrs. Stoppini, that cross might be a priceless antique."

"Good gracious," she murmured—to herself, not to me. "I didn't realize."

"There's something else."

The intense woman sitting across the room from me began slowly to come apart. Her severe expression ebbed away as signs of grief—a softening of her brow and the set of her mouth—crept in. The rigidity of her back and shoulders gave way, and she gradually settled into her chair. Her chin quivered.

"I'm sorry," I said quietly, regretting my decision to press her. But she surprised me.

"Please continue, Mr. Havelock."

I swallowed a bit of grappa. "There is a complete typed book-length manuscript. Written by Professor Eduardo Corbizzi."

She gaped as her thick brows rose in surprise. "Did you say 'complete'?"

I nodded.

She began to cry silently.

"I'm sorry, Mrs. Stoppini," I said again.

"Tell me about it," she said, pulling a lace hanky from her sleeve and dabbing at her streaming eyes.

"The title is *Fanatics*. Professor Corbizzi had been editing it when he . . . when he stopped." I hesitated. "Raphaella has read it."

"Good. The late professor would have been most gratified to know that an intelligent young woman like Miss Skye had read his book."

She blew her nose and continued to pull herself back together.

"Well," she sighed, making a final dab with her hanky and stuffing it up her sleeve, "an interesting conversation to be sure."

"It's not over yet."

"In that case." She held up the bottle to ask if I wanted more, and reading my refusal in my face, she topped up her drink.

"I have a few questions, if you don't mind," I said.

She took a slug. "Please go on."

"This may sound strange, but have you ever noticed the odour of smoke around the house? Or even outside?"

I kept my eyes on her face, certain that if she tried to be evasive or dishonest I'd notice.

"Not since the library was cleaned and the draperies and rugs laundered."

It was possible. Her activities in the mansion were mainly confined to her bedroom, the kitchen, and the room where we were sitting now. The spectre could reveal himself when he wanted. And to whoever he wished. Did the odour he left behind follow the same rule of ghostly physics?

I pushed on. "You've told me that toward the end of his life the late professor was very secretive, and that he asked you to stay away from the library. I get the impression that he was acting . . . um, in a way that was uncharacteristic."

I had almost said "acting crazy" but caught myself just in time.

"I . . ." She paused momentarily. "I used to love that library," she said sadly. "It was—is—such a beautiful room, so full of light. It was our custom each morning to take our coffee there before our breakfast. We would chat or read contentedly, surrounded by our books, discussing our plans to return one day to Italy and retire to a small village outside Florence. Our house there has been in the Corbizzi family for three hundred years. There is a small garden and a few olive trees on the rise beyond the yard. I regret to say it passed into other hands when the professor needed to raise money quickly last year for his research.

"There was a time, Mr. Havelock, when I would not have shared with you what I am about to relate. But you have proved to be a reliable and, may I say, a caring young man, and I feel that I can confide in you.

"During the last few years the professor began to act in a way that was, as you say, uncharacteristic. He was frequently agitated. He had begun a new project, his last book, he promised, his best and most important. I saw immediately that it was not like the others, which he composed at an orderly pace, working an hour or two each morning after breakfast, then again after lunch. He became obsessed, as if his life would have been rendered meaningless if he didn't finish the project.

"He grew increasingly secretive, retreating to the library behind closed doors. He made me swear to keep confidential all facts pertaining to his most recent work. Eventually he requested, then demanded, that I stay away from the room in which we had passed so many pleasant hours. He worked feverishly, often long into the night, as if desperate to reach some self-imposed deadline. Occasionally I would open the doors to see him asleep at his work.

"I feared for his health. He lost weight and his colour was not good. Sometimes I heard him talking to himself, at times remonstrating, as if he was arguing with someone. I looked forward to the day when that accursed book would be finished for good and all. But of course, he passed on before . . . I was about to say, 'before he brought the book to a conclusion,' but you've said it *is* finished."

"Did his change in behaviour begin as soon as he started the book?"

"Shortly thereafter. He was conducting preliminary research and drafting the outline when he told me excitedly that he had made some sort of breakthrough or discovery and it was imperative that he go immediately to Florence. It was subsequent to his return that he . . . changed. For some reason, the journey altered him, and he evolved from a kind and gentle man to a person possessed. He was frantic to finish the project."

"Did he bring anything home with him?"

"Papers. Notes from his research. Books. And something he refused to let me see. He kept it in the library, out of sight."

"So you don't know what it was."

"Not until today. I know now. It had to have been that cross."

Everything Mrs. Stoppini had told me fit with what Raphaella and I had deduced. Now I had to proceed cautiously. I couldn't let slip anything about the spirit haunting the library. If I did, Mrs. Stoppini would think I had flipped my lid.

"Mrs. Stoppini, there are two important—crucial—suggestions Raphaella and I want to make."

"Very well."

"But you can't ask why we're making them."

"Indeed. Well, Mr. Havelock, you *are* mysterious when the spirit takes you."

You're not kidding, I almost said, not realizing at first that she was using the word "spirit" in a different way.

"About the cross. If it is bequeathed to the university"—she nodded as I spoke—"please don't take it to Italy yourself. Don't let anyone take it. Send it. The second thing is that Raphaella and I are certain there is only one copy of the professor's manuscript. There should be a backup copy. We'd like your permission to take it out of the house to have it photocopied."

I had decided not to tell her that Raphaella had photos of each page, taken without permission.

"We hope you'll have it published," I said.

"Yes, Mr. Havelock, I agree. As I said, I was not aware that the late professor had completed the book. That fact alters my original intention to include it among his papers and add it to the bequest. I shall not do so. But I see no need to hurry publication. The manuscript will keep, I am sure."

Not if it burns first, I wanted to say but couldn't.

"In addition," she went on, "you are quite correct about making a photocopy. I shall lodge the second copy with my lawyer. He keeps a safe in his chambers. I would be most grateful if you and Miss Skye could attend to that task as soon as is convenient."

I relaxed a bit and took another sip of the grappa. We sat together for a few minutes in what Mrs. Stoppini would have called a companionable silence. I heard her sigh, then she spoke softly.

"In a way, Mr. Havelock, the late professor gave his life to that manuscript."

She didn't know how right she was.

II

IT WAS LATE AFTERNOON when I got home to find Dad assaulting the hemlock hedge that borders our yard, his electric clippers buzzing and clattering as he slashed away like a cavalier. Mom was relaxing in a chaise longue on the patio, spooning boysenberry yogurt into her mouth.

"How was your day?" she asked.

"Eventful."

"How so?"

"Tell you later. I gotta hit the shower. Make sure Dad still has all his fingers when he's done."

I stood under the hot water a long time, letting the shower sluice away the day's sweat and tension and trying to decide what had been more intimidating, the testosterone-charged atmosphere of the paintball camp or the mournful face of Mrs. Stoppini. I was pleased that she had opened up a bit. When I thought about it, I recognized that she had placed a lot of trust in me from the start—in certain areas.

Not that I blamed her for guarding her personal business. It was her unexplained behaviour concerning the secret cupboard that had weakened my trust in her and led me to wonder if, in a way, I was being used and purposely kept in the dark. Now I believed in her, and that made me both glad and relieved, because I liked Mrs. Stoppini.

I was getting into clean clothes when my cell rang.

"It's your companion," Raphaella said.

"Nice to hear your voice, Ethel."

"Hah-hah. What did she say?"

I sat down on the edge of my bed and replayed my conversation with Mrs. Stoppini.

"It must have been hard on her, going over the events of the prof's death again," Raphaella remarked.

"Yeah. There were lots of tears. But I got the feeling she was relieved, too, like she was unburdening herself."

"She'd been holding it all in since he died."

"Right."

"But you're certain she knows nothing about our favourite ghost?"

"I'm pretty sure."

"Good. And you got her permission to take the manuscript away and get it copied?"

"Yup."

"You're brilliant."

"Come over for supper. We can pick up a movie and flop in front of the TV for the evening."

"Okay. Who's cooking?"

"Dad."

"Oh."

"Come anyway. It's barbecue."

"Barbecued what?"

"I don't know. Some dead animal or other. I'll try to get Dad to throw some veggie burgers on the grill while he's at it."

When I came downstairs Dad was still raising mayhem in the yard, a clutter of hemlock cuttings at his feet. I dragged a chair beside Mom and sat down.

"How's the research going?" I asked.

"You haven't explained your cryptic answer to my question when you came home."

"You first."

"Are you still my confidential source?"

"Yup."

"Meaning anything I tell you can't be shared."

I nodded.

"Even with Raphaella."

"No dice, Mom. I tell her everything. Besides, she already knows most of it."

"All right. I'm not surprised. Anyway, I've contacted the Mounties through my lawyer. The laws relating to terrorist activity and suspected activity are pretty broad, so someone like me has to be careful about even possessing information affecting national security, because that can be interpreted as a crime. Protecting an anonymous source is very difficult. The old rules about reporters refusing to divulge a source don't really apply. It's all very unclear, and if it's unclear, the practical result is that the security forces have very wide powers to make my life hell."

"So you think these guys *are* terrorists?"

"I think it's possible. I *know* the Mounties will think it's likely. I can't tell the authorities about the cellphone—not yet anyway—without getting into legal complications. In the meantime, my lawyer has worked out a deal with the cops. My position is that an anonymous source warned me about some suspicious-looking guys at a hunt camp near Orillia. I followed up and got enough info for a story, and I want to go ahead. But I understand the cops' position that I can't compromise an investigation. So I'll agree to hold off. When the cops break the story, the basic facts will go out via the usual press conference. Once it's announced, I have the exclusive on all the details."

"That's great, Mom. You can continue your research so you'll be ready when you get the green light."

"Exactly."

"Will it go worldwide, d'you think?"

"Probably. For which I have you to thank."

"True," I replied, smiling.

"Even though you bribed me."

"If you want to play in the big leagues, Mom, you gotta be tough."

She laughed. "Right. My son, the hard rock."

"Anyway, go on before Dad finishes."

"The phone was the key," she continued. "By tracking down many of the numbers I've been able to identify some of the men. Most of them live in the Scarborough area. A lot of the calls were made to a particular mosque in the same locality. I'm beginning to piece together a scenario, but I have lots more research to do, including a trip to the city to confirm a lot of what I have."

"How does the drowned guy who was found up on Cumberland Beach fit into all this?"

"I'm coming to that. You were right about the link between the cellphone, the GPS, and the drowned man. There's been an information blackout on the corpse. Since the body was discovered there has been no further information about him—no name, no cause of death, no autopsy report. When I made enquiries I was stonewalled. The Mounties won't confirm or deny that there *was* an autopsy."

I remembered one of Mom's reporter's maxims: if the authorities refused to tell you something, it was because they had something to hide. Which demanded the question . . .

"Why?"

"Good question. One of the first things I did was follow the links. The dead man owned the GPS you found. The GPS took you to the camp, where you came across the cellphone. The info on the phone's memory card led me to the Scarborough mosque and the men I mentioned before. But there's more. It turns out that whoever owned the cellphone made dozens of calls to a certain very interesting telephone number. I pulled in a few favours and discovered that telephone number belongs to a cop. A Mountie."

"You're kidding."

"I'm not kidding. The Mountie was the drowned man's controller. The dead guy must have been undercover."

"Meaning he was also a cop."

"Or working for them as an informer. Feeding them intelligence. Or helping them to set up a sting. Everything you and I know—and more—the cops are also aware of."

"Meaning," I added with a shudder, "there's a good chance the undercover was found out by the gang and killed."

I recalled the night at the mansion, when I stood at the window and watched the thunderstorm tear up the sky. I had thought I heard a motorboat. Were the paintballers dumping the body of the murdered undercover man, not realizing that somehow his GPS had floated away?

"I wonder what the paintballers are planning," I muttered.

"You should stop calling them that. It makes them seem like innocent sportsmen. These guys are serious characters. They're in training. They were considered dangerous enough for the cops to infiltrate the group."

I thought of the paintball hits around the door and window of the cabin out at the camp, and of the leader, with his commanding air and the machine pistol hanging across his chest. But then I saw in my mind's eye the so-called sentry I had come upon that very morning. He didn't seem dangerous. He was a joke, playing at soldier with his music-player buds in his ears.

"The Mounties still don't know about the GPS and the cellphone," Mom said. "That's why I had you take the cell to your new workshop. It's evidence. If the cops turn on me and get a search warrant for the house to take away my files and computer and so on—and they've done it before to other journalists with pretty flimsy cause—I need the cell to be off-site where the search warrant won't apply."

"No worries on that score, Mom."

She pinned me with her eyes. "Why do I get the impression there's something you're not telling me?"

"The GPS is gone, like I told you. The phone is back where I found it."

Mom's pretty features clouded over. "That's what you meant by 'eventful' when I asked you about your day. I thought I told you—"

"Like I said, No worries."

"Please don't go near that place again."

The sound of Dad's hedge clippers died and we watched him trudge across the lawn, winding the extension cord into big loops on his way to the garage.

"Anyway, Mom, you haven't shared your theory. What are these guys planning?"

Dad came out of the garage and walked down the flagstone path toward us.

"Stay tuned," Mom answered.

III

NEXT MORNING, Raphaella and I went through the familiar routine—taking compulsory tea with Mrs. Stoppini, anxiously opening the library doors, every nerve vibrating—releasing locks to get into the secret cupboard. But this time, the spectre didn't appear. We left the mansion with the professor's manuscript at the bottom of my backpack.

With Raphaella riding pillion, I piloted the Hawk through the cool morning, turned in to the big mall, and parked near the front door of the office supply store. We walked inside, filled in an order form, then waited while a man wearing green braces with his purple trousers ran off a copy of the manuscript.

While Raphaella was paying for the service I dropped a few dollar coins into the shrinkwrap machine and sealed up the original manuscript. I slid the photocopy into the professor's file box. We left the store and rode to Mrs. Stoppini's lawyer's office on Colborne Street. We explained to the secretary who we were.

"Ah, yes," she said. "I was speaking to Mrs. Stoppini myself."

We handed over the package and made our way out the door—but not until we had watched the secretary put the package into the safe.

The sun had climbed toward noon by the time we pulled through the mansion gates. Raphaella and I went directly to the library and put the photocopy where it belonged. We sat down in the chairs facing the fireplace.

"One last duty," I said with no confidence whatsoever.

"Finding a way to make the spirit leave."

"For good."

We threw a few ideas around, including Raphaella's joking suggestion to hire a priest to conduct an exorcism. She was laughing when she said it.

"I don't think you can hire a priest, anyway. Besides, you're not Catholic."

No matter how many scenarios we spun, we ended up with the same problem—the gold cross.

"How about we separate the relic from the cross?" I suggested.

"Thereby accomplishing what?"

"Did you just say 'thereby'?"

"Sorry. Must have been the influence of the lawyer's office. But answer my question anyway."

"If we remove the atlas we dissolve the cult. No reliquary, no secret movement."

"But they don't actually *need* the reliquary. They can still hold meetings and worship the friar and hatch their plans. And really, none of that is our business. They have a right to believe what they want."

"True. Okay, why don't we post the atlas on an online auction. 'One fanatical monk's atlas bone. Previously owned. Slightly marked by events.'"

"'Be the first kid on your block to have your very own holy relic,'" Raphaella added, and began to giggle. "If we separate the relic from the cross, what do we do with the atlas?" she asked, suddenly serious again. "I don't believe it's holy, but it *is* part of a human being, however evil he was sometimes."

"Could we bury it?"

"Where?"

"A Catholic cemetery?"

"But would that solve anything?"

"I don't know."

"Me either."

"So," I summed up, "we're agreed."

"Yeah. We don't have a clue what to do."

"Exactly."

Five

I

OVER THE NEXT WEEK a lot happened in the part of my life that had nothing to do with the Corbizzi estate or the Renaissance ghost that had taken up residence there.

Raphaella was in constant demand. MOO was gearing up for opening night, with a full rehearsal schedule. The show was coming together well, she told me. It was looking and sounding good. Mr. and Mrs. Director were getting along. Between MOO and her responsibilities at the Demeter, Raphaella was run ragged.

I was bouncing down the stairs from my room one morning when my cell rang. A man introduced himself as Derek and said he and his wife had been looking at the walnut cabinet I had made and put on display in the Olde Gold showroom. My father had given him my cell number. Would I be able to come to their house and discuss a commission?

I rode out to their century home on Maple Drive, where

we sat by the lake in wicker patio chairs and worked out a deal for the cabinet and three more custom-designed pieces—two chests of drawers and a bookcase with glass doors. I agreed to come back with an estimate and preliminary drawings in a couple of weeks—they weren't in a hurry, they said—and left the patio with a deposit cheque in my wallet.

I practically sang out loud as I rode home. Finally, a real customer—and some cash flow. Finally, I could realistically hope that not too far in the future Raphaella and I would be able to find a place of our own and move in together. We had talked about getting married. The conversation lasted about five seconds, as I had expected. Raphaella thought marriage was an outmoded institution based on the idea that women were property or second-class citizens. "We don't need a piece of paper," she had said. "We know how we feel about each other." I didn't care one way or the other, as long as I was with her.

I came back into the house to hear a strange sound coming from the living room. Our TV set never saw action until at least six o'clock. I walked down the hall and got my second shock. My mother was watching TV. In the middle of the day.

Before I could say, "What's wrong?" she asked, "Heard the news?"

At the bottom of the screen a white banner crawled, almost shouting "Breaking News," while an overly made-up woman sitting behind a huge kidney-shaped desk was talking.

". . . confirmed that at least six men, including the imam of the Scarborough mosque all the suspects attended, were arrested early this morning in a coordinated series of raids in Scarborough and Mississauga involving security services and two police forces. The men, all Pakistani-Canadians, ranging in age from juveniles to mid-twenties, have been detained in connection with possible terrorist activities. More on this after the break."

Mom hit the Mute button on the remote.

"It's started," she said.

"Did you know it was coming?"

"I knew it would be soon. That's why I went to the city and checked out the mosque and some of the addresses I had acquired by using the phone numbers on the cell you found. I just drove by and took pictures. I already had their names."

"So you're all set to go?"

The sparkle in her eyes said yes. "I think so. There might even be a book in this."

On the TV screen, where the news reader had just been talking about suspected terrorists, a woman was earnestly demonstrating the wonders of a new brand of paper towel to her husband. The "more after the break" claim turned out to be a repeat of the announcement. Additional information was promised.

By the time the six o'clock news came on the kitchen radio, the arrest count had risen and the media had already dubbed the detainees "The Severn Ten," continually referring to them as Muslim men. The training camp had been discovered, thanks to an anonymous source, near Orillia.

"That's us, Mom," I exclaimed, earning a scowl from her and a confused glance from my father. He put down his knife and fork and calmly aligned them beside his plate of fish and chips.

"Why do I have the feeling I'm the last one to get the joke?" Dad asked.

Mom took a sip of her white wine and began to explain. She emphasized the reasons why she couldn't tell Dad what she had been working on. Now that the story was out, she could. Our plates were empty by the time she finished.

Dad looked at me, then at Mom, then he smiled.

"So you're not going to Herat, then," he said.

By eleven o'clock the training camp was being called "jihadist" and the men "Islamists." They had been plotting, the police said, to attack one or more targets in the city, including Union Station and CSIS headquarters. A huge cache of firearms, ammunition, and explosives had been captured during the raids. In addition, each of the detained men carried a copy of a manifesto calling for the establishment of an Islamist state and strict rule according to Sharia law.

"In other words, a theocracy," I murmured. "There's not much news left for you to break, is there, Mom?" I asked.

"Oh, we'll see," she said mysteriously.

II

AFTER DINNER I FLOPPED in front of the TV and flipped through channels mindlessly, unable to give my attention to anything on offer. I tossed the remote aside without turning off the set. On the screen two ego-warriors in black jump-suits and watch caps were going through the classic Hollywood "suiting up" scene—buckling buckles, zipping zippers, cinching drawstrings, slamming ammo clips into wicked-looking weapons, eager to shoot or blow up anything that got in their way—all this as uptempo music pounded in the background. It wasn't clear to me what they were fighting for, other than their own egos. As sparks flew and mangled bodies fell, my mind was constantly drawn back to reality and the radio newscast at dinner.

I was relieved that the whole issue had been resolved. The bad guys had been rounded up and Mom was staying put—for the time being, anyway.

Raphaella hadn't taken the camo-boys seriously, but now she'd have to. Mom had it right. There was nothing funny about them. I figured some of them—like the one I had seen taking a leak at the camp—were losers, but even losers can be dangerous. An explosion in an enclosed underground train depot like Union Station, with thousands of commuters packed onto the platforms or streaming up and down the stairways, would be a bloodbath, ripping countless bodies to shreds. If the terrorists had been able to carry out their missions there would have been blood on the walls in other parts of the city, too.

And all for what? An Islamist state based on Sharia law? In North America? How realistic was that? The camo-boys must have left their sanity out in the bush somewhere.

Of all the revolting, cowardly acts humans were capable of, planting a bomb and walking away to safety had to be one of the most despicable. Killing was bad enough. Murdering without even knowing or caring whose blood you spilled was worse. And suicide bombers? A bunch of cowards brainwashed by soul-dead manipulators. They boarded a bus or walked into a crowded market and thumbed a button, vaporizing themselves and tearing dozens of strangers to bloody fragments. They didn't even have the guts to stay around and witness the carnage.

Guys like the Severn Ten were not freedom fighters or soldiers of God. They were vermin who crawled out of the woodwork when the sun went down. They wanted a theocracy. Professor Corbizzi had warned that Savonarola had wanted a theocracy, too. Government according to the will of God. Different religion, same objective. As far as I knew, Savonarola had never planted a bomb and beetled home to wait for the body parts to fly, but he had called for the death of his political enemies, and the burning of "sinners" and their "vanities."

I picked up the remote and shut off the TV, recalling Raphaella's question in Professor Corbizzi's library not long ago. Was it the religion that was to blame or the people who practised it—the songbook or the singers? She had wondered if evil people used their religion as a cover for their own immorality, an excuse to kill and maim. The pope who signed the order to torture and hang and burn Savonarola would have said he was doing the will of God. He was also snuffing out a personal enemy who had urged reform of the Church and removal of corrupt men like him. If the camo-boys had succeeded in bombing Union Station they'd likely have shouted, "God is great!" but they would have meant "Aren't we wonderful!"

The news reports had harped on about the Severn Ten being Muslims, as if every Muslim in the country was a terrorist. It wasn't religion or holy texts that killed. It was people who read the books and used bits of what they picked off the pages to justify their deeds, the way the ancient Greeks in the old blue book of myths on my bookshelf had used the Fates.

"God made me do it" or "God wanted me to do it" was a lie.

III

FOR THE TIME BEING, MOO had taken over Raphaella's life. As stage manager she had to be on hand for each full rehearsal and every performance—a responsibility I'd have run from but Raphaella enjoyed. The show had a three-night run. Opening night found me backstage, sitting on a chair out of everyone's way. Although I hated musicals, I was energized by the performers in early-twentieth-century costumes who entered and exited according to Raphaella's cues and sang their comical songs with more enthusiasm than skill. In her all-black outfit and wire-thin headset, holding a clipboard in one hand and a mechanical pencil in another, she reminded me of the day soon after we had met. Frustrated by her ignoring me, I marched across Mississauga Street, bashed through the backstage door, found her working a rehearsal of the *Sound of Music*, and declared that I had loved her since the moment I first saw her. Amazed at myself for blurting out such a terrifying admission, I was even more thunderstruck when she dropped her clipboard and kissed me on the mouth in a way I'd never been kissed before.

MOO's opening night was a smash. The following shows sold out. As the cast and directors had hoped, they were invited to give a benefit performance for the World Youth Congress at Geneva Park, the conference centre on the east shore of Lake Couchiching. The producer consulted the two directors and the cast, who all agreed, and after a day's rest, Raphaella, the directors, and the musicians went out to Geneva Park in the morning to set up and do a thorough sound check.

"Want to come with me for the performance?" Raphaella asked me on the phone that afternoon. "You can give me a ride out and back."

I picked her up after an early supper and we rode out to Geneva Park, motoring through the Chippewas of Rama territory and past the busy casino. We turned off Rama Road, followed a tree-lined lane to a gatehouse, where we signed in and received photo-ID badges from blue-clad rent-a-cops, and parked in the lot nearest the conference centre, where the performance would be held. I noticed several security personnel in similar outfits near the main building.

Inside, teenagers of all sizes and shapes and wearing a wide variety of dress styles wandered around in small groups, obviously on a lull between laid-on activities, chatting in languages I didn't recognize. Chairs had been arranged in front of the stage. Music stands stood skeletally off to the side. Raphaella and I went backstage, where Mr. and Mrs. Director were arguing about something.

"I'd better get out of your hair," I said. "Maybe I'll go for a walk."

Handing me the PIE, she replied, "Take care of this for me? I forgot to leave it at home."

Raphaella had a rule that no cells were allowed backstage. People said they'd turn them off, then they'd forget. I shoved the PIE into my pocket and gave Raphaella a kiss.

"See you later," I said. Then, nodding toward the warring directors, "Good luck with the children."

A crew of groundskeepers were tending to the lawn and shrubs in the open area beside the main building, cutting and trimming and raking, looking overheated in their brown uniforms and baseball-style hats. According to the map in the pamphlet I had picked up at the gate, the centre occupied a forested peninsula intersected by pea-gravel trails connecting tennis courts, sleeping cabins, outbuildings, patios, and the beach. I followed the path toward the lake. At the shore I came to a boathouse and dock, where a security guard who looked as if she'd rather be just about anywhere else stood sentry. I continued along the edge of the water until I got to a stand of white pines. I walked a few steps into the green grove, the mantle of fallen needles springy under my feet, and sat down, leaning against one of the trees. The lake was bright with late-afternoon sunlight, shimmering in the still air, the green water along the shore fringed with spiky grass and sand.

Chiefs Island lay off to the southwest, between me and Wicklow Point, where Mrs. Stoppini was probably writing letters in her study or reading over a glass of Chianti, alone in her big empty mansion. No, not quite alone, I reminded myself, and shivered. The friar was there, too, lurking. I asked myself again how Raphaella and I could force the spirit to slink away for good, and as always I was stuck for an answer.

I opened the pamphlet I had picked up at the gate, curious about the World Youth Congress just under way. The teenage participants had come from all over the world, representing more than two dozen countries. No wonder there were rent-a-cops around, I thought. The congress brought the kids together to inspire "mutual understanding and cooperation between cultures," through activities like "team-building" and "goal-oriented tasks that encourage and reward collaboration." I hoped that meant the kids could have fun together and get to know one another by sailing, swimming, playing games, and generally horsing around.

I looked up when I heard boots scraping on the footpath. A man in a sweat-stained brown uniform made his way along the shore. Grass clippings clung to his trouser cuffs. He glanced at me and continued on without saying anything. He looked familiar, in a vague way.

I folded the pamphlet and slipped it into a back pocket, thinking the congress was a terrific idea. I liked it when people from different countries and cultures mingled. Lazy in the heat, I settled back against the tree and idly picked up a clump of dry brown pine needles. Dad had tried to teach me some arithmetic once, long before I started school, using pine fascicles. We were hiking the Ganaraska Trail, west of town, in a blaze of autumn colour, and he was rambling away about white and red pines, how their needle clusters were different. Five white, two red, he chanted, not realizing that I was barely paying attention. He plucked one fascicle from each kind of tree and pointed out that the red pine fascicle held two needles, the white five.

"Remember, the word 'white' has five letters, and the white pine has five needles. The word 'red' has three letters—two less than five—therefore red has two needles. And white times red makes ten."

How he imagined this convoluted logic would help me remember anything was beyond me—for a while, until I realized it had worked.

I checked my watch. The show would be starting soon. I got up and ambled back, using a different route. The trees threw long shadows across the trail. I passed through a cluster of sleeping cabins—old log structures that had been updated. The cabins were scattered across a pine grove. Whitewashed rocks delineated the paths leading from the gravel walkway to the ground-level platform at each cabin door.

White times red makes ten popped into my mind again. Ten divided by white equals red. Ten divided by red equals white. I chanted as I walked.

Ten.

At the edge of my vision, a brown blur. I whirled around in time to see a man hurry into the trees behind the cabin nearest the lake. It was the groundskeeper I had met at the shore, the one who had looked familiar. He was carrying one of those small foldable shovels. He hadn't noticed me.

Ten.

What kind of task would take a landscape worker into the bush? I wondered. Keeping the cabin between him and me, I worked my way around it until I could see movement in the maples beyond the pine grove. Where the ground sloped away to the lake he stopped, got to his knees, and began to dig. I crept back to the front of the cabin, my shoulder brushing the log wall.

Ten.

I ransacked my memory, frustrated. I couldn't place the man's face. Why did that number and the image of the face chase themselves around my brain box? Were they linked? I allowed my vision to play across the grounds and the tall white pines that striped the area with shadows. Around me, all was quiet. No one stirred in any of the cabins or along the walkways. Everyone was in the audience, waiting for the show to begin.

Ten.

In a dark corner of my mind, something clicked as a connection was made.

Ten.

The news reports about the suspected terrorists associated with the paintball/jihadist training camp called the men who had been apprehended by the police the Severn Ten.

And I hadn't paid enough attention to the details.

Ten had seemed right. I had seen exactly that number of camo-boys at the camp, and I had taken photos of some of them, including the leader. Ten men had been arrested in Scarborough and Mississauga.

But one news report had stated that an imam had been taken into custody as part of the conspiracy. Was the imam one of the men at the camp? Or should the total number of arrests have been *eleven*?

Had the cops missed one? Had one of the paintball-camp terrorists slipped out of the net?

Frantically, I snatched Raphaella's cell from my pocket. My hands shook so violently I could barely thumb the keys.

"Hello?"

"Dad, put Mom on. Hurry."

"What—?"

"Do it!"

My mother's voice came on a couple of seconds later. "Garnet?"

"Mom. You have the photos from the paintball camp on your laptop."

She caught the excitement in my voice.

"Yes, I still have them."

"Email the picture of the guy with the machine pistol to Raphaella's cell. Right away."

"Got it."

I disconnected. I stole a look around the corner of the building. The man was still at work, deep in the trees, digging. I stood quietly, listening to the air flowing in and out of my lungs. Once more I scanned the cabins, each with its path neatly bordered by white rocks, each with its single window and low platform before the door. I visualized another cabin, colourful paintball strikes around the door and windows, like acne.

The PIE vibrated.

I punched buttons. Opened the email. Mom had sent the photo. I zoomed in on the face of the camp leader. Take away his moustache, exchange the camo field cap for a brown groundskeeper's hat, and there he was.

I erased Mom's email and called her back.

"Listen carefully," I said in a low voice, trying and failing to hold back the adrenaline buzz. "He's here—at Geneva Park, at the World Youth Congress. I saw him."

It all made sense, I rushed on. Why did the terrorists access their camp by water, from Lake Couchiching down the Trent system to the landing? Because they intended to *attack* by water. Their target was Geneva Park!

And what had they been doing out on the lake during a storm that night? Rehearsing. Practising. Getting their timing right. Maybe landing at Geneva Park in the middle of the night, in a storm, when they wouldn't be seen, and burying arms and ammo right on the grounds. But they ran into trouble. A violent thunderstorm. An overloaded boat, maybe. A boat pitched around by savage waves. One of them—the undercover—fell out of the boat during the thunderstorm. Or his cover was blown and they killed and dumped him. His GPS floated free and washed up on the grounds of the Corbizzi estate.

"They planned to assault Geneva Park during the youth summit all along, Mom! I—"

"I'm phoning my contact at the cops. Hang up, Garnet. Right now. And get the hell out of there!"

I thumbed the Off button and shoved the PIE into my pocket. Then I heard a twig snap behind the cabin.

IV

I FLATTENED MY BACK against the logs and held my breath.

The terrorist in the brown uniform walked purposefully past the corner of the building, heading down the main walkway, his feet crunching on the gravel. He held the shovel in one hand and a gym bag sagging from its handles in the other. What weighed down the bag was easy to guess. Thoughts flicked on and off in my mind like camera flashes in a stadium crowd. A man twisted with hate carries a rifle into a Montreal school and massacres more than a dozen women. A couple of Colorado teenagers zoned out on self-pity make war on classmates, leaving a dozen dead. It seemed every country had its school shooting or equivalent, where twisted minds saw murder as a form of self-expression. But this guy was different. He was a fanatic calmly carrying out his version of Allah's will. Within minutes he would stroll into the main building, pretending interest in the show—your friendly lawn-care guy attracted by the crowd and the music. He'd find a good vantage point in the semi-darkness, put the bag down, whack a bullet clip into the machine pistol, lay out the extra clips in a neat line for rapid reloading, and let the gun make a statement that would ensure he'd be remembered for decades—and so would his cause. He'd open up on the crowd, screaming that God was great as bullets tore into flesh and bone, filling the air with a fine mist of gore. Within minutes the auditorium would be a slaughterhouse strewn with corpses, the floor a lake of blood. When the cops came for him he'd keep tossing grenades until he was shot dead. He'd be a martyr.

And Raphaella would be among the dead.

"Hey!" I called out.

He stopped about ten paces from me. His broad shoulders bunched. He turned slowly, his dark eyes hard and calculating.

What to say next? I scrabbled for words. Blanked. Stood like a fool, mouth open like a startled fish.

"Er, have you seen Mary?" I blurted, my heart battering my chest wall. "I . . . she told me this was her cabin. Number . . . whatever. But nobody'll answer. See?"

Moronically, I demonstrated by rapping on the screen door. I ransacked my brain for a way to delay him, but I had run out of ideas. He took a step toward me. He still hadn't uttered a word. Behind him in the distance I heard the opening cymbal bash of the overture for *Merrie Olde Orillia*.

"Don't," I pleaded. "They have nothing against you. They're innocent."

His eyes flared. His fingers tightened on the looped handles of the bag. Something came over his face—a shadow—and I could almost hear him asking himself how I knew that he was about to make the auditorium an inferno of gunfire and smoke. The dark unyielding eyes widened again. Did he realize I was the intruder who had come upon him and his followers in the forest outside Orillia, who had caused the arrest of his accomplices and the destruction of his plans?

"Think about it," I said desperately. "You can't do this."

He strode determinedly toward me. The hand gripping the shovel's handle relaxed and allowed the tool to slip through his palm until he could grasp the end of the shaft. I readied myself to shift quickly at the right second. But he fooled me. In one lightning-fast circular motion he flung the shovel. It whickered end over end across the space between us, small lumps of earth flying off the blade as it spun.

I flinched instinctively, twitching my head back and to one side a split second before I heard the sickening *pang* of metal on bone. Light exploded inside my head and I dropped like a stone to the platform. He was on me in a second, snatching up the shovel, lifting it high, and striking down toward my skull. I rolled onto my back and he grunted as the shovel crashed into the plank beside my head. He snarled, eyes smouldering with hatred and frustration. I brought one knee to my chest, and as he raised the shovel overhead, I gathered what strength I could and jabbed my heel into his balls.

He cried out and fell to his knees, desperately groping for breath. The shovel clattered to the planks. I scrabbled away from him and, struggling dizzily to my feet, stood swaying like a drunk, my vision blurred, my head ringing. Something streamed down the side of my face like hot syrup.

The terrorist fell forward onto one hand, the other clutching his crotch, choking as if the air around him had been sucked away. He turned his head, fixed his eyes on the gym bag. As if in slow motion I picked up the shovel, stumbled out of his reach. I had no doubt that if he got the tool I'd be dead in seconds.

"Don't move," I croaked.

Gasping and groaning, he crawled toward the bag.

"I said stop."

Still he fought his way across the bare ground, his fingers scratching at the soil. I raised the shovel and slammed the rounded side of the blade down on the back of his head. There was the clang of a frying pan hitting a stovetop. The terrorist collapsed and lay still.

I stood beside him, panting, searching for balance. Threw aside the tool and fell to my knees. Pressed my fingers against his neck. Found a pulse. Crawled clumsily across the dirt, blood dripping off my cheek, leaving a trail. Unzipped the gym bag and pulled it open. A machine pistol similar to the one in his photo lay on a bed of full bullet clips, a cluster of grenades at each end.

I staggered back to him as if struggling through thigh-deep water, my legs continually swept from under me by the roar of surf in my ears. I leaned close, caught the faint rasp of his breathing. Heard playful music in the distance, and crashing waves. Zipped up the bag, dragged it to a tree, and dropped it behind the trunk, desperate to hide it from him. Slogged back toward the cabin platform. Lowered myself to the planks to rest, just for a minute. No. Can't rest. Gotta find Raphaella. But I couldn't get up. I teetered on the edge of the deck, then toppled into the waves. Plunged beneath the water and down, the tiger-striped green bottom of the lake shimmering, lit by bursts of coloured light.

PART FIVE

The essence of fanaticism is that it has almost no tolerance for any data that do not confirm its own point of view.

—Neil Postman

One

I

I WAS STARING into the face of a monster.

Dark hair, spiky and dishevelled. A shaved patch across the skull from the right temple past the ear, a vivid stitched-up slash not quite hidden by a bloodstained bandage. A black eye swollen shut, puffed cheeks bruised and discoloured. Fresh scabs on nose, left cheek, and chin, bright red against pale skin.

I handed the mirror back to the nurse. "Call Hollywood," I croaked. "Tell them to hold off on the screen test."

I didn't remember much more of my semi-conscious ride in the ambulance than the banging of doors, being lifted and lowered, prodded and jabbed, but I recalled waking up briefly to tsunamis of pain rolling through my skull. Later—hours? days?—brain fogged by dope, I saw light in a window. My hands had sprouted needles attached to tubes leading aloft to plastic bladders of liquid—one clear, one dark red—suspended from a rack. A tall nurse stood beside my bed, unclipping wires from my head, removing sticky patches, pushing a machine out the door, coming back with a little white paper cup.

"Take these," she said. "You'll feel better."

"Raphaella," I mumbled.

Something squeezed my upper arm. I heard my father's voice beside me.

"She's fine. No one was hurt," he soothed. "Thanks to you."

Later, pain-wracked, I floated in a dream-like state. A small black-robed man drifted past. The odours of earth and moss wafted from the shore. Gunfire crackled in the distance. Something thick and wet was smeared on my face around my eye and over my nose and chin and cheek. Gentle fingers smoothed warm paste on my skin.

A commanding voice in the background. "Here! Who are you? What do you think you're doing!"

A face in the dark above me—the features, I would have sworn, of Raphaella's mother.

Now things seemed normal—almost.

"You'll be your regular, handsome self in no time," the nurse announced merrily, returning the mirror to the drawer in the nightstand beside the bed. "Let me prop you up a little straighter. You're drooping."

A motor hummed, then the nurse bashed enthusiastically at the pillows behind my head for a few seconds. "Comfy?" Without waiting for an answer she headed out the door.

"You have visitors," she called over her shoulder.

I had been in Soldiers' Memorial Hospital for two nights, and this morning I was beginning to feel almost normal, although the mirror had hinted otherwise. My head, still aching a little, had cleared. I was hungry. I guessed that was a good sign.

Raphaella came through the door first, a vision more healing than any medicine, wearing a fire engine red T-shirt and black jeans. My parents trailed behind her, smiling, wearing that parental expression that said "We're not worried about you; we just look like we are."

Raphaella leaned over me. I could smell her hair and her skin, and I felt tears gathering at the corners of my eyes.

"I want to kiss you," she said. "Where's your mouth?"

AS THE MORNING PASSED and we waited for the hospital's grinding bureaucracy to release me officially, Mom, Dad, and Raphaella brought me up to date.

"They got the guy," Mom began. She related that in response to her call the cops had employed a silent approach—meaning no sirens—as they descended on Geneva Park. The Rama First Nation officers got there first, finding two unconscious men lying in the dirt. They had cuffed both of us before more cops charged onto the scene in a cloud of dust. The bag holding the gun and ammo was discovered minutes later. By the time the ambulances arrived police had sorted out the good guy from the bad guy and I was on my way to the hospital. Where they took the terrorist, no one knew.

"You have a concussion," Mom went on, "and a bad cut on your head. Twenty-one stitches. You'll have headaches for a few days, but the doctor assured us you're all right."

"That shiner is a doozy, but all in all, no worries," Dad added. But his expression said "We were scared to death."

"None of us in the auditorium had a clue what was going on outside," Raphaella told me. "The show was a huge hit—the kids loved it—and with the music and the roars of laughter and the applause, it was mayhem in the auditorium. After the final curtain calls I went outside looking for you, and there was no hint that something serious had happened, that we had all been within an inch of our lives. Then I noticed a lot of cops moving around, a few hanging yellow DO NOT CROSS tape across the pathway to the cabins, and I realized something was going on. I still can't get my head around it. We could all be dead right now."

"We tried to call Raphaella to warn her," Mom went on. "But you had her phone, remember? I sent you the photo?"

"There's a publication ban on the details connected with the incident, ordered by a judge," Dad said. "The official story is that a man with a history of mental illness was arrested at Geneva Park. That's it. Your mom has been helping the police a little, and you'll have to give a statement in a few days, when you're feeling up to it."

"And after you've talked things over with our lawyer," Mom added. "We can discuss all that when you're home. I just hope the police don't find the cellphone with the terrorist's picture in it. That could cause us problems."

"The phone's safe," I said. "During the fight, it fell between the boards of the deck at the cottage door. I erased the image."

"And now, Annie," Dad said, "I think you and I should go to the cafeteria and have a cup of their horrible tea."

After the door had hissed shut behind my parents, Raphaella sat on the edge of the bed and took my hand.

"Your dad says you should get a medal. You're a hero."

"I'm no such thing."

I told her everything that had taken place after I left her in the auditorium.

"When I finally worked out who he was and what he intended to do, I was petrified. All I could think about was that huge room full of kids—and you—and pictures I've seen on the TV news when somebody goes into a school or someplace with a gun. I didn't know *what* to do. I said something stupid to him, and he turned around and hurled the shovel and hell broke loose. It was a fluke, the way it turned out. It could just as easily have gone the other way."

"Maybe your dad thinks you're brave because of what you didn't do."

"What's that?"

"Run away."

II

I HAD BEEN HOME a couple of days when the cops telephoned and asked me to come in to make a statement and answer some questions. By then my constant headache, the jungle drum beating in the background, had faded, although my face still looked as if I'd stayed in the boxing ring one round too many.

My parents were having their five o'clock glass of wine together on the patio when I got off the phone, and when I told them about the upcoming interview they exchanged glances. My dad was up to speed on everything by that point. Mom had been in a bad mood lately. I didn't blame her. A judge had clapped a total ban on publication of any aspect of the story. Mom's exclusive—at least for the time being—had gone out the window. So much for freedom of the press.

"We'd better go over this together," Mom cautioned. "When are you due at the cop shop?"

"Day after tomorrow at 10:00 a.m."

"I'll call Mabel Ayers and see if you can get in to see her tomorrow," Dad said, getting up and going into the kitchen.

"Do I really need to talk to a lawyer?" I asked my mother.

"I can't believe you asked that," Mom replied.

Long experience as an investigative reporter had left her with a schizophrenic attitude toward police forces in general. She respected cops, knew their jobs were difficult in ways the public did not understand, agreed we needed them. "They're unappreciated," she would say. But she had also seen cops fudge evidence to get a conviction and even lie in court, under oath. She had, within the walls of our house, renamed the RCMP the RCLC—Royal Canadian Lies and Coverups.

"You have to be prepared for what they're going to ask you, that's all," she said, putting down her wine glass. "They may try to trick you. And Mabel will be helpful."

THE NEXT MORNING she and I drove to the city and met with Mabel Ayers, a chubby middle-aged woman with a small, messy office and a phone that rang constantly. The morning after that, I drove over to the OPP headquarters and met with three inspectors who represented, together, eleven letters of the alphabet—CSIS, RCMP, and OPP. The

Rama First Nation cops who had arrested the paintball terrorist weren't represented.

I was nervous. The two males wore dark blue suits, one with a red tie and one with a red-and-blue tie. They were clean-shaven, their hair clipped short. The woman—OPP—had on a dark grey pantsuit and wore her sand-coloured hair short. They sat across a big table from me, each with a newish file folder and a pad and ballpoint pen. It seemed more like a business meeting than an interrogation. Mom had warned me to keep my wits sharp. I jumped right in with the question Mabel had told me to ask first.

"Are you recording this interview on audio or video?"

RCMP frowned, then exchanged glances with the others. "This isn't a formal interview, Garnet. And no, we're not recording you."

"On video *or* audio," CSIS added. "Now, Garnet—"

"So I'm not under investigation?"

A look of irritation crossed CSIS's face.

Mom had warned me that they'd call me by my first name, and she had been right. It was a technique to make me feel at ease so I'd trust them, and at the same time it emphasized that they were in control. They had introduced themselves using surnames only, but I was Garnet.

OPP tried her luck. "Garnet, this is just a chat. A conversation. We think you can help us fill in a few blanks, that's all. Okay?"

I nodded.

Under questioning, I related that I had taken a walk around the grounds of Geneva Park, waiting for the show to start, when I noticed a man in a groundskeeper's uniform emerging from the woods with a shovel in one hand and a duffle bag in the other. When I asked him what he had been doing in the woods he attacked me.

"I was just being nosy, I guess. I didn't expect him to clobber me."

From the time he bonked me with the shovel I didn't remember much, I told them, except that I was mad and wanted to hit him back. I answered their questions truthfully but volunteered nothing. They didn't ask me if I'd ever seen the guy before. Why would they?

"Is he hurt bad?" I asked.

"He'll live. Do you remember opening the duffle bag?" the woman enquired.

"No."

"Or putting it behind a tree?" one of the men—CSIS—asked.

"No."

"So," RCMP summed up, "you had no idea that you had saved the lives of a couple of hundred people?"

"No."

I had been afraid they'd grill me about Mom's phone call to the cops, the one weak spot in my story. But she had said in her formal statement that she deduced the youth summit had been the terrorists' target all along, and with the show opening that evening—which she knew about because her son's girlfriend was stage manager—she alerted police out of caution. Her version of events sounded pretty thin to me, but she emphasized that we had to stick with it. I guessed it had satisfied them because my interview came to an end with no hint that they were sceptical of Mom's version. In unison the three inspectors got to their feet, and when I followed suit they thanked me for coming and wished me a speedy recovery from my injuries.

Just as I turned toward the interview room door the CSIS inspector said, "It's quite a coincidence, though, isn't it?"

I almost laughed. How often had I seen this same ploy in detective movies? The bad guy thinks he's fooled the detective with his lies. The polite cop thanks him and is about to leave when he stops, as if a stray thought has struck him. He turns and says to the suspect, "Oh, one more thing. It's not important, but . . ." Then the bad guy, his guard down, spills the beans.

But I hadn't told any lies. I turned back toward the three suits, stood silent and waited.

"Your mother is an investigative reporter," CSIS went on. "She's the one who broke the story about the Severn Ten. She appears to have a lot of information about them."

"And here's you," RCMP continued, "the son, who just happened to be on hand to prevent the massacre."

"Yeah, well, Orillia's a small town," I said, and walked out the door.

Two

I

MOST OF THE KIDS I had gone to school with saw graduation as an escape hatch. They couldn't wait to leave Orillia in their dust. For them it was a small town, practically a village, narrow and unexciting, with nothing new to offer. They had explored all its possibilities long ago, and living here was like being condemned everlastingly to read and re-read a dull book. As graduation neared they became restless, eager for a future that would be rosy only if it was lived somewhere else. I had been just as fidgety—not to get out of town but to get on with my plans for the future.

I liked the familiarity of Orillia's streets and parks and lakes, the sense of being on well-known ground, a part of things. And on days like today, when the sunshine poured like honey out of a clear blue sky and the breeze from the lake carried the scent of vegetation, hinting of adventure, I only had to imagine myself slogging through the traffic-racket of Bay Street in

Toronto, the skyscrapers forming a shadowy canyon where the funnelled wind flung grit and bits of fast-food wrappers into my face, to know I was where I wanted to be.

It was funny, in a way, the notion that drama and excitement only occur somewhere else. Raphaella and I had had our share of adventure and mystery—and fear—without leaving town, when we were caught in the fallout from events that happened near the African Methodist Church more than 150 years before. My scrape with the paintball terrorist was more proof—as if we needed it—that being a sleepy little town didn't make Orillia immune from the wider world. And our unanticipated crash course in the Italian Renaissance fanatic, Savonarola, made the prospect of a one-day whirlwind bus tour of Florence, Italy, seem dull in comparison.

I thought those thoughts as I drove the van toward Wicklow Point to begin my first day back at work since Geneva Park. I hadn't been able to ride the Hawk lately. My face was still too swollen and tender to fit inside my helmet, with its tight safety padding. I was glad to get back to my normal routine, and I was looking forward to making a start on the designs for the pieces commissioned by Derek and Liz. My unfinished task—the inventory—hung over my head like a cloud of mosquitoes, but I had to see it through, and I would, with Raphaella's help and, I hoped, with*out* the interference of the spectre.

Getting rid of him permanently was another problem altogether.

I drove through the gate and down the shady lane to the shop and parked in the usual spot under the birches, then went to the back door and knocked.

"Good gracious!" exclaimed Mrs. Stoppini, wide-eyed and frozen in the doorway like a black mannequin, her bony hand on her cheek. For a split second she seemed unable to move, then she exploded into action, grabbing my arm and hauling me into the kitchen and bundling me into a chair. She slammed the door and alighted on the edge of a seat, staring at my face.

"I scarcely recognized you! What on earth—? Don't tell me you have had an altercation!"

"An accident," I fibbed. It was half true, I supposed. "I'm fine. I know I look awful, but—"

"Indeed!"

"I'm okay. Ready to get back to work."

Over the inevitable cup of tea and brioche or two, and amid Mrs. Stoppini's clucking and fussing and peering at my banged-up face, I told her about my new commission. I said I planned to spend the mornings working in the shop and would continue the inventory during the afternoons when, on most days, Raphaella would join me. Now that MOO was history, she had more time. She'd arranged to run the Demeter in the mornings and then come to the estate.

"Most satisfactory," Mrs. Stoppini pronounced.

Before I went out to the shop I walked down the hall to the library, eager to see if there had been any changes over the past couple of weeks. The corridor was quiet, and for the first time in what seemed like ages, it smelled of floor wax rather than smoke. I took a quick peek inside the library doors. Everything seemed as we had left it, undisturbed. The room was quiet and almost, if I hadn't known better, inviting.

I left the room and headed for the shop and my drawing board.

THE NEXT FEW DAYS passed without a ripple. The late-summer weather was hot and dry. The breeze off the lake flowed into the library as Raphaella and I toiled away, making good progress in the boring notation of book titles and authors' names into the database. Once we had reached the alcove our progress had slowed to a crawl as we unshelved, examined, and noted the details Mrs. Stoppini required from every volume. We worked together, one dictating, the other typing.

At times we could barely detect the uniquely unpleasant smoky odour we had grown used to. On other days it was strong enough to be an almost physical presence. What all that signified, we didn't know. The spectre never appeared and we didn't complain.

Hanging over us was the unasked, unacknowledged question: What should we do when this assignment was complete? Walk away and say nothing about Savonarola? Casually tell Mrs. Stoppini, "We're done. It was fun, and by the way, there's a vicious ghost in your secret cupboard"? And speaking of the spectre, where was he, anyway? Why was he being so quiet these days?

Without having to give voice to our thoughts, we were certain that we were on track for a showdown.

And we were right.

11

As if it was in sympathy with the mood inside the Corbizzi mansion, the weather turned unseasonably nasty. A cold front lumbered down from the north and soggy grey clouds rolled in over the lake and settled down for a long stay. Rain came and went on gusty winds, ticking drearily against the window glass. Raphaella and I talked about lighting a small fire to chase out the damp air and cheer up the place, and I had got as far as carting an armload of scrap wood in from the shop. But we decided the room was the wrong place for flames.

I was thinking about taking a break when my cell rang. I listened, then closed the phone.

"What's *zuccotto*?" I asked Raphaella.

"An Italian scooter?"

"I don't think so."

"An Italian painter?"

I shook my head. "Mrs. Stoppini just invited us to share a piece with her in the kitchen."

"I have always believed," Mrs. Stoppini said as she poured strong tea into china cups, "that a generous helping of *zuccotto* brightens up even the dullest day."

It turned out to be sponge cake filled with hazelnuts, almonds, cream, and chocolate. Raphaella tried a bit, chewing with an angelic look on her face.

"I think I've died and gone to heaven," she rhapsodized dramatically. "Mrs. Stoppini, this is divine."

Mrs. Stoppini smiled her thin-lipped smile. "One tries." She glanced at me. "And your verdict, Mr. Havelock?"

I chewed slowly, swallowed, pressed my lips together, and tried to look pensive.

"Well . . ."

Mrs. Stoppini's brows dipped in toward the bridge of her nose.

"Come on, Garnet," Raphaella urged. "Don't keep us in suspense."

"It's so delicious," I intoned, "it ought to be illegal."

Mrs. Stoppini tried not to look pleased. "Indeed."

We all had a second piece.

Raphaella patted her tummy and said, "Bad idea to feed us, Mrs. Stoppini. Now I feel too lazy to work."

"More tea," our hostess stated, filling Raphaella's cup. The teapot thumped as she set it down. "Mr. Havelock, if you will permit me, I have a request."

Raphaella and I settled back in our chairs. "Fire away, Mrs. Stoppini," I said.

Mrs. Stoppini folded her hands in her lap, drew in a long breath, and began. "I have been in contact with Ponte Santa Trinita University in Florence with respect to the late professor's will. As executrix of his estate, I have decided to act upon a certain part of the bequest as soon as possible. To that end I enquired of the university, and the relevant persons there were kind enough to send details by mail."

Was she being obscure on purpose? I wondered. I flipped a glance at Raphaella, whose eyebrows lifted almost unnoticeably. She didn't get it either. Not yet, anyway.

Mrs. Stoppini got up and glided out of the kitchen in her creepy way, returning almost immediately with a bulky manila envelope, which she laid on the table beside my plate. The envelope had foreign stamps on it, along with a few post office imprints and stickers.

Taking her seat, our hostess went on, "I wish to ship one of the, er, objects in the library to Italy—the university—as soon as possible."

"The cross," I guessed.

She nodded toward the envelope. "There are strict but simple procedures regarding the shipping container required, along with suggestions for insurance, method of shipping, and so on. These latter issues I will handle myself."

She paused.

"I see," I said.

"I should be most grateful, Mr. Havelock, if you would consent to construct a suitable container for the object in question. Of course, I shall pay for the required materials and for your services."

Her decision didn't surprise me. Raphaella and I weren't the only ones who would be happy to see the cross off the premises, although we *were* the only ones in that kitchen who knew it was a reliquary. Or that it was, as well as a valuable artifact, a bundle of trouble.

"I'll agree," I said, "if you'll let me name my price."

"Very well," she replied with obvious relief. "That is acceptable. And what is your fee?"

"Another piece of *zuccotto*."

"HMM," Raphaella mused.

"Hmm, indeed," I replied.

We were sitting before the fireplace as the gusty wind outside fitfully grumbled in the chimney. Behind us, beyond the window, legions of clouds marched across a sombre sky. I felt as if we were being shoved toward an inevitable confrontation with the spectre—a feeling I had been almost successful in ignoring for the past week or so. Mrs. Stoppini's decision had brought Raphaella and me back to our main problem.

"What do we do?" I asked, throwing myself into a chair before the hearth.

Raphaella lowered herself into the other club chair. "We don't have many options, do we? Comply with Mrs. Stoppini's wishes, crate the cross up, and wash our hands clean of the whole issue. Or tell her it's a reliquary with a resident ghost—"

"A murderous ghost."

"And let her take responsibility. The way I see it, because we know what the cross really is and what its dangers are, we're responsible if anything bad happens when it's sent away."

"I agree. There's no way we can sidestep this one."

We stared silently at the coals for a while.

"On the other hand, if the haunting is connected to the professor's manuscript, as we believe . . . I don't know where I was going with that thought."

Raphaella got to her feet. "Well, I know where I'm going," she said. "Back to work."

"Unless . . ." I continued.

"Unless what?"

"I've thought of this before, but I pushed the idea away. It's too . . . frightening."

Raphaella nodded. "I know what you're thinking. Go ahead and say it. Get it out in the open."

I nodded in the direction of the fireplace. "We could take the atlas from the reliquary and burn it."

Raphaella sat back down. My statement lay between us like a sleeping dragon, too horrible to examine closely because we were afraid of what it might mean.

It would be like killing Savonarola all over again, I thought.

Raphaella shook her head, as if I'd spoken aloud. "He's been dead since fourteen ninety—what was it?"

"Eight."

"Right. He isn't alive. Therefore we can't kill him."

"But it would be sacrilegious, like desecrating a grave."

"How much respect is owed him? He probably killed Professor Corbizzi. Or contributed to his death. He wants to destroy the professor's book. And look at his record."

"I still don't think I could bring myself to do it."

"Me either."

"But you said—"

"I was just playing devil's advocate."

"Good choice of words," I said.

III

ON THE WAY TO THE SHOP the next morning, under skies that showed no sign of allowing the sun to peek through, I stopped off at the lumber store and bought a sheet of thick plywood and some spruce planks to make a frame for a shipping container. The packing foam would be delivered in a few hours.

With the directions from the university in Florence—translated by Mrs. Stoppini—laid out before me on my workbench, I started to work. The guidelines were straightforward and pretty simple. I needed to build what was essentially a wooden box with interior braces capable of holding the cross upright and immobilized so as to withstand rough handling and vibration. The space around the antique would be stuffed with synthetic packing. I didn't tell Mrs. Stoppini that there would be a stowaway in the crate.

By working full tilt I had the crate ready by lunchtime. I brushed it clean of shavings and sawdust, hung my apron by the door, and left the shop, taking a deep breath of the soggy air to clear calculations from my head.

I had just stepped onto the patio when I saw him on the shore of the lake, by the willows, just as I had weeks before.

The setting suited him—the backdrop of grey waves and greyer sky was a perfect frame for his black robe and dark, disfigured features. He stood motionless, if "stood" is the right word for a spectre that seemed to hover just above the ground like an evil thought, his cape undisturbed by a wind that lifted the willow branches nearby. His ravaged face was trained in my direction, the swollen eyes dark in their sockets, as if he were reminding me of something. I held his stare, fighting to control my breathing. He glowered at me, fuming, radiating anger and hatred.

"So I guess today's the day," I said to myself as an icy shiver crawled up and down my spine. The reckoning. The showdown. Today the atlas bone would be sealed up and sent back to Florence.

"Or not," the ghost's malign glare seemed to say.

Then the wind gusted and his form broke up like oily smoke and drifted off along the shore.

I gulped. The vision had lasted a few seconds at most, but the impact was like someone had cracked me on the head with a plank. I took a deep breath, pulled myself together, and went to the kitchen door.

Three

I

RAPHAELLA ARRIVED IN TIME for minestrone soup and panini stuffed with egg salad salty with chopped olives. The three of us ate in silence. Mrs. Stoppini seemed preoccupied—and sad. Raphaella's face showed the tension I felt. The moment she saw me she knew that I had seen the apparition.

After lunch Raphaella and I lugged the new packing crate from the shop to the library and set it onto a blanket we'd spread on the alcove table. The pleasant odours of glue and freshly cut spruce were swamped by the acrid stink of smoke hanging in the room. I returned to the shop for the power drill, screws, a jar of adhesive, and the strips of felt I had cut earlier for the surfaces where the braces would be in contact with the cross. Through the window I noticed whitecaps forming on the lake. Wind-thrown rain began to patter against the glass.

Raphaella was setting up in her usual spot, turning on her laptop and pulling pens and pads from her backpack.

She placed the computer on the movable lectern I had made. We planned to retrieve the PIE from under the cabin deck at Geneva Park once the police presence there had died down. She didn't seem to miss it much.

"I can feel his presence," she said.

No need to mention who "he" was.

For what I hoped was the last time, I went through the familiar procedure. Put the first brass key in the lock and open the alcove cupboard. Reach inside, press the knot, wait for the click as the catch on the hinged bookshelf section released. Pull open the heavy door. Insert the second key and open the secret cupboard.

I peered inside. Each object—the cross, wooden box, *Compendium Revelationem*, manuscript file, and felt-wrapped cross—was just as we had left it. I turned toward Raphaella. She nodded encouragement. I lifted out the antique reliquary, laid it on the table by the crate, and pushed the cupboard door closed, leaving the key in the lock.

I had never experienced an earthquake, but the tremor that seemed to rise through the floorboards under my feet must have been similar. Raphaella stopped typing for a moment and gripped the edges of the lectern. The shudder beneath us subsided. I unwrapped the cross and carefully slid it inside the crate, snug against the braces securing the base and the horizontal beam. The fit was perfect. Inside the box the glass dome glowed as if lit from within.

The floor under me trembled again.

I removed the reliquary and stood it beside the crate, then began to paint quick-dry glue on the felt strips, using the brush attached to the inside of the jar's lid.

Whack!

The door of the secret cupboard flew up and the file folder tumbled to the floor beside me. I concentrated on applying the strips of cloth to the braces in the crate, pressing hard with shaking hands. Raphaella went back to tapping keys. The rain beat harder against the window. I glued the last piece of felt, then picked up the file folder from the floor and placed it on Raphaella's table.

Above my head a book sprang straight off the shelf, fluttered like a confused bird, and crashed to the ground. A second one followed. Then, volume by volume, the entire row of books streamed into the air and plummeted into a heap at my feet.

Raphaella shrieked, pointing to the fireplace. Behind the safety screen the pyramid of scrap wood I had set there the day before burst into a fierce blaze.

Forcing myself to work methodically, not to give in to fear, I tested the crate, finding that the glue had set. I gritted my teeth, clamped my jaws shut, muttered, "Here goes," and gently but with as much determination as I could scrape together seated the gold cross in place. I slid the lid on and, glancing around, picked up the drill and a couple of brass screws.

"Garnet."

The forced calm of Raphaella's warning tore at my nerves. I whirled around to see her staring wide-eyed toward the other side of the room. The spectre stood by the escritoire, radiating hatred, his hood covering all but his blistered, ruined face. The air was thick with a miasma of burned cloth and wood and broiled, putrid meat. Savonarola raised his arm under the singed and rotted cape, pointing.

The folder on Raphaella's table quivered. The string slowly unwound itself from the paper button. The folder suddenly sprang toward the ceiling, spinning end over end, spilling pages like feathers from a burst pillow. Sheets filled the air, a blizzard of paper streaming toward the fireplace, where every single page slipped behind the screen, flared for a split second in a tiny soundless explosion, then expired in a puff of black ash. In minutes the manuscript was gone.

With a sweep of his skeletal arm Savonarola pointed toward the alcove. An avalanche of books poured from the shelves, battering the heavy crate, sending it crashing to the ground, knocking the lid off. The cross broke free and tumbled among the fallen books. The table shook violently, rose from the floor, hung suspended for a second, then shot toward me, ramming my shoulder and knocking me to the ground, pinning my legs. A heavy book whacked against my head and I collapsed in a daze, craning my neck to keep my eyes on Raphaella.

She cringed by her table, mercilessly pummelled by flying books, struck repeatedly on her shoulders and head. She held up her arms to protect herself but the torrent knocked her to the floor, where she lay on her back, paralyzed with terror, her chest heaving. I heard a rumbling and a clatter, turned to see the chairs by the hearth tip and tumble across the floor, coming to a thumping stop against the doors.

The spectre began to float toward Raphaella, slowly, relentlessly, as if savouring what he was about to do. "Don't!" I shouted, but he continued to glide toward her. Raphaella stirred, raised herself onto her elbows, crab-walked backwards, her eyes on Savonarola's black form, until she bumped against the east wall.

Thin rivulets of flame, capillaries of fire, seeped from under the frayed black robe of the ghost and streamed toward her. She stared, wide-eyed, as the fire encircled her.

"Garnet!"

I struggled to free myself from the weight of the table and books, fighting to catch my breath. Something crashed into my shoulder. The crate lid spun toward me in a vicious arc. I ducked just in time and it smashed into the wall beside the window.

Savonarola stopped in front of Raphaella. He raised his arms. The robe fell back to reveal bones poking through burnt flesh. His piercing gaze bored into her.

"Don't!" I pleaded again. "Take me! I'm the one you want!"

The spectre didn't so much as turn my way. I remembered again how Savonarola had despised women—creatures to be lectured or scorned, originators of sin, agents of Satan. I hauled myself to my knees and tried to crawl over piles of books toward Raphaella. The flames around her crackled and smoked.

She cringed in the shadow cast by the dark spectre looming bat-like above her. Then, as quick as a thought, the terror suddenly left her face. She seemed—unbelievably—calm. She stared at Savonarola's destroyed face. Her voice came, firm and strong.

"You can't."

The wraith seemed to shrink back a little.

"You know you can't," Raphaella said.

As if suddenly starved of oxygen, the flames around her shrank, flickered, and died, leaving no marks on the floor.

Raphaella looked my way.

So did Savonarola.

I knew what I had to do, but he was way ahead of me. I scrambled among the jumble of volumes on the floor, hurling them this way and that, glimpsed the sparkle of a red jewel against a gold background, and hauled the heavy cross out of the pile. Fumbling in my pocket, I yanked out my knife and opened it, my hands trembling violently.

"Garnet, look out!"

Savonarola flowed toward me as fire veined from his robes and across the floor, like lava seeping from a volcano. I jabbed at the clips holding the glass dome to the base of the cross. In my frenzy, I broke two of them. Pried up the others. Thumbed the dome free. It clattered across the floor. With fire searing the bottom of my feet, I snatched the atlas from its cavity in the base of the cross.

I clawed my way toward the fireplace, the stench of the spectre in my nostrils, the searing fire around me, the five-centuries-old bone clutched in my hand. I heard Raphaella scream a warning, felt myself snatched into the air and hurled forward. I slammed against the mantel and fell to the hearth, knocking the screen aside. The fire scorched my face, singing my eyebrows. I thrust my hand over the flames and dropped the bone into the heart of the fire.

A prolonged, ear-splitting howl of rage and despair battered the room.

From behind, something grabbed me, pinning my arms, and hauled me away from the fire. I fought back with the little strength I had left.

"Garnet!"

It was Raphaella, holding me in her arms. We stared into the fire, at the bone resting on the coals in the centre of a forest of flame, afraid that if we took our eyes off it, the atlas would disappear. It smoked, glowed reddish orange for a few seconds, turned white hot, seemed to quiver. Then it flared and died and crumbled to a powdery ash and was lost among the coals.

Together, we felt the weight of his presence behind us. Still on our knees, we turned. He was in the centre of the room, a black cloud of evil, arms raised, his bony fingers pointing accusingly at us. Books cascaded from the wall behind him and thundered to the floor. The window imploded, showering us with glass. Savonarola glowered at us, his distended eyes wide, his devastated face twisted with frustration and hatred and rage, his ravaged mouth a black oval as he bellowed again. He glided in our direction on a raging sheet of fire. But as he crept forward, the fire's intensity was already waning. His body began to lose power and substance, its colour fading. His physical presence wavered and then he seemed to dissolve like cooling vapour into the air around him, until he was gone.

Raphaella and I embraced like two shipwrecked sailors clinging to each other for life and warmth, the upended furniture, disintegrated window glass, and Professor Corbizzi's books strewn like flotsam on a beach. We looked around the room—the evidence of violence everywhere—searching, not quite believing our eyes.

"He's gone," I whispered.

"Gone for good now, I think."

"And he didn't get the professor's manuscript."

Four

I

WIND AND RAIN GUSTED into the room through the damaged window, clearing and freshening the air. The fire in the grate had dropped to embers. A thought struck Raphaella and me at the same time.

"Mrs. Stoppini!"

"I'll go," I said, jumping to my feet.

I took the stairs two at a time, ran down the carpeted hall toward her suite. Her door was ajar. Out of habit, without thinking, I slowed to a walk, stopped at her threshold, and put my head through the door. I could see the foot of her bed. Two black-stockinged feet, soles toward me, unmoving.

She was snoring softly and rhythmically. She had slept through everything. I retraced my steps to the library, slowly and quietly this time, and closed the doors behind me. If she woke up, I didn't want her to see the room as it was.

Raphaella had gathered a few rugs from around the

library and spread them over the fallen books under the windowsill to protect them from the rain. We brought sheets of plywood from the workshop and nailed them over the destroyed windows. I retrieved a metal bucket, a dustpan, and a brush from the garden shed, and we went into the house again.

"I won't feel confident that he's really gone until I do this," I said, scooping up the embers and ash from the fireplace, brushing up all the dust, and dumping it into the pail.

When Raphaella was satisfied that not a molecule had been left behind, I carried the pail outside and dug a hole behind the shop and dumped in the ashes. I trudged across the sodden lawn to the lake, scooped up some water, lugged the pail back to the hole, swirled the water around the inside of the pail, then poured it into the hole.

"Let there be no remains to tempt the relic hunters," I murmured as I filled in the hole and tamped down the dirt with a shovel.

Back in the library, Raphaella had begun to pick up books and stack them on the trestle tables. The entire alcove had been stripped, along with a couple of hundred volumes from the south and east wall. I hauled the crate back onto the table, then picked up the cross and reattached the glass dome, bending the unbroken clips into place. I fitted the cross inside, pushed the packing material into place, and screwed on the lid.

"The rain's let up," I said. "Maybe we'll see the sun today after all."

Raphaella plunked an armful of books on the table and forced a smile. "I think we can put everything back in a couple of hours," she said. "We already have the columns labelled, so we can organize the books by topic first, then alphabetically, then reshelve them. I—"

"Stop." I took hold of her hands. "We're okay," I reassured her, seeing the frenetic energy in her eyes, the aftereffects of our ordeal. "We came through it. It's over."

Raphaella began to cry—first tears, like the patter of rain that heralds a storm, then a full-on gale of sobbing. I held her tightly, holding back aftershocks of my own, blinking away the image of Raphaella on her back on the floor, encircled by flames.

"I thought I was going to lose you," she spluttered against my chest, "when you were down and he went after you."

"It takes more than an ugly little monk with a bad attitude to put me out of commission. Even a firebug like him."

Raphaella laughed. Sort of. "We ended up burning him after all," she said, wiping her eyes with the heels of her palms.

A ring sounded.

"What was that?" she exclaimed.

"My stupid cellphone."

"I do apologize, Mr. Havelock, for failing to provide your afternoon refreshment," Mrs. Stoppini said, a little flustered. "I was reading in my room and must have dozed off. I slept the afternoon away!" There was a moment's silence as Mrs. Stoppini composed herself. "I shall have tea ready in seventeen minutes."

Mrs. Stoppini didn't seem upset when we told her about the library window. "I didn't realize the wind was that strong" was all she said.

She told us she'd call a glazier to have it repaired as soon as possible. She'd also contact the shipping company to pick up the crate, which Raphaella and I had carried to the foyer at the front of the house. After a quick cup of tea Raphaella and I returned to the library and got to work putting the place back in order.

"Let's take a break," I suggested after an hour or so. I led Raphaella to the chairs by the fireplace. "I've been thinking," I said.

Throughout the afternoon something had been scratching away at the back of my mind, like a mouse in the attic. I had been reviewing the battle with Savonarola's ghost. Not that I had wanted to. I couldn't help it. But there was something I couldn't explain. It seemed that when the spectre was about to burn Raphaella, somehow she had warded him off. How?

"You can't. You know you can't," she had said. She had been desperate and terrified, but she had uttered those words with something like confidence. What prohibition would someone like Savonarola recognize, no matter how much he thought Raphaella deserved to be burned alive? I could think of only one. It was an unbreakable rule that had applied through the ages to condemned witches and female prisoners bound for execution. As an ordained priest, Savonarola had been obliged to follow it.

"You persuaded him not to kill you," I said.

Raphaella nodded. Her eyebrows rose.

The library was silent for a moment.

"Is it true?" I asked.

"He would have known if I'd been lying."

I felt the world shift under me.

Raphaella smiled tentatively. "So what do you think?"

"I think that next to you, this is the best thing that ever happened to me."

Her smile widened. "I knew you'd say that."

She came and sat on my lap and snuggled close, her head under my chin.

"Well, we're all set, aren't we?" she said. "We have no money, no place to live, and a baby girl on the way."

I didn't ask how she knew it was a girl.

II

THE NEXT MORNING, still reeling a little from the events and the news of the previous day, I walked downtown, planning to have a coffee at the Half Moon and then drop in at the Demeter and see Raphaella.

She and I were entering a new phase of our life sooner than we had planned. People we knew would soon be abuzz with gossip. Critics would tsk and complain that we were too young and irresponsible. Children bringing up a child, they'd declare. Ruining their future. I didn't care what uncharitable opinions they'd spit out. Raphaella *was* my future.

"What happened to your face?" Marco asked when I sat down at the end of the coffee bar near the kitchen.

"It's a long story."

He nodded. "Understood. A latte, then?"

"A macchiato today, please, Marco."

He smirked. "I see the Corbizzi family's having an effect on you."

I drank the coffee, chatting with Marco as he made a mini-pizza from scratch. Who ordered a pizza at 9:30 in the morning? I wondered as he repeatedly tossed the dough into the air, spinning it into shape.

"Hear about that business over at Geneva Park a while ago?" he asked.

I fibbed. I was getting tired of pretending, but the cops had made the publication ban clear. "I don't think so."

"'Parently some guy went berserk with a rake or shovel or something. Started wailing on a guy he didn't even know. They hauled him away in a straitjacket."

"Oh, yeah. I think I remember now," I replied.

Marco's remarks proved the cops' and spies' disinformation campaign was working. Now I knew why I had never been asked to make a formal statement the day I met with the three inspectors. My fight with the leader of the Severn Ten—Eleven—had never happened.

"Prob'ly a disgruntled employee like you hear about on TV all the time. He was with an outfit that took care of the lawns and flowers. That's what you get for hiring outsiders," Marco concluded, crumbling mozzarella over the pizza. He was always put out if people from outside the community were contracted.

"I heard they took him straight to the loony bin at Penetang. They say he escaped from there six months ago and was living in the woods."

Orillia. Where a story was never accurate for long. I couldn't resist.

"Must have been hard landing a job with a landscaping company from outside of town if he had been living in the trees."

Marco grunted his agreement, then used a wooden paddle to slide the pizza into the oven.

I said goodbye and left the cafe, heading for Peter Street and the Demeter. I was surprised to find Mrs. Skye behind the counter. Raphaella was supposed to be on duty. Mrs. Skye was ringing up a sale, placing jars of vitamins and supplements into the customer's environmentally friendly shopping bag.

After the vitamin lady had shuffled out the door, Mrs. Skye leaned back on her prescription table, arms crossed on her chest, scrutinizing me.

"Raphaella will be in later," she volunteered. "She wanted to sleep in today."

Did Mrs. Skye know? I wondered, searching her face for clues. She must have read my mind.

"Somehow," she drawled, but without the usual edge in her voice, "I don't see you as a father."

"Yeah, well, I guess we'll both have to get used to the idea."

Then, like a miser handing over his last penny, she said, "I suppose Raphaella could have done worse."

"I love her, Mrs. Skye. I'm not going to apologize for that. To anybody. And I'm proud we're going to have a baby. And I'm glad it's a girl."

A single tear trickled down the edge of her nose and onto her upper lip. Her face softened. This is what she looks like when she's not mad at the world, I thought. Then I realized something.

"It *was* you."

She swiped the tear away with the back of her hand. "What? What was me?"

"In the hospital," I said, hardly able to believe it. "I *did* see you."

She shrugged. "They weren't treating your contusions properly. All those drugs they gave you, but no simple healing salve. Typical of the medical establishment."

I felt a grin creep across my face. "Raphaella was right. You *are* warming up to me."

"By slow degrees," she said.

Five

I

Between the mansion and the lake, the leaves on the outer edges of the trees showed a tinge of colour—red for the maples and yellow for the willows. The air was crisp and clear, the way it is only in autumn, and the lake glowed its characteristic green under a perfect blue sky. In a few weeks, leaves would be drifting down like multicoloured snow.

Starting today I was the caretaker of the Corbizzi mansion until it was sold in the spring. Mrs. Stoppini had instructed her lawyer to piece off the coach house and a bit of ground, and to maintain both a right of way down the lane and a narrow strip giving access to the lake. My lease was extendable after the three years were up, with an option to buy if I wished—and if I ever had the money.

I was looking out the shop window across the yard to the place on the shore where I had found the GPS. Chief's Island was a dark green brushstroke in the distance. Behind me, in the light of the window, Raphaella sat in a lawnchair reading a book with lots of health-food advice for expectant mothers. Nearby, next to the spray booth, rested the second of the three pieces commissioned by Liz and Derek—the smaller of the two dressers—ready to be stained. The design for the bigger chest of drawers lay on my drafting table. Derek had kept his promise. He had been happy enough with the bookcase that he had recommended me to some friends, and I had a few new orders already.

My cell rang. I turned to see Raphaella earmark her page and take the call. She nodded. "Thank you, Mrs. Stoppini," she said, and disconnected. "The airport limo will arrive in approximately twenty-two minutes," she announced in an uncannily Mrs. Stoppini–like voice.

"Duly noted, Miss Skye."

All day Mrs. Stoppini had been giving us regular—and totally unnecessary—progress reports. She had called to declare that she had finished loading her steamer trunk. That the padlock had been locked. That the suitcases were packed and ready. That all of the windows in the house were closed and secured.

Raphaella and I crossed the patio and joined Mrs. Stoppini in the kitchen. Her trunk and bags stood ready by the door. She insisted on wearing her long shapeless coat and her hat—a beret-type thing that drooped over one ear—while she waited, as sharp-edged and angular as ever. Her lipstick had been applied over an even wider area today.

After apologizing that under the circumstances she was unable to offer a light refreshment, she continued, "I received welcome news from Florence yesterday. The purchase of the apartment I was seeking has been finalized and the place will be ready for me when I arrive. I shall go there directly from Amerigo Vespucci airport. The apartment is not far from the university. It is on the third floor of a centuries-old building on the Piazza della Signoria. It is quite spacious, with a guest suite."

"But that's—" I cut in. The Piazza della Signoria was the city square where Savonarola had been executed.

"I beg your pardon?"

"Er, a beautiful square I heard . . . er, read."

The thick black eyebrows rose. "Quite," Mrs. Stoppini agreed. Then she continued her train of thought. "Miss Skye, Mr. Havelock, I should be most grateful if you would consent to visit me for at least a month, after I am settled and before you"—she nodded to Raphaella—"find travel inconvenient. Nothing would give me greater pleasure than to escort you through some of Florence's art museums and architectural treasures."

She stopped. She took a deep breath.

"I shall miss you both deeply. But if I have your visit to look forward to . . ."

She swallowed. And blinked. Then she straightened her already rigid back and regained her composure.

"Winter in Florence is not the most clement of seasons, but . . . May I expect you, then, in Italy?"

Raphaella and I exchanged glances. Raphaella nodded, her chin quivering.

The grille on the kitchen wall buzzed. I got up and pressed the button to let the airport limo in. A few minutes later a black van appeared in the window and drew to a stop near the Hawk.

"Your ride is here," I said unnecessarily.

Two burly men in blue nylon company windbreakers took charge of the trunk and the bags, then climbed back into the van. The driver made a three-point turn and waited, his engine idling.

Mrs. Stoppini was struggling to hold on to her composure. She whispered something to Raphaella, who hugged her, earning a startled look. Then Mrs. Stoppini stepped toward me, her hand extended.

"I shall hold you to your promise to visit me in Florence, Mr. Havelock."

I shook with her but didn't let go of the bony gloved hand. "Thanks for everything, Mrs. Stoppini. For the shop lease and the delicious lunches, and for introducing me to macchiato, and for introducing me to Professor Corbizzi's books, and especially for teaching me that in civilized countries cappuccino is never served after twelve o'clock."

The ghost of a smile crossed her lips. Before she could escape I wrapped my arms around her stick-like body and squeezed.

"I've been wanting to do that for a long time," I said.

"Indeed," she replied. And she climbed into the waiting limo, rapped on the back of the driver's seat, and was swept away.

We watched the van disappear around the bend in the lane.

"You didn't say that you'd told her about the baby."

"I didn't. She just knew."

"You don't mean—"

"That she has the gift? No. I would have picked up on that. But she's a very intelligent and observant lady."

"I'll miss her."

"Not nearly as much as she'll miss you."

II

ON THE EVENING of October 27 it snowed—the earliest blizzard in fifty years. By the time I unlocked the shop the next morning, the storm had marched on, leaving a watery sun in a cold grey sky.

I spent an hour snow-blowing the lane and shovelling the sidewalk to the front door of the mansion, then the path between the kitchen and the shop. As I did at least twice a week, I walked through the house, checking the window latches, the faucets, the radiators in each room.

And as always I spent a few minutes in the library, whose doors were now left permanently open. At last Professor Corbizzi's favourite room was the way Mrs. Stoppini had wanted it—stripped of every last book, rug, and article of furniture. The majority of the collection had been taken away by a dealer. The alcove books, the Savonarola medal, the priceless copy of *Compendium Revelationem* had been shipped to Ponte Santa Trinita University in Florence. Mrs. Stoppini had even asked me to "do something" about the secret cupboard, and so I had locked it one last time, disabled the mechanism holding the bookcase section in place, removed the knot from the outside cupboard, and plugged the hole with wood filler, smoothing and staining it to make it invisible. No one who was unaware of the secret would ever discover the empty cupboard.

A couple of days before the blizzard I got a letter post-marked "Firenze." *Fanatics* had been accepted for publication, Mrs. Stoppini announced in her cramped, angular handwriting—fountain pen on thick, creamy monogrammed paper—and the book would be off the press next summer.

"I shall, of course, send copies to you and Miss Skye immediately the book is available," she concluded. "I have taken the liberty of dedicating it to both of you. I know the late professor would concur."

The sun had come out, filling the library with dazzling light reflected off the snow. This must have been how the room looked when Professor Corbizzi had first entered it, full of plans and ideas to fill it with books and to carry on with his work, driven by his commitment to warn his readers about fanatics who use religion as a veil for their hatred. Now that the publication ban on news about the Severn Eleven had been partially lifted, my mother was, in her own way, carrying on his work.

I left the house and returned to the shop. On the bench, awaiting assembly, were the cherrywood pieces I had fabricated to make a cradle. I put on my apron and went to work.

AUTHOR'S NOTE

In 2009 at least nine million people were displaced from their homes and communities owing to religious intolerance.

—*Harper's Magazine*, November 2009

Fanatics is a work of fiction. Except those noted below, all happenings and characters are imaginary.

The events in the life of Girolamo Savonarola (1452–1498), as described in *Fanatics*, conform to the historical record. The manner of his death follows eyewitness accounts.

The "Severn Eleven" incident is very loosely based on the activities of the actual "Toronto 18," who trained in a rural area near Orillia, Ontario, planned several terrorist attacks in the Toronto area, and were arrested in June 2006 and charged with various crimes under the Anti-Terrorism Act. As of this writing, a number have been convicted.

I found the following books useful in my research:

Seward, D. *The Burning of the Vanities: Savonarola and the Borgia Pope*. Sutton Publishing, 2006.

Martines, L. *Fire in the City: Savonarola and the Struggle for the Soul of Renaissance Florence*. Oxford: Oxford University Press, 2006.